On the Trail of the
RUTHLESS WARLOCK

Lynne Armstrong-Jones

Lynne Armstrong-Jones

Tellwell Talent
www.tellwell.ca

ISBN
978-0-2288-2173-1 (Paperback)
978-0-2288-2174-8 (eBook)

Table of Contents

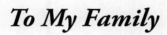

To My Family

CHAPTER ONE

The Attack

The sun was bright and comfortably warm as the sorceress made her way along the path, astride a grey donkey. The weather made the day pleasant enough, but the young woman considered herself fortunate indeed. She had completed her long days and nights of study in the Tower of Giefan, and was in the process of making the short journey west for her final Tests and Completions, in the Hidden Caves of the Abufan.

Yes, all of this was enough to bring a smile to her face, yet there was more. For her sister, Carlida, was nearby with her nomadic tribe, and the sorceress, Creda, would have an opportunity to visit with her! It had been a few years since they had been together, so this seemed nothing short of wonderful!

Hmm. She pondered as she bobbed slightly up and down atop the little beast. *How old are my nephews now?*

Her jaw dropped open suddenly. Could the younger one be *eight* years now? She sighed. It had definitely been too long. But it was time to be positive. After all, she shouldn't be far away now. She could see a large boulder up on a hill not too far from here, and that should be the one which her sister had told her to watch for, in the note which she had had delivered to Creda at the Tower. It described the rock quite clearly, with its surface like a man's face that kept the children entertained. They plodded steadily until the rock was quite visible at the top of the small hill. She pulled the little donkey to a stop.

If we are close, why do I not hear the children at play? Where is the sound of supper being prepared?

Why was it so eerily, deathly silent?

"Go, Portar! Go!" She urged the little donkey forward, a frown creasing her forehead. Something was awfully wrong. It was so silent, so silent. She scanned the skies for carrion-eaters and was relieved that she saw none.

But then ... *something*. A smell. Just a hint, just a tinge. But it was there. That sweet scent of magic. But it was so faint. Hastily she urged Portar to the side of the trail, and tethered him there with trembling hands. She was at the spot at the bottom of the hill which her sister had described. Her sister and her people should be just beyond the bushes ahead. Creda pushed the bushes aside and stepped beyond them. Now she knew why the carrion-eaters were not circling in the sky. They were here. Feasting.

The sorceress moved forward, avoiding the birds. She was holding her breath as best she could, yet still the smell of death was strong. One of the birds screamed at her, something red hanging from its beak. It did not wish to share its bounty with her, or anyone else. Creda was barely able to make out what it was beneath the fluttering bodies. Then, finally, she saw something which was not feathered –

A hoof.

The air rushed from her lungs as she stopped holding her breath. Relief flooded through her – relief that the carcass did not belong to any of her sister's people. But there was something else. She knew that she might need to make use of her power ...

Creda stepped past the feasting birds, past more of the bushy growth. She gasped. This was where her sister and her people had been. Not one of the small tents still stood. Pottery, food and clothing were strewn about the area. There was not one person to be seen ...

She moved toward what had once been a tent. Now it resembled nothing of a home. Now it was simply coarse, tattered, dirty material, crumpled and partly stretched across the ground.

Although the sight set her trembling, a brownish-crimson stain attracted her attention. Creda knew what she had to do. Her lips moved as she quietly recited the words of the spell she needed, her fingers seeking her amulet in order to focus the power which resided within. Now. Open. She was open to receiving whatever messages the crimson had to share –

She stooped beside the flattened tent, the fingers of her right hand reaching toward the stain while her left hand touched her amulet. She felt the recent warmth of life …

I was a man of the nomadic village. Suddenly there were raiders on horseback, hoofs pounding the ground. The attack was so sudden that I barely had time to grab my sword before the raider was upon me. The man – or was it some sort of beast – lunged with his ax. I parried the first blow –

But a scream from behind had me whirling. Mara! One of the raiders had seized her and was pulling her up onto his horse. She struggled, and I stepped towards them.

But the raider did something to her – I couldn't see what – and my dear Mara slumped forward as though dead! I screamed, but my cry was lost in the midst of dozens of others. A sharp pain penetrated my back and shoulder from behind. My arm was suddenly icy cold, and my hand could no longer grasp my sword. Everything seemed to be spinning— I could no longer focus – but I wasn't dead.

Silence returned. The man's story had ended – at least, as much as his spilled blood could tell. Creda sighed. There were other bloodstains in the area. When she consulted two of them, they had similar stories.

And this story seemed clear. Those in the Tower – as well as the people of the town – had all heard of it. There was one who attacked and took all of the prisoners alive. Those of the Tower had discussed the possibility of having their sorcerers and sorceresses coming together to stop this evil, yet the Tower Superiors had not reached any consensus.

Of course, there was no urgency to do so when the reports of the attacks had not come from anywhere in the vicinity. But this was the first time that such an attack had occurred so close to the city. The urgency was here. Now.

Creda closed her eyes, fingers once more cradling her amulet. She was picturing her sister. And that vision sparked determination. It was time for some sort of action.

"Oh, Portar. *Please!* I know you're tired, but we have *got* to hurry!" She was standing in the roadway, clutching the reins in her hands, pulling and begging the old donkey to move.

They *had* to move along! The shadows across the roadway reminded her of the approach of evening. They needed to at least reach the outskirts of the City of Espri before darkness enveloped everything completely.

But how to convince the donkey of this? He had already devoured the treats she had brought along in case of this. She looked at his white muzzle, his yellow teeth as he seemed to chuckle at her. His large brown eyes twinkled. Creda sighed, and reached out a hand to touch his muzzle. She felt a peculiar closeness to him. She had noticed this before with other animals, but when she had mentioned it to one of the Superiors, the response was simply a puzzled expression. Perhaps Creda could use this rapport to urge Portar along ... but she wasn't sure *how*. This certainly wasn't something taught at the Tower –

"Now. Portar, *please*." Once more she pulled on the reins, but the donkey wouldn't budge.

Creda hadn't thought about whether or not this might appear ridiculous to someone else – at least, not until she heard hoofbeats approaching. But suddenly the memories of the villager flooded her mind, and she reached for the knife which she had sheathed at her belt --

But when she saw the rider approaching from the way she had come she tucked the blade away. He certainly did not at *all* resemble the villager's memory of those who had attacked the nomads. This is not to say that he did not have the look of one who would be capable of attacking someone, for he was clad as a warrior, with his head protected by a helmet, and his broad chest by thick hide. He wore a long, thick brown cape which would quite adequately ward off the evening chill –

Yet it was not adequate to keep the rather large, very muscular arms from view. He pulled his horse to a stop – rather dramatically, it seemed to Creda – and shoved his helmet back far enough on his head to allow him to scratch at his dark hair with a thumb, and smiled, lips twisted in a wry grin. The man peered down at the sorceress and her creature, his dark brown eyes crinkled with laugh lines at their corners.

Creda's first impression was one of arrogance … and yet, there was something appealing, somehow, about this warrior.

"Good thing I happened to come along," he was saying in what appeared to be a serious tone but was not. "Dire situation you have here, Sister." He clicked his tongue. "Yes, I'd hate to think of the two of you spending the entire night at such an impasse, and cold it will be getting now that winter is not far off."

Creda tried to think of something to say – some sort of clever retort – but nothing would come except for stammering and stuttering. This only seemed to make the warrior grin all the more, as he dismounted and began to rummage through a sack which hung from his saddle.

"Yes, indeed," he continued. "Quite a spot. But you are fortunate, dear Sister, to have the fighter known as *The Dreaded One, The Quickest and the Bravest, Ad Bellum –*"

"*Ad Nauseum?*" Finally, it was Creda's turn to smile wryly.

"Hmmph," was all he muttered as he extended a large arm to help her to mount his steed. He held the reins behind him in one hand and held the other one toward Portar with a carrot in his hand.

The donkey's brown eyes widened and his nostrils flared. Fatigue forgotten, he eagerly followed the outstretched hand, grabbing a bit of carrot.

As the little group made their way along the trail, Creda was looking at the tall, dark-haired fellow, wondering what age he might be. She saw no grey in his dark hair, yet the crinkles at the corners of his eyes suggested he must certainly have seen his share of years. She listened to him as he nattered on about his great exploits, and how, now that the wars had ended in the northern provinces, he'd come further south to find employment.

He had said nothing about the village. He must not have seen it ...

"Um – what may I call you?" She knew that she must interject. "*The Quickest and the Bravest* is a bit cumbersome, after all."

"Oh. Well, I am known by many names."

I can only imagine, thought Creda. But she said: "And which do you prefer?"

He glanced over his shoulder at the sorceress, his wry grin quite evident again. But he returned his gaze to the path ahead as he said, loudly enough: "Fornico."

Creda sighed. She was not the innocent eighteen-year-old – or younger -- that some were when they had recently completed their Tower training. Creda had had a bit of experience with life before she had turned to the Tower, and she had known people in the past who displayed such bravado. Most had been seeking to intimidate others or perhaps to make themselves feel more important.

Another sigh escaped her. This matter was too pressing. It must be dealt with.

"If you don't mind, I will call you Nico. And there is something which I must know."

Nico turned, and stopped the two beasts. He looked up the sorceress. Her hood had fallen back, exposing light brown hair tied at the nape of her neck, the sun revealing yellow gleams amid the brown strands. Her pale blue eyes revealed serious concerns, as she adjusted her green robe, pulling it more tightly around her. He gave her a courteous nod. The look of bravado had left him.

"Nico, on your journey in this direction, did you – did you notice anything strange, anything amiss?" Creda began to tremble as she once more recalled the destruction of the village.

"No, Sister. I saw nothing as important as what seems to be occupying your thoughts. What is it, Sister?" His voice was very soft.

"You didn't come by way of the valley, then?"

"No, Sister. I took this roadway all the way from the ridge through the mountains. What is it, Sister? And is there another manner in which I might address *you*?"

Despite her concerns, she couldn't help but smile. For all of his bravado, there seemed to be some sincerity within. "Yes, Nico. You may call me Creda. And – and what happened in the valley is something fearsome. The valley is just south of here, and to the west. The other side of the foothills. One must take this road east, then south, to find it. I – I was planning to meet my sister there this afternoon …"

Creda paused, a lump forming in her throat. Nico studied her face for a moment, then took a place immediately beside where she sat, urging both beasts forward from here. "Tell me, Sister Creda," he said gently.

She told him. She told him everything. She told him of the stories which had been spreading from the southern counties and provinces. She told him of the rumours – how it was said that a ruthless man of magic drew his power by drinking the blood of his prisoners while they still lived. But she also told him the facts, as she knew them to be. She told him of the bloodstain, and the truth that it had shared. Although there had been no indication from it of anything about the drinking of blood, it was true that there were no victims' bodies left behind. No dead bodies had ever been found after attacks such as these.

Creda stopped, and dragged a sleeve across her damp eyes. She was suddenly very aware of the steady thumping of the hoofs against the dirt amid the silence.

"Sister Creda," said Nico softly, "we've not heard of the like of this in the far northern counties. This is a matter of concern for sure. I've fought many a foe but none fitting the picture which you've just painted! But, if this man of magic is so powerful, how can he – or maybe it – be stopped?"

"I have no idea."

CHAPTER TWO

The Prophecy

"I thank you, Nico, for your escort all the way to the Tower. I certainly did not intend for you to accompany me all this way past the inn! What – what payment were you anticipating? I haven't much –"

But he shook his head as he helped her to dismount. "Nothing, Sister Creda. I only hope that you and the others of the Tower can find a way to defeat the evil you have described. I know nothing of sorcery." His white teeth flashed as his smile once more lit his face as he nodded in the direction of some passersby. "Dear Sister," he continued, "I'd rather fight with my *sword*! All the best to you, gentle lady." He bowed, rather dramatically.

"And to you, Nico." She watched him for just a moment as he led Portar to the stable for her, but then she turned to hurry up the steps. Her mind was once more on the seriousness of the task ahead of her, for she must alert the Superiors to the attack in her sister's village. She reached for the handle of the heavy door –

"Sister Creda!"

She turned, startled, to see Nico grinning from the stable doorway, passersby eyeing him curiously. "Wh – what is it, Nico?"

"Tell me, Sister Creda. Are all the ladies of this area as fair-haired and blue-eyed as yourself?"

From another man, this might have seemed forward or inappropriate. Yet somehow from Nico it seemed innocent and nothing more than curiosity – except for the degree to which he was enjoying the attention from the passersby.

Despite her anxiety, Creda had to laugh. "No. There are all colours here, although perhaps not as many dark-haired ones like yourself as you might find further north."

"Ah, well then! 'twill be an interesting visit! Thank you, dear Sister." With that, he gave another of his grand bows.

She returned his smile and turned her attention back to the heavy door. She closed her eyes and focussed. In her mind she could see the enchantment as a golden key which placed itself into the lock. She pushed open the door and hastened inside …

For those who knew only the rumours of the lives of those who resided and learned inside the Tower, the sight would likely have lived up to their expectations.

The Four Superiors sat before the others around their small table, deep in thought, while they gave consideration to the horrific details which Creda had provided. Creda watched them anxiously from the students' table, Sister Bedano to her left. Sister Bedano was a younger acolyte, a few years behind Creda in her studies. Brother Ruten sat to Creda's right. Although younger than Creda, he had also reached the end of his studies and had been preparing to leave soon. But such plans might be pushed aside if travel had become too dangerous.

And so they sat in silence, faces haggard with the heavy news, and looking even more so because of the long shadows cast by the candle flames which flickered in the drafts.

Finally, Superior Veras spoke, the candlelight giving her short auburn hair an almost magical reddish glow. "I can see no way, Brothers and Sisters. I had hoped that the rumours were exaggerated. This is some enchantment we have not seen the like of before –"

"Or *is* it?" Superior Ante interjected, her crackling voice reminding all of her advanced years. "We do not know for certain if the stories are true! It may be only another power-hungry dog taking prisoners so they'll do his will. 'twould not be such a difficult spell to make the victims think that the raiders were unusual!"

"Sister Creda? What think you of this?" It was Superior Xyron, seeking, as always, to examine all details from all possible points of view. His fingers toyed with the greying whiskers of his beard.

Creda sighed. She had been through the memory again and again, yet there seemed so little certainty about what she had witnessed. "I – I am sorry," she whispered. She pulled the long, wide sleeve of her robe down low over her fingers to fight the chilliness of the Tower. Or, she wondered, was she shivering at the thought of what they might be facing if the rumours were true? She watched how the flames' glow brought the deeper shades of green in her robe to life. How black it appeared in the shadows –

And black would be all of their futures if they didn't take some course of action! But she knew that the Superiors were anxious to do what was politically wise. The King had always been supportive of the Tower, and certainly all who learned and resided here wished for this to continue! But matters relating to power struggles between the area leaders were the army's responsibilities. Yet, on the other hand, if this was a powerful *sorcerer–*

"I think – I – I," she began, then felt a need to stop and lick her dry lips.

"Continue, Sister Creda," urged Superior Ante gently, her brown eyes watering in a waft of candle smoke.

"I realize that it is not my place to take part in any decision," Creda continued, "but I believe that we must know what we can of the truth, and soon! If there is any truth in the rumours, then we must find a way to stop this! The safety of our people may depend on it!"

There was silence in the room. Then Superior Xyron ceased toying with his beard and gave a deep sigh. "I agree," he whispered.

But Superior Mettor, as usual, was strong in his disagreement. He shook his head, more vigorously than would seem necessary, his long white hair shaking from side to side. "We cannot. We can*not* –"

"We cannot *unless* there may be a situation of such severity that there is no recourse," put in Superior Veras.

Creda and Bedano exchanged looks. Could these four never agree on *any*thing?

"Excuse me, Superiors," said Brother Ruten, "but if the rumours may be true, there is need to make great haste."

Creda and Bedano once more exchanged looks. Slender Ruten, with his reddish-brown hair and always trying to say the correct things, reminded them both of a sly fox. But, at this moment, Creda was most grateful for his interjection.

Superior Mettor, his jowls waggling, exhaled sharply. "It will tax our powers greatly –"

"Not as greatly as we may be taxed if the stories are true and we have done nothing," put in Superior Veras firmly.

"I agree," said Superior Xyron once more, his fingers again beginning to stroke his beard.

"At my age," began Superior Ante, her wrinkled visage proof of her many years, "it is I who shall be facing the greatest risk. But I am convinced of the severity of the situation. Let us begin then. Are you with us, Mettor?"

Mettor was exhaling once more but nodded a hesitant consent.

"And – what of *us*, Superiors?" Sister Bedano asked uncertainly. It had been many years since this ritual had been carried out. It had certainly never occurred since Creda and her companions had come to be Tower-trained.

Superior Ante shared a gentle smile. "Sister Bedano, Brother Ruten, Sister Creda. This is a rare occurrence. You are free to leave if you wish, although I tend to believe that you will learn much if you consent to stay and witness. Sister Creda, considering your recent contact through the victim, I would ask that you remain. Bedano, Ruten?"

They nodded their agreement, Ruten enthusiastically, and Bedano with a touch of hesitance.

"Very well," began Superior Ante. "Sisters and Brother, bear witness as we seek to combine our powers and harness them so that this can be utilized to call upon the Seer to assist us."

With that, she reached out a hand to each side, her fingers seeking contact with the temples of Superior Veras and Superior Mettor. As she did so, they did likewise, each one seeking contact with Superior

Xyron's head. They sat around a square table, one person at each side. It was not difficult for them to reach one another.

Neither was it difficult for the three observers to make their own contact. Creda was a bit surprised to find that Brother Ruten's fingers had made their way over to grasp hers. She looked toward him. No longer did he seem to resemble a fox, for his brown eyes were wide, and he had lost his confident look –

Creda redirected her attention to the Superiors. She could *see* their power now. From one to the other it crept along, like a silver lightning bolt suddenly tamed and carrying out commands. As it moved from Superior Ante to Superior Veras, its colour changed from silver to more of a glimmering deep blue. Then, as it made its way along Superior Veras's arm to Superior Mettor's head, it suddenly became green. From there it snaked along to Superior Xyron, where it became azure as it continued to Superior Ante. All was still, save for the shimmering light which seemed to physically link the Superiors –

And Ruten's fingers, which seemed determined to break completely through Creda's flesh.

Suddenly, there was a rushing sound, almost as the winds will rise before an approaching storm. The rushing sound became louder and louder, and harder for their ears to bear – yet, strangely, only stillness did they feel …

Then, slowly, silence returned to the little room. Creda opened her eyes hesitantly, yet all that she saw were four older people clad in robes which seemed to glow a rainbow of colours. The people sat quietly around an ancient-looking table. The only unusual aspect was the white light which seemed to glow from each one of them. Each gleamed a brilliant whiteness as though surrounded by a halo of utmost purity. The four individuals no longer shared physical contact, as this was no longer needed.

The room was very, very still. Then, in complete unison as though from one body, they began to repeat the Sacred Words: *"Oh, Great Seer, hear us! Help us. Bring us thy wisdom. Help us so that we may use our blessings to preserve and keep all that is Sacred. Oh, Great Seer, hear us!"*

Over and over they repeated the Sacred Words. Creda found herself mouthing them and could hear Ruten as he softly repeated them.

"How strange," whispered Bedano into Creda's ear. "We are witnessing something that has occurred so rarely that at one time we thought that its use was only a rumour. And now its purpose is to dispel or confirm yet another rumour ..."

Creda shook her head at the irony of the situation. But she regretted doing so, as she was becoming somewhat dazed and dizzy. It seemed that the room was slowly being turned onto its side – very, *very* slowly ...

And it was filling with smoke. Creda tried to check the candle flame, but it, too, seemed somehow to be moving independently of everything else in the room. And the Sacred Words were being repeated more and more and more loudly.

The room stopped moving, and Creda was able to determine that there was no smoke in the room. It *couldn't* be smoke – because it was all collecting in one place ...

On the table immediately in front of the Superiors. And it was – it was *silver*. No, *gold*. No – it was like looking at a rainbow which was steadily moving, twisting inwardly upon itself.

And it spoke -- in a delicate, whispery tone which seemed to confirm its ethereal nature.

All four Superiors appeared to be bathed in an eerie white glow as the Seer cast its light upon them.

"You seek to destroy that which no man can! No man is safe from this warlock." The light seemed to shine more brightly as the thing before them spoke, then fade slightly when it paused.

The four Superiors sat motionless, hearing but not fully comprehending the words.

"Is – is there *no* way, Great Seer?" Superior Ante's voice was little more than breath.

"No man can defeat this warlock! But there is a One. That One shall be given the Way by the Witch of the Great East Wood. But, heed me well, no man can defeat this warlock!"

The glow began to fade then, as though the tenuous contact had been stretched to its limit. As the continuously twisting and turning colours started to languish, the Seer became smaller and smaller ... until there was only a tiny flicker of light like a candle flame suspended in the air.

Then, as quick as a flash, it too was gone.

The white light which had illuminated each of the Superiors also faded, leaving the four once more maintaining contact. The processes of such important acts needed to be reversed gradually, rather than simply stopped. And so an azure glow seemed to become a colourful serpent as it glided from Superior Ante to Superior Xyron, then green, it moved from here to Superior Mettor, then deep blue to Superior Veras, and finally silver, returning to Superior Ante –

Who moaned audibly, and slumped forward, her face against the table.

The spell was broken. Quite broken.

Concern for Superior Ante had taken the immediate attention of the other Superiors. The pupils had to settle for being urged to seek their beds, as they would need ample rest for the morrow. And so it was that they had no explanation of the Seer's puzzling words, nor any opportunity to ask questions of the Superiors.

But ... *beds?* How could they think of such after what they had witnessed! It was true that they had received training in how to relax themselves in almost any situation so that they would always be able to obtain the rest that their bodies required in less than desirable situations. Yes, they knew how. But ... *tonight?*

The three found themselves seeking the quiet and open which could only be gained from the top of the Tower during dark hours. Frequently during their years in the Tower, they would find solace there – sometimes with the knowledge of the Superiors and, sometimes too, not.

And so Sister Creda, Brother Ruten and Sister Bedano now stood, despite the cold, seeking comfort by gazing upward at the twinkling stars, or downward at the now almost empty streets of the surrounding city. Across the square was the Palace, and somewhere inside of it, the Prince, who, it was said, was extremely handsome to look upon.

Ruten, as usual, was the first to find his voice. "So then, Sisters, how are we to interpret what was said?"

Bedano spoke in a trembling whisper, "Did you not hear, Ruten? It said that no one can defeat this enemy!"

"But then why did it *also* say that there was a *One* who should seek council with the eastern woods-witch?"

"There is *One*, yet there isn't," murmured Creda. Her mind felt filled with a jumble of a thousand confusing images and voices.

"It said – it said that *'One shall be given the Way'*. But if the 'Way', then, is not the way to destroy this enemy, what can it be?" Ruten's voice, too, was uncharacteristically soft.

"And what about poor Superior Ante?" Bedano sounded anxious as she pulled her cloak more tightly around herself.

"It was too much for her," Creda sighed, shaking her head. "What if – what if this is all for naught? What if – what if this has cost Superior Ante her health or even her life, and we cannot defeat the enemy anyway?"

"Oh, don't despair, Creda. It will certainly not help matters if we begin lamenting over situations which we do not know enough about."

She returned Ruten's gaze. "You're right," she said. "I shared the villager's experience. And my sister and her family have fallen victim. We must do everything that we possibly can."

Ruten placed a hand on Creda's shoulder and gave it a squeeze. "Well," he said, "if we're to find the answers to our questions on the morrow, I guess we should try to get some rest." With a nod to the others, he headed toward the door.

Bedano began to follow him, then suddenly turned back. She stepped to Creda and put her arms around her, hugging her tightly, then turned back toward the door.

Creda found herself once more seeking comfort from the patterns of the stars above in the night sky. Would she be able to find such peace inside of her spirit and mind tonight?

CHAPTER THREE

The Prince

The singing was beautiful. A choir of angels, perhaps? So lovely. And the warmth upon her face was glorious -- glorious in contrast to the cold throughout the rest of her –

And then another voice – a familiar one –

Creda opened her eyes to see the face of Superior Veras surrounded by a tremendous golden glow. For several seconds, Creda hovered in the mystical world between sleep and wakefulness, uncertain of everything …

But it was the morning light of the sun which gave the Superior her wonderful halo. And the music was that of the birds who sang their praises of the morning's warmth and light.

"Sister Creda," Superior Veras said gently, "I am pleased that you were able to gain some rest, but I hope that you will not find yourself ill from being out so long in the cold air!" She extended a hand to Creda, helping her to sit upright on the wide bench, then helped her to stand. Creda began to follow her to the door, then suddenly remembered –

"Superior Ante! How does she fare?"

Superior Veras stopped, her hand on the door handle. She turned to face Creda, her smile dropping from her face. "Superior Ante has been sorely taxed by the energy needed to achieve contact with the Great Seer. Whether she can recover or not – well, we are not yet certain. But my dear, we all have great risks and challenges in our lives. Especially now." She managed to force a weak smile, and stepped though the doorway, beckoning to Creda to follow.

Her words echoed inside of Creda's mind: *especially now … especially now*

She went to her room to wash, and to change her robe, thoughts of what had transpired tumbling through her already jumbled mind. Weariness and anxiety were her companions as she made her way to the room to which Veras had bade her come.

"Enter, Sister Creda," came the deep, clear voice of Superior Xyron through the open doorway. He looked tired this morning as he motioned to her to sit – this time at the larger, round table which was usually considered to be a place for the Superiors only.

Creda sat upon the wooden chair, her nostrils happily appreciating the steam which rose in front of her. Bread, cheese and honey were quietly passed about the table. To her right sat Superior Veras, and to her left Brother Ruten. Superior Xyron and Superior Mettor were immediately across from her, and Sister Bedano at Ruten's side.

Finally, Superior Mettor began in his gruff baritone. "Sisters and Brother, first we should tell you that Superior Ante still lies *very* weak in her bed. Considering her advanced age, we cannot be certain of her complete recovery. But we must deal with the other situation immediately. Superior Xyron will explain our plans. Xyron?"

Superior Xyron stroked his beard a moment, then spoke: "We have decided that we must seek the assistance of the Witch of the Great East Wood, as directed by the Prophecy. As there may be questionable value in myself, Superior Mettor or Brother Ruten going, we three shall remain here to counsel the Prince and assure the best care for Superior Ante. Sister Bedano, you have not as yet completed your studies and therefore must remain as well. Sister Bedano and Brother Ruten, the two of you can assist in welcoming our new students when they arrive and helping them to become accustomed to our routines."

"Superior Veras," he continued, and he turned to meet her eyes with his, "Superior Veras will leave as soon as possible for the eastern wood, as shall you, Sister Creda. We shall speak to Prince Yurmar as soon as we finish here and seek some guards to accompany you."

He stopped then and studied their faces. "Questions?"

Creda and Bedano exchanged looks. Ruten appeared all-knowing, as was usual.

"Superior," Creda began, feeling awkward at needing to ask a question when the Superiors seemed to understand so much more than she did. "Forgive me, but did the Prophecy not say that no one could defeat this warlock?" Superior Xyron once again shared eye contact with Superior Veras. It was Veras who spoke: "We must always remember, Sisters and Brother, that *every word* spoken in a Prophecy must be carefully considered. The Great Seer does not speak with unneeded detail. It indicated that *no man is safe from this warlock*. Therefore, we will not send male Superiors, nor you, Brother Ruten. The *One* must be a female human being, or something else. Doubt still clouds your mind, Sister Creda?"

She could feel her cheeks grow uncomfortably warm, and she wondered if they were uncharacteristically pink. Being older, and with more life experience than either Brother Ruten or Sister Bedano, Creda felt as though the others expected her to be more understanding of most circumstances. She sighed. "Forgive me. I –I thought that *man* and *mankind* could sometimes refer to females as well –"

Superior Veras nodded. "That has been the way at times. However, the Great Seer speaks with very exact detail. Although we cannot be completely certain, it would seem that, should no living being be destined to destroy or stop this warlock, we would have been told precisely that. What else could the *One* be?"

Silence once more filled the room – but this time it seemed as though it hung there like an ominous, black storm cloud.

Sister Creda found herself continually adjusting her green robe, ensuring that the hood hung just so over the upper part of her forehead, and that no parts of her might be inappropriately displayed. But she was no young girl! Every time she checked her appearance, she became angry at herself for doing so. She was a Sister of the Tower of Giefan – even more so, since she was due to complete her examinations soon! She was not some young peasant girl to become giddy at the thought of seeing the Prince! She sighed, wishing that this could be over …

Superior Veras, beside her, heard her and misunderstood. "Do not be anxious, dear Creda. He may be royalty, but he is still a human being inside – although I would truly be more comfortable if it were the King or Queen we could see! This is so very important! Indeed, I hope that the King and Queen are safe in *their* travels!"

"Hmm," Superior Xyron was musing from Creda's other side, "as the Palace Sorcerer is a male, his value, too, might be questionable should their Royal Highnesses themselves come upon this warlock."

"Ah," added Veras, "but the Prophecy only states that no man can *defeat* him. In view of this, men should certainly prove valuable in interfering with him, and perhaps injuring him and therefore saving the lives of others –"

"Perhaps, then, I should come with you," suggested Superior Xyron, his fingers yet again seeking to stroke his beard. Creda could not help but wonder if there might be any truth to the rumours that he and Superior Veras had, at one time, been more than close friends. His eyes sought hers once more as he spoke.

"But Xyron," said Veras with a shake of her hooded head, "should this warlock venture within the city limits, the people will most certainly need you here."

Xyron sighed. He was obviously not comfortable about Veras venturing forth without him. He gazed downward, toying with a loose thread on the sleeve of his robe. In the sunlight which beamed into the palace waiting chamber, the multi-coloured Superior's Robe of Competence glimmered like a never-ending rainbow.

Their musings were interrupted by the approach of a servant.

"Superiors, Sister," the servant nodded to them respectfully. "His Royal Highness, Prince Yurmar, will see you now. Please follow me."

They followed the tall gentleman down a short corridor. He stopped before a large open door –

Beyond this was the largest room which Creda had ever seen. She was well accustomed to the austere life in the Tower. Never before had she witnessed such luxury as afforded by these deep carpets and shiny surfaces. They were invited to enter, and walked forward upon a rich, red rug which appeared as though it had threads of pure gold throughout its long length. And the *Prince* ...

He sat casually upon the throne – which was itself quite a sight to see, with its intricate patterns and designs engraved so deeply into the rich wood -- on an angle, one foot hanging over the arm while the other leg stretched out before him. Long legs they were, for he was, indeed, a tall young man. And his hair was like spun gold. The sunlight which gleamed through the windows seemed to make it sparkle, while auburn streaks shone through in places. He had pale brown eyes. To Creda, they seemed to be a rather fascinating colour, as they almost matched the hues of his hair.

The Prince wore no crown, and his golden thatch was rather disheveled, as though he had hurried here. Actually, it was rather obvious from whence he had come, for he wore riding boots and breeches and still held his crop in his hand. He wore a serious expression upon his face and his impatience revealed itself in his continuous tapping of his riding crop against his thigh.

A gentleman introduced them to the Prince, and the Superiors greeted him and thanked him for seeing them so soon.

"You were riding, Your Highness." Veras stated this, rather than asking a question.

The Prince gazed at her silently for a moment. "I have been told something of the reason for your visit, Superior. Please advise me of the reason for all of this haste."

"Yes, Your Highness. We believe that you would be wise to think twice about riding for pleasure outside of the walls of Espri during the next while."

He changed his position to sit correctly upon the throne, his eyes still fixed on those of the Superior. "We have had word of the attack upon the nomads' village not far from here. What can you add to what we already know?"

Veras nodded. She gestured to Creda, who stood beside and slightly behind her. "Sister Creda witnessed the damage yesterday and brought news of it to us. She identified some sorcery about it and we of the Tower spent the night seeking knowledge."

"What can you tell me, Sister?"

At first, Creda found her heart beating harder as the Prince turned his eyes in her way, but quickly her mind was filled with images of the attack upon her sister's people. "Have you heard the stories of the *warlock*, Your Majesty?"

"Surely there are many warlocks about. But I have heard some stories about one who seems ... different."

Creda nodded. "I fear that there is such. And it was quite definitely his raiders who destroyed the village. This is the closest that they have ever come to our city. It would appear that this warlock may be no longer satisfied with what he has found in the areas south of here."

The Prince said nothing. He no longer gazed at the sorcerers and sorceresses, but stared blankly into space ... or looked at something inside of his own mind.

Creda continued: "He does not kill his victims. He takes them alive." She swallowed. The silence in the room seemed to hang ominously in the air.

It seemed as though no one in the room dared to speak, or even to breathe. Veras and Xyron explained the Prophecy then, as the Great Seer had explained it to them.

When the Prince spoke once more, it was to the servant who stood at his left. "Grendan, give the order to sound the horn to gather in our citizens who are outside of the city gates. And close the gates. And double the guard, especially those who watch the distance from the tops of the walls. And ring the chapel bells. I want the citizens to convene in one hour. I shall head up to the balcony to tell them something of the danger of attack. But – everyone in this room – heed me well. We shall *not* tell the populace of the stories of this warlock. At least not now. We do not want the people of Espri in a panic. We are to be ready to defend our people and keep them safe."

With that, he rose, nodded to those of the Tower, and headed toward a door across the room. But he stopped, turning back to face them. "You two sorceresses cannot go without protection and assistance. We need most of our army here, but we will seek volunteers and will spare some of our army or guards to travel with you."

One hour later, Superior Veras, Superior Xyron and Sister Creda stood at the front of the large group of townspeople, in front of the Royal Balcony. There was much chatter, and some of the folk had heard about the attack upon Creda's sister's people. Some had tried to gain information from the sorcerer and sorceresses, but they explained that it was the Prince's responsibility to explain, not theirs. Finally, Prince Yurmar appeared. He stood erect, emphasizing his ample height. The crown which he now wore gleamed golden in the sunlight, giving him the appearance of a god with a halo.

He explained the situation carefully and confidently, omitting certain details which might draw attention to some of the more horrible rumours being circulated. When he mentioned the involvement of sorcery, several of the townsfolk gasped. He motioned to Superior Veras and Sister Creda. "These are the sorceresses who shall search out this magician before he can become more of a threat to our kingdom. As it has been prophesized that a male will not be the one to defeat this evil, these Sisters of the Tower will go. But they will have need of protection. Most of our army needs to remain here to protect our city and countryside, but I seek brave fighters to assist these two. Our own soldiers are free to offer their services should they wish. Of course, any who join this expedition will be compensated at its conclusion. Now, who will offer to assist in this great mission?"

Creda watched the Prince in fascination, wondering how anyone could not join them after such an eloquent speech. A murmur was making its way through the crowd. Creda was suddenly aware that there seemed to be hundreds of eyes on her, and on Superior Veras …

But that was all that was happening! Stares and murmurs, murmurs and stares. And not one individual made any move to offer his or her services –

Until one voice finally spoke. It was a loud and overly confident voice –

And one which Creda recognized …

"What? Will not one citizen speak? What sort of people *are* you, anyway?"

The crowd began to open to let the man through, almost as a wave in the sea might move as a ship makes its way through.

A strong and well-built warrior stood in front of the Prince's balcony. He had his large hands on his hips, as though taunting others. He was tall, as was the Prince, but this warrior was much heavier and broader through the chest and shoulders. His hair was as dark as night, and his skin had a light brown tone. He wore thick hide across his chest for protection from spears and daggers.

He glanced toward the sorceresses, and Creda returned his look. He winked at her, and she couldn't help but smile in return. Creda felt, rather than saw, an inquiring gaze from Veras.

The man looked around himself at the townspeople, and up at the Prince on the balcony. He bowed respectfully. "Good thing I happened to be coming this way," he said loudly. "Yes! I am a warrior and a good one. And I offer my services to assist these good Sisters. Come and join me! You need have no fear, for you will be serving with a great and experienced fighter! I have been called *The Quickest and the Bravest, Strong and Bold, Might and Right —*"

Creda swallowed. *What if someone asked him which name he preferred?* If he said *that* name, how could she explain it to Superior Veras? But there was silence. Creda let out the breath that she hadn't realized she'd been holding —

But it was the Prince himself who asked: "And what shall *we* call you, soldier?" The Prince was smiling kindly at the warrior.

Creda looked over at the warrior, her mouth agape.

He smiled and nodded in her direction before he turned back to the Prince. "Some call me *Nico*, Your Highness."

CHAPTER FOUR

The Journey Begins

It was a beautiful day when the little group set out. To Creda, it seemed almost *wrong* that they should be venturing forth on such a challenging and horrific mission, while the sunlight warmed them and accentuated everything around them that seemed good. Even the steady *thump-thumping* of the horses' hoofs could not drown out nor even muffle the wondrous twitterings of the birds which flew overhead or stopped to rest in the tree limbs.

But she reminded herself that it might be that she was simply more sensitive to the creatures than other people were. Certainly, there had been indications of this in the past.

"Sister," said a voice from beside her.

But Creda was still lost in her musings and failed to reply.

"Sister," came the voice, more urgently this time.

This time Creda was a bit startled, realizing that this was the second time she'd just heard this voice. "Yes, yes. I – I'm sorry, sir." She turned to look at Joul Zann, a palace guard who had left his post in order to offer his services to their quest. Creda couldn't help but wonder at first if his decision had been influenced by Nico. But since that time, the Prince had proclaimed the gentleman to be captain of the group – and now Creda wondered if Nico – with all of his bravado – was comfortable with this.

"Please, Sister," he nodded politely. "We had best move more quickly if we hope to reach the town by nightfall."

"Yes, of course. My apologies, sir." Creda clucked at the mare to hasten her trot. Captain Zann was quite correct. They certainly *did* want to reach the town of Edgewood before dusk. Apparently, this was to be their last opportunity for a while to eat their meals and sleep indoors. Zann was now speaking to Superior Veras, no doubt suggesting to her, too, that they should make haste. Zann had the air about him of someone who was accustomed to having others follow his orders. Creda looked around for Nico, but then remembered that he had ridden ahead. It seemed that Nico preferred not to be in the same vicinity as Captain Zann, and she wondered how their group would fare if there were two among them who both preferred to lead …

Creda held the reins more tightly as her mare picked up the pace. She glanced over her shoulder at the four behind her. Two from the Royal Army and two from the city. They were all armed, yet the sorceress couldn't help but wonder just how effective a group of eight might be against the likes of this warlock they had to face.

Nico had rejoined their group, and Creda watched as he guided his black stallion so that he rode beside Veras. He leaned closer to her and said something to which she responded with a merry laugh. In all of the time that Creda had been learning from her Superior, it had been a rare occurrence to hear Veras laugh so heartily. What could Nico have possibly said to a *Superior* that was appropriate, yet so humorous?

And, considering the gravity of their mission, was such gaiety suitable at all? Creda snorted and urged the mare to move even more quickly.

Superior Veras sighed. As accustomed as she was to keeping her feelings to herself, the stiffness of her joints from the long ride was beginning to become more painful. She had been adjusting her position as much as possible, yet still some parts were beginning to ache. Yet she tried to keep a relatively cheerful countenance, knowing that she had skills which could affect the states of mind of the others in the group.

The moon was making an appearance against the darkening blue of the sky. Its brightness was certainly welcome, although it added an eerie look as thick clouds moved slowly across its face.

All was very quiet, the only sound the thumping of the hoofs upon the dirt. As the darkness increased, so did the evening chill.

A sudden *screech* had her heart jumping, and Creda cried out, just ahead. Veras was about to urge her mount forward, but Nico had guided his stallion over to join the Sister. Vera could see his broad smile when he turned his head to look at Creda. She could not hear his words, but he laughed, and began to hum a tune. It was a well-known tune, the words of which were rather bawdy.

Veras chuckled but wondered what Creda's response might be. As Nico left her side, Veras moved up to take his place. She gazed over at the Sister and opened her mouth to speak but decided against it. Creda was not the typical young apprentice, after all. She had had more life experience than most …

At long last, the small company reached the town of Edgewood, saddle sore and dusty. The townspeople would likely never know how very welcome their lights had been when Captain Zann first pointed them out against the blackness of the night. Fortunately, the one inn was not full, although it seemed quite abuzz with activity. It seemed a sharp contrast to the quiet of the Tower to which Creda had become accustomed. As they took their horses to the stable, Creda couldn't help but wonder if staying with the horses might be more restful than being in the inn. But the group was in need of food and drink, and proceeded to the Hound's Tooth, the inn's pub.

Nico was in his element. He whispered into the serving girl's ear, making her laugh as she gave him a playful cuff on the cheek. Some of the younger men in the room seemed to think this was great sport and cast admiring eyes in Nico's direction.

The first serving of ale was quickly drained, and the second washed the mutton down the thirsty throats of the escort. The Superior and Sister quietly supped on their breads and cheeses and sipped their tea. Although they were both quiet, Creda couldn't help but notice that Superior Veras frequently cast her eyes in Nico's direction, smiling. Creda had memories of inns such as this, but she was of no mind to share them at this time. She looked forward to retiring to the room upstairs which she would share with the Superior. She closed her eyes and rubbed her head with her fingers …

Suddenly, the laughter and banter at their table ceased, although it continued in other areas of the large room. Creda opened her eyes and looked, wondering what was happening. Those of their escort were all gazing at Veras. Creda had not been listening, and wondered what the Superior could possibly have said –

Nico spoke first, choosing his words carefully. "Superior Veras, our opponent is this fearsome?" He was looking downward into his tankard of ale, his face serious.

Veras regarded him for a moment, then turned to gaze at the faces of the others around the table, seeking to include each one as she spoke. "This warlock may very well be the most fearsome foe that some of you have – or ever will – face. There have been many rumours about what he has caused to happen, unfortunately, and one can never be certain how much of what is *said* may actually be true. But we *do* know that he has taken many innocents alive, using an army which may involve some sort of sorcery. In order to accomplish these actions, he must be a powerful warlock indeed." She paused, once more ensuring that her eyes met those of each of the others at their table. "We must all be quick and sharp as we continue our journey, and we must begin now. If any of you have second thoughts about accompanying and assisting us, you may head back to Espri tomorrow."

Captain Zann had also been scanning the faces of those in the group, and now spoke: "We shall abide by your words, Superior Ver—"

But the *screech* of a chair leg against the wooden floor interrupted him as Nico stood. "Superior," he said in a voice that seemed louder than necessary, "I believe that you are correct. I will not allow myself any more ale this night – and I will seek my bed now, to be well-rested tomorrow. Good evening, ladies." His eyes met Veras's for a moment, and he strode confidently from the room.

Zann stroked his thick brownish moustache, then suggested that the rest of the retinue follow suit. Good nights were exchanged as the group made its way to the stairs leading to the private rooms.

Their room was small and simply furnished, which was comforting in its similarity to the rooms of the Tower. It supplied their simple needs, offering two small beds, basins of water with cloths for washing and drying, and a warm fireplace. There was a mirror above one of the water basins, and Veras watched as Creda attempted to work her fingers through the tangles of her now-unbound brownish hair, which glittered with gold tones in the light from the fire. She took a step in the Sister's direction, and the floorboards groaned. Creda started at the sudden noise, and Veras put a reassuring hand upon her shoulder.

"I'm sorry, Creda. I didn't mean to frighten you!" Although Creda had demonstrated the skills necessary to be a competent sorceress, Veras knew that she needed t0 help Creda to become more confident in view of the possible challenges awaiting them.

The younger woman turned to face her. She forced a smile, although her pale blue eyes looked tired. "I'm all right, Superior Veras."

"Yes. From now on, Creda, we should call each other simply by our names. Or perhaps *Sister*. Do not refer to me as *Superior* again – at least, until this business is complete."

"Why, *Veras*?" It seemed odd to refer to her instructor -- her mentor -- simply by her name.

Veras's green-blue eyes had a faraway look about them, as though her mind was seeing – or was imagining -- what the future held. "Well, should we be overheard by any of the warlock's raiders, or anyone associated with them, it would be wise not to let them know that one of us has achieved the level of Superior. If they think that we are simple sorceresses, they might be less prepared to deal with the level of the skills which we might bring against them. We must ensure that this is explained to the others as well. We should tell them that this is also the reason that we are wearing simple brown robes instead of those usually worn by sorceresses and superiors."

Creda nodded thoughtfully, but glumly.

"But Creda, tomorrow we will be in search of the Witch. Once we have met with her, we should have more answers." Veras smiled encouragingly.

"Or more questions," offered Creda with a wry smile.

Veras nodded in response to Creda's words. "Yes. Now we had best make use of our training to prepare ourselves as much as possible for what tomorrow will bring." Veras sank down to sit upon the worn rug which covered part of the rough floor. She had unfastened her jaw-length auburn hair, and she pushed a strand back behind her ear. Then she took her amulet into her hand, closing her eyes. Creda joined her. They shut away from their conscious minds all images of the rabble downstairs, the dusty road, the beauty of the bright moon somewhat spoiled by the dark clouds which had skittered across its face. And there, just beyond lay their enchantments stored carefully away, each in its own compartment, awaiting the touch of their spirits ...

Their amulets seemed to buzz with life. They vibrated and were warm in the hands of the sorceresses.

And the necessary words came forth, as though of their own accord: *When the moon's face shines down upon the shadow of the golden orb, so ye shall find the answer ye seek.*

Veras opened her eyes and reached for one of the candles. Creda pulled the golden chain of her amulet over her head and held it so that the amulet hung just to the right of the moonlight from the window. Veras leaned forward to adjust the position of the candle. Its light needed to shine from behind Creda's amulet, so that the amulet's shadow lay in the path of the moon's glow. Veras reached a hand to grasp Creda's so that the physical contact could enhance the union of their thoughts.

Then, before them, a thick, dark wooded area slowly began to take shape. At first the images were quite faint, and they could see the room's furniture through them easily. Gradually, though, the vision took a stronger form. They could smell the sweet scent of evergreen and hear the faint rustles of the colourful leaves while the breezes gently stirred them.

When they looked behind them, there was more forest. They could barely see the moon shining down through the thickness of the tall trees above.

An owl hooted suddenly, and Creda's heart jumped in its place –

Instantly Vera was able to send a message of soothing tranquility. She took a deep breath, and, in their joined state, Creda automatically followed. Calmness enveloped them both. Now they could see better in the darkness ...

They were in a small clearing. They searched the area for landmarks which would assist them in finding their way on the morrow. A boulder to the left, and a path behind them, but also one ahead

They stepped forward, the breaking twigs making small cracking sounds beneath their feet. Ahead was a bit of glowing light, although its source was still cloaked in blackness. They made their way slowly through the growth, until they reached the base of a cliff. High above them was the source of the glow ...

It was much more than just a glow in the dark, though. The two sorceresses knew that it represented the end of the first leg of their journey – and the answer, hopefully, to some of their questions.

But the question now was -- how would they get up there?

CHAPTER FIVE

The Wood

Nico stood just outside of the stable, rubbing his large hands over his mount. The horse enjoyed the contact and tossed his head before pushing his long nose against his human companion, snorting contentedly. Nico relished the feel of the beast's strong, muscular body, as well as the friendship which the two shared. They had been together for several years.

A gust of wind distracted the man, and he turned his face upward to study what the sky might tell him. The clouds above were twisting and writhing as they passed across the sun before exposing its rays again. More clouds were following, and there seemed to be increasingly grey ones beyond –

A motion over his shoulder caught his eye, and he turned to see Sister Creda standing in the stable doorway with the reins of her mare in her hands. She, too, was scanning the skies, and her forehead was puckered in a frown.

Smiling broadly, Nico stepped in her direction, his mount stepping behind him. "Sister," he said loudly, "no need to look so worried! We have a mission to complete, and the weather won't be a problem. Anyway, why worry when you have an escort the like of *this* one? Ha!"

She smiled, and led her mare out of the stable, thanking Nico for his assistance as she mounted. The bay mare was certainly not a large horse, but Creda had become well-used to little Portar. Yet she appreciated the complacent and calm nature of the little horse in contrast to the donkey's almost constant opposition! She reached forward to pat the mare's neck.

"Is everyone ready? Is everyone here?" It was Joul Zann's voice, as he looked around from one to the other. Satisfied with what he saw, he began to lead the little procession.

They left the hustle and bustle of the town and entered upon the peacefulness of the surrounding countryside with its farms and endless grasses. Rolling hills were ahead, as though to remind them that they would soon be approaching the edge of the mountains. A low rumble had several of them glancing upward to see the ominous presence of increasingly grey clouds. They were swirling even more now, twisting and turning as they wormed their ways inside of each other, then outside once again.

They were just in sight of the edge of the Great East Wood when the rains came. Luckily the rain came lightly at first, almost like a falling mist. Those that had them pulled their hoods lower over their faces. Fortune remained with them, for they arrived at the shelter of the trees before the rain began in earnest. It was much darker here, but at least it was not so wet.

Zann waited for the rest of the group to catch up to him. "All right," he said, his eyes scanning the group, "we will be going into thicker undergrowth, and will have to ride the path in single file. Make certain that some of you are near to the Sisters at all times. Their protection is of the utmost importance."

So into the dark forest they moved, Captain Zann in the lead. Bramble bushes grew in abundance. Care had to be taken when avoiding the lower-hanging branches, as the group could not always see what it was which they might brush up against. *Darkness, dampness and uncertainty ...*

They had ridden for what seemed to be an awfully long time, yet still all that greeted them were tall trees and endless shadowy areas. Initially, their spirits had been lifted by the chirping and chattering of the birdlife, but for the last while all that they'd been hearing was the steady *plop-plopping* of the horses' hoofs –

Veras shared a glance with the young man who rode behind her. She remembered that his name was Vander. His young face looked very pale in the darkness which seemed everywhere. The Superior gave him a confident and encouraging smile, knowing the importance of helping the others to keep their spirits up. When she turned to face forward once more, she was pleased to see the Captain motion to her to move towards the front of their line to join him. He advised her that there was a clearing just ahead, and they urged their mounts forward, eager to be free of the dense and damp growth.

A relieved sigh escaped the Superior. She closed her eyes and took a long breath of replenishment. Then she smiled at Captain Zann, and he nodded in return with a smile of his own. They were dismounting when the others joined them in the clearing.

"Step carefully," advised Zann. "The grasses are wet." He had tethered his mount to a tree branch, and the others followed suit.

Veras stood beside Zann and appeared to be waiting for their attention. The group turned to her, anxious to know what was to come. "From here," she said gently, in her quiet but confident voice, "we shall follow this narrow path a way. Then we shall be at the base of a cliff. Bring rope and whatever else you might have with you to assist in our climb. It does not appear to be a high climb, but it might be an awkward one."

She and Zann entered the thicket, quickly followed by the others. There was a continued need for care and caution, as the thorny bushes along the edges of the path seemed hungry to seize and hold anything that might come in contact with them. From up ahead, Creda heard Veras mutter something in an uncharacteristic tone, then saw that Nico was helping to disentangle her brown robe from the prickly growth.

Soon the mists around them becoming more and more thick and wet, they arrived at the base of the cliff. Their destination lay ahead ... and *above*. Through the cave's entrance gleamed an eerie light. If not for the shadows and the grey of the sky, it might have been easily missed by someone searching for it.

As Creda gazed upward, no matter what the challenges might be within that cave, it seemed inviting if there was a warm fire inside of it. She noticed Zann, Veras, Nico and two of the others in discussion. As she moved closer, she wasn't surprised to hear that they were talking about different possible ways of making the climb.

"What if we went back a little distance from here and headed up where the climb is less steep?" Vander suggested. "From there we could cross at the top, then make our way *downward* where it's steepest …"

There was continued discussion regarding this. Several voices spoke at once initially, and their hushed quality reflected the tension of the situation.

Zann raised his hand, palm toward the group in a bid for silence. "Vander's suggestion has merit, as do some others. What is *your* opinion, Nico?"

Nico looked up from lowered eyes, regarding the faces of those around him. After a few seconds he raised his chin, confident as usual. "I agree that it can be done. Some should remain here to care for the horses, and the supplies which they carry. Those of us who have climbing experience should accompany the Sisters."

Zann was nodding, considering while he stroked his thick, brown moustache. "Yes. Sisters, we may be able to avoid the muddier areas if we climb the less steep and grassier area, as Vander suggested. If the going becomes very difficult, can we count on you for your assistance?"

Veras was silent a moment, a look of sadness crossing her face. She smiled at Creda, then turned to the Captain. "Creda and I are seeking to face the warlock who has caused all of this turmoil. We don't know when or where that will be. Our energies for spell making must not be spent unnecessarily. You must count on us only for assistance in dire circumstances."

Concern clouded Zann's face while he listened. But he pulled himself to his full height and looked confidently at those surrounding him. "Very well. Vander, I know that you have experience in these hills. You will join me and Nico in accompanying the Sisters. The others will remain here, with Ferren in charge. You know the signal, Ferren, should you need to contact me."

"Very well, Captain," agreed Ferren. Her short brown hair bounced up and down as she nodded.

Vander, Zann, Nico and the Sisters headed along the trail until they saw a break in the brambles.

The break was very short, though, and with a sigh, Nico unsheathed his sword and prepared to hack at the prickly branches which blocked their way. He turned to Veras and gave his usual confident grin. "Little did I know that my first adversary would be undergrowth!"

Vander and Zann joined him, and Veras drew her knife, nodding at Creda to follow suit. The two women began to make some headway against the thinner branches. After a time, Creda could see a grassy section of hill not far ahead. She pointed it out to Veras, and the two renewed their efforts with greater enthusiasm.

They exchanged glances when they heard a shout from Nico. Unable to see him from where they stood, they followed the direction of his voice. Veras cleared some of the higher branches –

He was stopped just inside some thicker, taller growth. Sweat poured down his face, despite the chill in the air. His dark hair looked even blacker with moisture. He dragged the back of his hand across his forehead.

"Not much farther, Sisters. Just up ahead the growth thins out. Watch your steps, there. I nearly tripped over that root."

Creda felt as though she was burrowing her way through a tunnel in the midst of thorny walls. As the incline became steeper, she found herself puffing and panting. But, at last, the bushy growth became less dense until it was mainly high grasses and rocks past which they made their ways.

A large hand was extended in her direction, from above. She took it without hesitation and felt herself being pulled easily upward and onto a rocky ledge. Nico's other hand then grasped her elbow and pushed her behind him to stand beside Vander, while he leaned forward to assist Veras.

After so long amid bramble bushes, the group was grateful to be on a fairly large ledge which afforded a view of the surroundings.

"Beautiful, isn't it?" Nico leaned close to Veras to whisper into her ear. He gave her a warm smile, and she returned it, her eyes holding his for a moment. "Sisters," he said in a louder voice, we'd best move along now." He nodded toward Vander, who turned to lead the little procession toward where they knew the cave to be.

But, as pleasant as the view was from the ledge, the weather was *not* pleasant. The sky was grey, allowing only a bit of hazy glow to reach them. And the drizzle continued, leaving puddles and slippery places along the rocky ledge. They each took a turn slipping but helped one another regain their footing. Even Nico faltered on one occasion but needed no assistance.

"Vander!" It was Captain Zann's voice. "No! Vander, come back!"

Nico moved to go after him, but Zann stopped him. Nico turned to Veras. "Sister!"

Veras swallowed hard, shaking her head, but shouted, "Vander, do NOT approach the cave!"

Vander had not seen the reddish glow across the mouth of the cave, as she and Creda had in their vision. He had not witnessed the look of it, like a glittering veil. But he knew that he should certainly not head in its direction!

She called to him again, as loudly as she could: "Vander! Do not approach the cave!"

But the terrible cry told them that it was too late.

CHAPTER SIX

The Witch

At first, Ferren had appreciated the responsibility of being in charge. But, as time went on, they heard nothing except for a few snorts from the horses and the steady drumming sound of the rain in the trees. She began to wonder what it was like for the others, who had gone to explore the way to the cave.

CREEE CREEE CREEE

The piercing cry seemed to fill the entire wood and the sky beyond. Yet they saw nothing –

Her blade drawn, Ferren exchanged glances with the other two, and, swords held before them with two hands, they walked slowly around the area, eyes alert for any movement, any more unusual sounds –

"There!" Tavis extended a shaking finger, pointing upward in the direction of the grey sky.

A huge, winged creature soared overhead, moving in the direction of the cave in the side of the hill. The greyish creature gleamed silver in what little light managed to find its way through the thick cloud cover. It had a large beak and talons ...

For a heartbeat, Ferren was torn – torn between gratitude that the thing was up *there* and not down here in their midst, and frustration that she couldn't get to the thing and do her duty in defending the Sisters –

Nico was holding his sword in his two large hands, breathing deeply in preparation to battle the hovering, crimson-eyed beast for Vander's life – although at the present Nico couldn't see much value in the life of the stupid young man.

A hand was on his arm, pressuring him to keep his sword down. He glanced to his left to see Veras, whose own eyes were on the creature which hovered just above them.

"Enough damage has been done already," she said softly. "This is the Witch's protection against trespassers, and Vander has alerted it."

Reluctantly, Nico lowered his weapon. If Ferren felt torn down below with the horses, then Nico was quite uncomfortably so. Here he stood, watching a fearsome beast threatening a member of his party, and the sorceress was bidding him not to interfere. How he detested magic! How had he gotten himself into this? How was he to defend stupid Vander?

The sorceress stepped past him, gazing at the creature just above and in front of them. Her fingers sought the touch of her amulet as Creda came to her side.

Although Nico had lowered his sword, his hands still gripped it firmly. He was tense and ready in case the thing made a move to harm the Sisters or Vander.

Veras and Creda worked to enact a *Spell of Protection*. They would create a barrier of magic between the beast and Vander. They had both accessed the power which lay inside of their amulets, and had repeated the words in unison, but the situation just wasn't right for the spell to work. There needed to be adequate room between the attacker and the one needing protection, in order for the spell to be enacted. But neither the creature nor Vander had knowledge of this, and the creature continually lunged at the young man, who responded to this threat by slashing at the thing with his sword.

Confusion was suddenly gripping Creda. There was a strange familiarity about it. She'd seen something which she *couldn't* have seen --

She could not have *seen* Vander as he thrust his blade in *her* direction. She *couldn't* have ...

A shrill scream once more filled the air –

And Creda *felt* it! And *anger – fury at this puny human who would dare threaten his mistress! Kill him he would! Again, he lunged at the human*

No!

Suddenly she was Creda again, seeing through her *own* eyes. Yet still she felt the creature's anger, his desire to kill –

He collected himself for one final lunge, for Vander was by now quite spent. The flying beast's curved beak parted as he gave a victory shriek, his talons moving in to seize his victim –

NO!

The creature hesitated, its strange red eyes fixed on Creda. Creda gasped –*the beast had received her thought!* The beast hovered for just a few heartbeats of time –

But it was *enough* time. When the creature returned his attention to his victim, he saw the human surrounded in a glow of deep blue – the colour of Veras's power. He leaned forward to peck at this strange mist.

Nico was watching Creda. She had been swaying, unsteady, but was now standing solidly once again. Veras's fingers were still on her amulet, and now Creda took her own in hers as well. Nico watched as the two sorceresses whispered together in deep concentration. All else was quiet. The creature flew upward and soared away, across the sky.

Creda was swaying once more. Quickly, Nico placed a hand on each of her upper arms to support her. "Are you all right, Sister?"

The sorceress took a deep breath, and placed a hand on top of one of Nico's. "Yes," she murmured. "I – I'm all right now. And so is Vander."

Veras, too, was regarding Creda with interest. She looked into Creda's eyes, her own face reflecting confusion and puzzlement.

So, thought Nico. *All did not occur as it was supposed to. This business of spells and magic is certainly not without its faults.*

Veras turned to speak to all of them. "We must approach the Witch immediately. We have an apology to make!"

Although Nico believed that it should be Vander who made the apology, he held his tongue. Such decisions belonged to the Sisters. "Come then," he said, and began to make his way up the small incline to the level ground near the cave's mouth. Part way up, he extended a hand behind to Veras.

She took his hand and he pulled her to the level ground, where Vander still sat not far from the mouth of the cave. Surrounded by the blue fog of Veras's protection spell, he looked quite unhappy. Veras reached forward toward the top of the fog, and suddenly it was gone. Vander clambered to his feet, quite shakily. He opened his mouth to speak, but the looks upon the faces of those around him had him shutting it again. The others were gazing toward the cave mouth, and he did too.

Beyond the transparent reddish glow which covered the expanse of the cave entrance, they could see her.

The Witch of the Great East Wood –

And she did not look pleased.

A formidable figure she appeared, her dark eyes reflecting the scarlet energy which flickered as it shielded her entrance from intruders. She was an older woman with grey streaks through her long, brown hair. Older yes, but she had a look of great strength about her, for she stood tall and erect – not bent over her staff as some legends would have a witch appear. Had the Sisters come here many years ago, no doubt they would have found a woman close to being, perhaps, beautiful, for her features were not unattractive even now.

She was standing with her arms crossed, silently. It seemed as though she might be studying them.

Captain Zann opened his mouth to speak. He was, after all, the leader of this group. But Veras made a noise in her throat to gain his attention, giving him a stern look, and he closed his mouth once more.

Veras was extending a courtesy, for when a sorceress faced one whose magic was considered superior, one must always allow the other to speak first. She was, therefore, paying the Witch a compliment, which would seem to be a good way to begin --considering that a member of their group had been caught trespassing upon this property.

Having scanned the faces of those in front of her, the Witch settled her stern gaze on Veras. Finally, she spoke. "So. You have come and intruded upon my cliff. What right have you to venture here?"

Veras bowed politely, her heart pounding. "Forgive us," she said in a soft voice. "Please forgive our very rude intrusion, oh Mother of the Great East Wood. Forgive our escort for upsetting your sentry – he will be dealt with. Mother, we Sisters are here to speak with you of a very urgent matter. We are here at the direction of the Seer –"

At this, the Witch's eyes narrowed. "You have had contact with the Seer?"

Veras nodded gravely. "Myself, with the three other Superiors of the Tower of Giefan."

"You reached the Seer," repeated the Witch, her eyes becoming unfocussed. She no longer regarded Veras, nor any of the others, for it seemed as though she might have been considering a memory, or some other contemplation. Then she cast a glance around the little group and turned her brown eyes once more to Veras. "You may enter, Superior."

Veras sighed slightly with relief, once more bowing her head respectfully. "I would ask, Great Mother, for permission to have Sister Creda join us."

The Witch hesitated a moment, eyeing Creda, but nodded her consent. Almost like a curtain parting, the reddish coating across the entrance disappeared down through the centre until it was just wide enough for the two to walk through. It crackled and glowed as the two seemed to walk directly into the red energy ...

CHAPTER SEVEN

The Segment

Nico still seized his blade with both hands. That – that woman, or *Witch* or whatever in blazes she, or maybe *it* was – had done little to inspire his confidence. How had he ended up on a quest such as this? He'd served in many a battle, but they'd been human against human, human against beast –

Sorcery -- *sorcery of all things!* What had he been thinking of when he decided to join this quest? He'd always avoided anything to do with the magic arts. How could a man fight something he didn't understand? He'd served his share of kings, not caring about their beliefs or principles. But he'd always avoided the palace sorcerers and sorceresses. Yet he knew the answer to his question. When he thought about the reason that he was here, he saw Sister Creda's face, at the moment when she'd told him about the attack on her sister's people. And now she and Veras were inside with that –that *thing* and he was powerless to protect them! All he could do was stand here, grasping his sword and doing nothing – like a damned fool!

He gazed at the hazy redness covering the cave mouth. Veras had made it very clear that they must not interfere …

"Curse all magic and sorcery," he spat, and turned away.

Vander remained still, trembling. He swallowed hard, avoiding making eye contact with the big man who was regarding him with distaste and anger. Nico moved close to him and opened his mouth to speak –

"Nico," said Zann quickly, as he stepped between them. "I've already spoken with Vander. There is nothing more need be said." But his eyes met Nico's, and he saw that there was something more behind the anger of those dark eyes.

Then suddenly the something was gone –

Nico spat once more, then chuckled. He looked again at Vander, then laughed aloud. "So! Early in the mission, yet I'll warrant you've found enough adventure already! Ha!" He moved away from the cave's entrance, strolled to the edge of the cliff, cupping his hands around his mouth. "Hey, down there! Not a bad bit of entertainment, eh? Well, you can relax now – I'm afraid there'll be no more excitement for a while at least!"

He chuckled again, moving back from the edge and under the overhang near the cave's mouth, which offered a bit of shelter from the continuing drizzle. Pulling his cloak around him, he dropped to sit beside the entrance to the cave, his back against the rocky wall. "May as well get a bit of rest while we can," he suggested to the other two.

Zann nodded his agreement, although he glanced once more at the cave mouth. But he dropped beside Nico, pulling a bit of dried meat from a pouch. Vander gazed at the other two, but continued to sit where he was, contented not to move – at least, not until the trembling had stopped.

Veras cast a glance back at Creda as they entered the cave. The younger Sister was staring in wonder at their surroundings. It was quite a contrast to the outside. The warmth was delicious. There was no hint of dampness nor chill. Somehow, the cave seemed alive, not an old, dank place in rock. There were a few birds which twittered contentedly about the area, and the fire in the centre quite adequately heated the entire cave – which seemed almost neverending, with all of its exits and entrances to and from this large room.

The Superior kept her eyes on the Witch, anxious that she be alert to all clues from their hostess. They must observe all correct protocol. They were relying on the Witch's assistance, after all. At a nod from the Witch, Veras sat upon the woven rug not far from the fire, and glanced at Creda to ensure that she, too, complied.

Creda sat, her eyes upon the Witch, fascinated. She had never seen a Witch before, only heard rumours about their appearances. The Witches had split away from the sorcerers and sorceresses many, many years ago. The Witches had felt that the palace sorcerers and sorceresses were quite wrong to use their skills for the political purposes of the kings and queens, and they also disagreed with those of the Towers, who developed and used their skills for use among the common folk, regardless of political affiliations.

For the Witches believed that those of sorcery were forgetting the most important application of magic there could be – that of sustaining Mother Earth, Mother Nature Herself, without whom none of the folk of the world could exist at all. And so it was that the Witches sought to maintain the important balance of life for all creatures, to ensure that Nature's children could exist without constant interference from the folk, with their burning and pillaging and wars and weapons and blood –

Yet they had a higher purpose too. Should one trained in the magic arts become more powerful than necessary and seek to use enchantment for selfish purposes without regard for the greater good, the Witches would take action. They felt it quite appropriate that they combine their powers to keep such a one from causing imbalance and harm to life in this world.

The Witch turned, offering warm cups of steaming liquid, which, she said, was brewed from the needles of the evergreens. She waited patiently while they sipped, seating herself upon a nearby wooden chair.

While she sipped from the cup, Creda felt a wonderful warmth spread inside of her. It seemed like she must be glowing. She looked over at Veras, and the smile upon the Superior's face told her that she was sharing the experience.

The Witch smiled once more, and the motion seemed to sweep years from her face. "If you feel replenished sufficiently, good Sisters, I would like to combine my power with yours, so that your memory of the Great Seer might be reproduced. I wish to know exactly what was shared with you."

Veras nodded, placing her cup on a rock beside her. She was eager to do this. This was a very important part of their visit. Once they had done this, the Witch would *truly* understand their mission. But she thought of Creda who had never done this before. She turned to the Sister, and squeezed her hand, giving her an encouraging smile. Together, each reached for her amulet with one hand while the other sought contact with the hands of the others.

The room began to fill with pale blue mist. It emanated from the area immediately surrounding them, then it expanded and spread until it was a thin, transparent haze which filled the cave entirely. And, amidst this, the eerie figure of the Seer appeared. And there were the words again: *No man can defeat this warlock! But there is a One. That One shall be given the Way by the Witch of the Great East Wood. But, heed me well, no man can defeat this warlock!*

Although silence now filled the area, it seemed to Creda as though the words echoed, over and over, throughout the cave.

Finally, the Witch spoke. "And so," she said softly, a deep sigh escaping, "it is now, then. The time has come."

"Yes, Mother," said Veras, equally softly. "It appears that the warlock's raiders have ventured within a half-day's ride of Espri. It is no longer only a problem for those in the farthest south. You have heard the Prophecy. What say you, Mother? What is the *Way*?"

The Witch said nothing. She seemed to be deep in thought, idly stroking the feathers of a small, brown bird which had come to perch upon her finger. The bird twittered softly, turning its head to study the two visitors.

Veras took a long breath. Her heart was pounding, yet she must not be rude. She must allow the Mother time to consider. The Great Witch had tremendous knowledge, and they must wait as long as necessary for her to share it. After all, they were powerless without her help. But ... but surely the Mother must know that time was of the essence! Veras sighed.

Her heart beating even harder, Veras spoke: "We cannot be certain, Great Mother, but we believe that the *One* is likely to be either of us. The other Sister Superior was rendered ill by her contact with the Seer, and all left in the Tower are an apprentice Sister not yet ready for any testing, and the menfolk. And ours is the only Tower within this realm and those just beyond …"

The Mother remained quiet, then cast a sad glance in Veras's direction. "There was a being, a long, long time ago. A being which thirsted for power as though it was the substance of the air to fill its lungs. Whether demon or sorcerer, or one of great trickery, my kind did not know."

She rose now, the little bird fluttering away to take perch elsewhere. The Witch fingered a small pouch which hung from her rope-like sash. A faraway look was in her eyes as she continued. "I know something of what this being *was*, not necessarily what it is at this time. However, let me say that his acts – and I shall refer to it as a man because that is the form which it took – caused him to be banished from what was once called the Witches' Cove. We Wood Mothers assumed the responsibility for his banishment. Once he was gone, certain – certain *signs* told us that his power may well have been underestimated. We, too – long ago – sought the advice of the Great Seer, despite the great danger such a combining of similar strong powers can create. We were told that there was nothing to be done until there was *One* who was prepared to defeat this warlock, which is what we now assume it to be."

The Witch began to wander about the room now as she spoke, deep in her remembrances. But now she turned, and redirected her gaze toward her visitors. Her eyes were filled with a strange mixture of sadness and anticipation. "For so long I have known of his cruelty and savagery. Yet I had to wait. Only the *One* could defeat him – and I could do nothing until the *Way* was clear." Again her eyes met theirs.

Veras was once again aware of the pounding of her heart. "Forgive me, Mother, but was there nothing that could be done to protect the innocents?"

Creda added: "It has been said, good Mother, that he takes prisoners alive so that he can drain them of their lifeblood –"

The Witch chuckled, but with bitterness. "That is not the truth, Sister. Somehow, he manages to interfere with their energy, yes. But not through drinking blood. I do not know exactly what he does, but it is not that. *Those* beings my people and yours put to rest many generations ago. And, Superior Veras, you must bear in mind that one way he has acquired greater energy has been through stealing from such as yourself the very spells you seek to use against him. No. I could do nothing. The Prophecy dictates that the *One shall be given the Way by the Witch of the Great East Wood.* And now, *you* are here."

Veras rose to her feet, Creda following. The Superior stepped closer to the Mother. "Now, Mother. Now that we are here, can you tell us which of us is the *One*?"

"Yes," the Witch replied. "And no. Good Superior Veras, is it wise for you to know? Although the Prophecy has said that the *One* can defeat the warlock, do not believe for a flash that such will be less than extremely difficult! Even the magical energies of the *One* might be redirected by the warlock, should he discover in advance the *One*'s identity. All must be carried out with great, great care."

"Then – what is the *Way*? Pray, tell us, Mother. Sister Creda and I will be the *One* together if that is what is required."

The Witch began to smile then. Her shoulders sank lower as she visibly relaxed. She tilted her head back and gazed upward in the direction of the cave's high, rocky ceiling, calling out in a strong, contralto voice. "Ah, Sisters, dear Sisters of the Woods. Sisters of the Glades and the Mountains. Sisters of the Coves and the Deserts. *It is time!* The *Way* is here! The *One* shall bring the end to the ruthless warlock! Hear me, Sisters! The *One* shall come!" As she shouted upward, great flashes of lightning flew upward and outward from her fingertips – reddish beams which travelled in straight lines. When one struck the cave wall, it veered off at a sharp angle to strike another surface, then another – until the entire cave was filled with crimson streaks of energy –

Finally, she raised her hands above her head, still shouting joyfully to her kind. The scarlet rays began to bounce from one side of the wall to the other, up near the ceiling's highest point. Their travels became slower and slower until they finally began to curve inward. At last, a great reddish, glowing ball sparkled above her head.

"Sisters," she called, "heed me well. It is time for the *Way*. Watch, my Sisters. The end has come. And the beginning is at hand."

The entire cave started rumbling then, as though an earthquake was starting. Veras and Creda clung to the furniture while the Witch, undisturbed by all of this, stood happily, arms outstretched. Finally the glowing ball began to pulsate as though it were a living thing. Inside of it, they could see two sections of a talisman twisting, turning, coming together to form half of a completed form, then pull apart once more –

The ball began to move, slowly at first –

Then it flew to the entrance, and was gone.

After a few curses from the men who waited outside, all was still once again. Together the Sisters stood, eyes on the Witch as she slowly came to them. She looked very satisfied now, as though something wonderful had been achieved. Creda felt foolish. She had so many questions swirling inside of her. "Forgive me, Mother."

The Witch's eyes met Creda's. They seemed very brown, very warm and lovely now. Indeed, her whole face, her whole *being* seemed several years younger. Even her hair and clothing appeared suddenly less soiled, and newly tended to. "Yes, Sister," she said with a smile.

"I – I … but what is the *Way?*"

Still smiling broadly, she sat upon her wooden chair, and motioned to the Sisters to sit upon the carpet once more. "Dear Sisters, there is a section of the warlock's talisman inside what is known as the Icetombs, in the far north. When we banished him, we shattered his talisman, but he managed to keep one piece. This warlock's power is, somehow, sufficient for him to have hidden his talisman segment in the Icetombs, even though his place of banishment was far, far from there. When we contacted the Seer, it was able to offer only one bit of information which might be of help. The Seer indicated *at this time, the talisman segment is not visible to the human eye.* But you must find it. And the other two segments I have sent out for you – one in the lowest of the Three Great Peaks, and the last in the largest cavern in the rocks at the northern end of the Sea of Extremes. Now, ask no more questions. Nothing more matters. At the base of this cliff, and past the clearing just below, there is a cave large enough to give you shelter. Go now, rest and sup while the rains continue, for when they cease, you must go."

Somewhat in awe of everything that had transpired, Veras thanked the Witch heartily. She accepted the small red pouch inside of which was one of the four segments into which the warlock's talisman had been broken. Hopefully, the pouch would eventually house the complete talisman. Veras held it reverently in her hand, then slipped the string holding it around her neck. The pouch was always to be worn around the neck of one of the Sisters. They turned, once again facing the red glow of protection across the cave mouth, and stepped through.

The faces of the three men were filled with questions. Vander opened his mouth to speak, but Veras shook her head. "No questions now, please," she said softly. "There is a shelter below that we must find first."

Back through the mists, the drizzle, the cold wetness, the brambles they slowly made their way. Back to the others who waited among the trees. Although anxious to hear all, the escort was contented for the moment to know that they were about to be led to an escape from the constant moisture. It was, of course, just as the Witch had said. The cavern was just past the clearing, and quite well-hidden by a large boulder. If they had not been told of its existence, they would no doubt have simply passed it by.

It was wonderful, indeed, to step inside, and out of the rain. There was even room for the horses, who seemed pleased to pause just inside of the entrance. Soon two fires had been lit, although they were kept small to avoid creating too much smoke.

Veras and Creda sat silently upon thick blankets, leaning against the cave wall. Veras closed her eyes and took slow, deep breaths, willing her body and spirit to take a bit of time to rest and regenerate. Although she attempted to find that level of relaxation which would take her into the world of sleep, she was unsuccessful. And so she focused on relaxing her body and her mind as much as she could. She was dimly aware of the sounds around her, but focused on her breathing rather than their sources.

Nico watched as Zann began to assign duties for supper preparation. Their eyes met, and Nico turned his back. He walked over to the horses and checked each one, ensuring that each was settled and away from any rain that might get past the boulder that blocked the wind. He ensured that each had food to nibble on while tethered just inside the cave entrance. Murmuring to Thunder, he ran his hand down the strong, black flank. He stroked his mount's nose, murmuring still. "Curse this weather, Thunder. We have a quest waiting for us, but we're stuck here. We'll be all right, though, won't we boy. There's a good lad."

He turned his attention from the horses, eyeing the others. When he saw that Sister Veras appeared to be sleeping, he smiled. She certainly must need it! By the stars above, they'd need her guidance, her apparent fearlessness. Beside her, Sister Creda looked tired and pale. And ... sad. He turned his gaze to the rest of the escort. Zann, he thought, was doing an acceptable job thus far. The other two who had volunteered from the army – a woman called Ferren and a young man named Sohn – seemed to be applying themselves to their tasks, their expressions serious. Tavis and Vander, the young men from the town, appeared to be arguing quietly.

Nico sighed. What were they to face next? The sudden, unexpected appearance of the Witch's creature had left them rattled. And Veras had not as yet said anything about what the Witch had told them. He had to do whatever he could to hold this escort together, to ease the fear and tension.

A long sigh caught his attention. He turned in that direction to see Creda, who met his eyes with hers. She glanced at Veras, then pulled herself to her feet and moved toward him. She stepped past him to stand close to her mare, reaching out a hand to stroke her reddish-brown neck. For a few moments the two stood silently, eyes toward the horses, the only sound that of the steady drumming of the rainfall past the entrance. Even Nico found some enjoyment in the peacefulness of the moment ...

"Uh – um, excuse me Sister." It was Tavis who had joined them. "Can you tell us what – what ... anything?"

Creda blinked. She reached to feel the little pouch which hung from her neck with the talisman inside. Veras certainly hadn't seemed to mind giving it to her when she had asked to wear it. Creda tried to find some words which might suffice –

"Why can't you just tell us *everything*?" The young man's fair hair was disheveled, his grey eyes intense.

Nico raised a hand to bade Tavis to stop. "The Sisters will tell us what we need to know when we need to know it," he said firmly. *Is this typical of the young men from the town? Demanding and thoughtless?*

Now Zann, too, stepped toward them. "Tavis, please show the Sisters some respect."

Ferren, too, had moved closer to the others. She would take her cues from Captain Zann. Although she, too, would like to have some questions answered, she would give the Sisters all respect.

Veras opened her weary eyes and regarded the group. She sighed. "You have a right to your questions," she called over to them, "as well as some answers." She rose to her feet, one hand upon the rocky wall for support. She blinked. Perhaps she *had* been asleep, for she certainly felt as though she was now somewhere between wakefulness and dreams. She passed a hand through her jaw-length hair. Adjusting her robe, she took a moment to clear her thoughts before approaching the others. She smiled, "let us all come sit around one of the fires." Veras returned to where she had been resting near the wall to retrieve her blanket. This she took to the fire and put the blanket down on the ground to sit on. Gratefully, she accepted a steaming mug from Vander. She drank deeply of the hot tea, savouring the feel as the warmth replenished her inside.

Nico sat beside her, helping himself to a mug of warmth, as the others began to join them.

Veras did not need to give terribly great consideration to her words. She had had past experiences in dealing with a mixture of people of the magic arts and those unfamiliar with, or even hostile to them. Truth was always what needed to be shared. The only question was how much of that truth might be appropriate for the situation and those in it.

"My friends," she began in a voice as soft as rabbit's fur. "You have every right to your questions – just as Sister Creda and I have every right to the answers. And that means that it is our responsibility to give you that knowledge and only that knowledge which is essential for you to have at this time."

"But – but why keep something from us?" It was Tavis again, his pale skin and light brown hair suggesting that his place of origin might be near Creda's.

Veras shared a look with Creda before she continued: "Tavis – all of you. Should something unforeseen occur, as you know it might, too much knowledge could be a danger to you. Should someone or something pursue us – someone with skill in enchantment – he or she could easily grasp the truth from your tongue before you'd even spoken! Such a one would also be able to determine quickly if you sincerely do not have the answer being sought, and therefore simply let you be."

"But – but wouldn't it be likely to simply strike us down in that case, rather than keep us alive to try to find the information?"

Veras couldn't help but grin wryly. "Tavis." Her voice was very firm as she continued. "Which would you truly prefer – to be killed quickly because of your innocence, or to be tortured until you die in agony as your attacker seeks to glean from you all that he or she *thinks* that you know?"

The silence in the dingy cave was broken only by someone's hard swallow.

Veras nodded as though she'd heard a spoken response to her question. "I will tell you *this*. We have a segment of a talisman. An item of sorcery which, when complete, shall give us the power to defeat the warlock. And complete it we must. In order to do so, we must find its missing sections. I will tell you now only that the *Way* will be treacherous. You are about to face dangers the like of which you may only have imagined – for these will be directed at you from the natural elements as well as from the world of enchantment."

For a moment, the determination which had been causing her heart to pound harder waned, and a feeling of grief threatened to replace it. Veras closed her eyes, focusing on the importance of the mission before them. "We must defeat this warlock," she said firmly, the determination once more found. "All who accompany us must be willing to die for this cause – and be willing to trust the judgements of Sister Creda and of me utterly and completely, and do exactly as we bid, without question. All right, then." She stopped, her gaze lost in the fire. "Honestly now, which of you is ready to leave this mission and return home?"

After a moment, it was Nico who spoke. "It's clear to me that *all* of us are ready and willing, Sister. Let's make a pact – now, together. A warrior's oath." He spoke firmly and confidently.

Veras smiled at him broadly. "An excellent suggestion, Nico. Let us, then!"

"Who shall speak?" Vander asked.

"We *all* will!" Nico declared, white teeth gleaming in the light from the fire. He held out his hand, palm downward, over the fire, and grinned at everyone expectantly.

Creda reached out, having to stretch to compensate for her small size, and laid her hand atop his. Veras placed hers upon Creda's, then Zann, then Sohn, Vander and Tavis. Ferren's eyes met Zann's. At a nod from her captain, Ferren followed suit. Veras's eyes had caught the hesitation. This was information she would keep in mind for later.

"I, Nico," came the big man's strong voice, "shall die if need be, defending Sisters Veras and Creda in their quest to defeat this warlock. I shall do everything in my power to free the land from his scourge. I shall follow every order from the Sisters, never questioning their words. This is my pledge."

They all, then, repeated the pledge.

When they sat back at last, all was silent once again. But then Nico threw back his head and chortled heartily, his laughter echoing from the walls.

The rest exchanged somewhat awkward glances, yet Nico's smile somehow seemed to reach inside of Creda, seize her anxiety, and thrust it firmly away.

CHAPTER EIGHT

Heading North

The light from the fire made flickering shadows across the walls. All was quiet in the cave. They had supped with good appetite after the oathtaking. Pleased with himself, Nico entertained the others with his attempts at sleight of hand – some of which was rather good, he thought, while some sufficed at least for a bit of laughter.

Ferren lay back upon her blankets, sighed, watching as the shadows danced and swirled across the ceiling. This was to be, it seemed, a strange mission, indeed. Hearing Sohn stir beside her, she turned to him and whispered: "What think you of this quest?"

The young man rolled over, changing his position beneath his covers. In the shadows, his blanket seemed to be arranging and rearranging itself. He spoke softly: "I think that this is such to be experienced only once in a lifetime, then to be talked about and shared in the inns forever."

Ferren grinned wryly. *Once in a lifetime*, indeed. She'd served with Captain Zann before. He was a good man, and she trusted him. Yet when she thought about what might lie ahead for her, she trembled, and was not sure if this was from excitement – or something else.

Creda, too, lay awake amid blankets. As she hadn't rested earlier, weariness was begging her to close her eyes and sleep. Yet her fingers could not seem to bear parting for long from the talisman segment.

Again she touched it through the soft material of the pouch, felt the smooth curve of the outside edge, and the sharper ones where it had been shattered –

Suddenly a warm hand was touching her upper arm. "Dear Sister," whispered Veras, "give me the talisman. It weighs too heavily upon your spirit."

Creda was only too glad to pass the burden to her Superior.

If the grey and drizzle of Edgewood had seemed like an ominous beginning to their trek, then this morning should seem like a promise that everything would change for the better. They were awakened by the lively honking of migrating geese, just as the reddish gold of dawn began to light the sky.

Creda lay somewhere in the misty space between waking and slumber. Her body jerked slightly from time to time, as though she was dreaming. Yet, as she began to consciously realize that she was no longer asleep, she also realized that it wasn't just the *sound* of the birds' excitement which she was experiencing –

She was sensing the excitement *itself. She was feeling what the geese were feeling, as though she was one of them* …

She shook her head vigorously to clear it, to help her to come back to herself. "Veras," she spoke softly, torn between wanting to speak with her Superior, yet at the same time not wishing to disturb her rest.

"Mmm," Veras murmured, sighing. "Yes, Creda. I'm awake."

The Superior's whispery tones were not very convincing. Creda opened her mouth to speak, then closed it again. But Creda could hear Veras roll over, pulling her blankets with her. "Creda? What is it?" Veras's voice was close to Creda's ear.

"It – it happened again, Veras. This time it was the geese," she said softly, not wishing for any of the others to overhear. It wouldn't do for them to know that she was…*different.*

It was fortunate that those in the cave were in various states of waking. There were still shadows in the cave, and Veras could feel free to frown with concern without Creda seeing. She did not wish to alarm Creda, but throughout her years of training and practising the arts of enchantment, she had never heard of such an ability before she had met Creda. Veras could not even imagine being able to see life through the eyes of creatures – and without using any spells at all! She recalled Creda's experience with the Witch's protective creature. "Creda, when you were – when you were experiencing the geese's situation, were you able to come back to yourself without difficulty?" It wouldn't do to lose Creda entirely if she were unable to break away from one of the beasts!

"There was no difficulty."

"*Good*. As long as you are able to control your involvement in these experiences, perhaps there might be some way of your skill being useful – although at this time I am not sure how ..." Her voice faded. It was disconcerting that someone at Creda's level might have an ability which Veras – a Superior – knew nothing of. She hoped sincerely that this might prove to be an advantage ... and not something which would further complicate their important mission.

Creda sat up, running her hands as best she could through her shoulder-length light-brown hair before tying it at the back of her neck. A thought thrust its way into her mind. She frowned. She didn't want it there, but it was insistent. *What might Carlida be doing this morning?* She was alive. There had been no dead bodies in the deserted village. But sometimes life could be worse than death ...

As the sunrise continued to light the cave, Nico was eyeing the Sisters across his mug of steaming tea. He poked at the fire in front of him where he sat upon a rock nearby. *What were the Sisters discussing? Whatever it was, it seemed to have left a gloom on their faces.* "Sisters," he called over to them.

They glanced across the cave in his direction, both sitting now and preparing themselves for the day ahead. He gave them both his best smile, well aware of how white his teeth looked against the deeply tanned colour of his skin. He smiled warmly at Creda, then met Veras's eyes and lingered there a bit. "The tea is hot, the biscuits nicely warmed, and the cheeses – well, satisfactory, although you are welcome to share my dried meat if you are so inclined."

He watched Veras return his smile, the auburn waves of her hair attractive in their disarray. She eased herself to her feet, extending a hand to assist Creda. "We would be more than happy to join you, Nico, in a moment." She smiled again in his direction, and he nodded, his heart suddenly beating just a bit faster. The Sisters disappeared behind a large rock on the far side of the cave to ready themselves, and Nico, like a gentleman, averted his gaze and once more poked the fire with a stick. He nodded a greeting to a few of the others, who came to sit at the other side of the fire.

He felt movement beside him. He poured hot water over the tea leaves, passing a mug to Creda. "Veras says we're to head northward," he said softly enough that the others near the fire wouldn't have heard."

"Yes."

"Have you ever been north before?"

"No."

"How *far* north are we to go, Sister?"

"Well ..." She hesitated, unsure how much information to share at this time.

He didn't wait long for her to speak. His tone was very serious, and again he spoke in a voice which was obviously for her ears only. "It can get very cold if we venture far north this time of year. We must get warmer clothing and more blankets along the way."

"Very well, Nico. We'll be fortunate to have you with us. The area may well be familiar to you."

Her tone was light, yet Nico's face bore none of his usual joviality. He let go a long breath, prodding again at the flickering flame. "Where are we headed? *Exactly.*"

"Nico, I – I'm not sure –"

"Creda, I *know* the north, or at least a good deal of it. It can be dangerous, especially to those not familiar with its – its challenges. If you tell me where we're headed, I can start thinking about how best to keep you safe."

Creda glanced over her shoulder. *Where was Veras?* "Nico, remember what Veras said. We're dealing with powerful sorcery. Should we be interfered with, and you have knowledge, this warlock or one of his army may be able to take it from you. Or you may well be tortured for the information –"

"I do not fear either pain or death, Creda. I've already had my share of the first, and seen much of the second – come close to my own more than once." His mouth was open, as though to say more, but he closed it again.

Creda studied his face. He looked uncharacteristically serious. She turned to regard the members of the escort, some of whom were preparing the horses while others broke their fasts or tucked away blankets. She spoke in a whisper: "The first section of the talisman is housed in something called the *Icetombs*."

Icetombs, Nico considered. Of course! He gave a quick snort. Rumour had it that no one could enter there and live, hence the name. There were rumours of some strange sorcery, too, but there were always tales about magic when something involved the unknown. It could be simply that the weather so far north was treacherous, and the exterior of the Icetombs extremely slippery. Yet he had known people foolish enough to try to get there, try to enter, simply because of the challenge … or maybe the strange beauty of the thing …

He had never heard, though, of anyone returning from the challenge.

"What is it, Nico? Is there something about this place that we should know?"

Now Nico laughed, his tone once again lighter. "It's *my* turn, Sister. This time *I'll* decide what information to share with *you*. Turnabout is fair play, right?" He chuckled. "It will be, though, much, much colder. Dangerously so. I'll talk to Zann and ensure that we pass through Turning Point –"

"Turning Point?"

Nico rose. He gazed down at her. "It's called Turning Point because it's the last chance for travelers to turn back before they hit the *real* cold and treacherous going."

"And – the Icetombs are beyond this." She was shivering slightly, apparently from the thought.

Nico's hand touched her shoulder, gave it a gentle squeeze. Then he was gone. The sun shone beautifully as they made their way back to the open road. Zann urged them to move more quickly. The horses were eager, too, to enjoy the chance to stretch their legs. Creda urged the mare into a gallop. Yes, no doubt the horse was enjoying this, after having been penned up in the cave –

There it was again! Somehow, Creda *knew* what the horse was *feeling*. She closed her eyes in an effort to explore the strange sensation –

And gasped. Suddenly, she was seeing the world entirely through the mare's eyes! She could see the other horses ahead, smell the dust of the roadway and the greenery around them, hear the pounding of the hoofs against the ground, feel the satisfaction of stretching cramped muscles. It was wonderful!

Creda opened her eyes, shook her head and pushed the sensation away. Yes, in a few seconds she was herself once more. Then a thought struck her. Not all powers developed at the same time. Sometimes skills which had been difficult to master could suddenly seem to make sense. Perhaps this was happening with this skill for Creda. But why would she develop this particular skill when none of the others in the Tower had any experience with it at all? She sighed. If only there was some way of making use of this strange ability …

The mare, being newly acquired, had not yet been given a name. Now Creda had one. She smiled. There was a term used to describe that closeness between Sisters or Brothers when they were in such complete and total contact that all they were was shared: *Ingemma*.

"I shall call you *Gem*," she said, reaching forward to pat the beast's red-brown neck with its black mane. She liked to think that the mare was pleased, although she knew that she was quite likely simply happy to be using her muscles.

That night they slept under a beautiful blanket of stars and a glowing moon. They'd travelled many leagues that day, and the inactivity was more than welcome. Yet, lying amid her blankets beside sleeping Veras, Creda found herself still quite awake. She'd enjoyed the beauty of the stars where they winked downward from the dark sky, but now she turned her gaze in the direction of the glowing fire.

Captain Zann was serving the first watch. He seemed deep in thought, the shadows cast by the dancing flames making his face look longer and more fatigued than usual. Something about him touched Creda ...

She rose, wrapping her blanket around her, and crossed in his direction, stepping carefully in her stocking feet. He didn't hear her approach. As her body blocked the moonlight from him, he sensed nearness, his hand quickly seizing the handle of his sword as he began to stand. But a smile lit his face, twisting his thick brown moustache upward at the corners, when he saw the Sister.

"I'm sorry if I startled you, Captain."

He settled back down upon the log which served as a bench. He motioned to her to join him. "Sleep escapes you, Sister?"

"For now. Do you mind company?"

He shook his head, his grey eyes regaining their twinkle. They sat silently for a time, watching as the flames leaped and danced, flashing yellows and golds and reds, almost as though solely for their entertainment. Creda's training had taught her much about observing people and reading their feelings while watching their movements and their postures. Perhaps she could help Captain Zann –

"Captain," she whispered, not wishing to disturb the quiet of the night. "What do you hope to find through accompanying Sister Veras and me?"

A long sigh escaped him. It seemed that Creda's question had managed to direct his thoughts toward somewhere he'd rather not visit. "Why do you ask, Sister?" He did not look in her direction, but prodded the fire with a long stick.

She studied his long face as he continued to gaze into the flames. "Because you have a need to tell me."

He sighed. Still he did not look at her. But he whispered: "Yes."

Yet he remained silent, still poking at the fire with his stick. Creda redirected her gaze toward the thin clouds which passed leisurely across the gleaming moon.

"I – I *had* to come." He turned his face toward Creda, shared a quick glance with her, then looked back at the flames.

Creda watched as the blazing fire cast shadows which added to the sadness of his look.

He continued: "I remember well what you told us of your sister and her people. And I, too, am hoping that a loved one might be saved from that monster."

His words brought back images of Carlida to Creda's mind. Yes, they must both cling to hope.

He spoke again: "My – my wife. My wife had ventured to the southwestern counties in search of better seedlings for the garden. She hadn't gone terribly far. She was only to have been gone one full day …"

Creda didn't need any powers of enchantment to hear, to feel his hurt, his loss. Although the Sisters were to use their skills sparingly, and not waste their energies, surely …

She touched his shoulder, relaxed her mind, and sent this to him, bringing him a feeling of peace.

"Then," he continued, more calmly now, "some of us rode out there to try to find her – and we found the destruction. I told the Prince, and he was uncertain what to do. Then you found what you did, so close to our own city. And action had to be taken."

"We must find this warlock and destroy him."

"Indeed, Sister Creda. Do you truly have the means, Sister?"

From somewhere deep inside came determination and certainty. "Yes." Then, after a moment, she added: "Please, you may call me Creda."

He nodded, turning his eyes to meet hers. "In the name of the sorrow we already share, and the unknown which we will both face, you may call me Joul."

Ferren rode comfortably, her eyes on the captain's back just ahead of her. Every once in a while she scanned the distant forests, the tall grasses off to the west, and the road over her shoulder. Any movement could mean an enemy. Yet she'd seen nothing, and now allowed herself simply to enjoy the ride from time to time -- as best as she could, considering the seriousness of her mission, the request from the Prince himself. The air was cooler, but the breeze was from the south, bringing with it a welcome hint of warmth –

She heard the nearby pounding of hoofs, and turned to find Nico riding beside her.

"Enjoying the ride, soldier?"

She eyed him, disliking that grin which always seemed to be stuck on his face. "Yes."

"Good! It'll get colder, so enjoy it while you can!" He laughed.

Ferren didn't reply. Resentment slid through her like a fiery snake. Why did this man always have to pretend that he knew *everything*? She could feel his stare. Well, that was *his* problem. She wasn't required to make conversation.

"What's wrong? A soldier like you wouldn't be feeling something like fear, now would she?"

She shot him an icy glare. "Not at all," she said evenly.

"Well," Nico replied, pulling his mount closer so that he lean in to her, "you might be *wise* to harbour a bit of fear, soldier. It may bring you caution when you need it."

He clucked to the stallion, and galloped ahead. He slowed Thunder's pace when he saw that Veras, Creda and Zann had stopped their mounts just ahead. Zann was shielding his eyes with his hand, staring northwest, where Creda was pointing. "What is it?" Nico asked, although he suspected that he knew what it was.

"There." Joul pointed. "A thin line of deeper blue where the greenery meets the sky."

Nico laughed heartily. "Good! The edge of the lake. Turning Point is only a few days' ride ahead then! We'll sup and sleep in an inn soon!"

He turned back to the others, motioned to them to gather round. "The lake is not far," he said loudly, "which means that Turning Point is within a couple of days. But," he said more seriously, "as we come closer to the lake, we will also be heading more directly northward. If not for the bit of south wind, we'd already be feeling much colder than we are now. But colder we'll be getting! Much colder. In only a few days. Take time to ensure that your blankets and cloaks are within easy reach. Heed my words!" But then his easy smile was back as he urged his stallion forward.

Was this blasted, arrogant man never wrong? All had happened, it seemed, just as he had been saying. Ferren eyed the lake. Large it was. Although she had done some travelling as a soldier, she had never been as far north as this, and she had never seen any body of water so blue, so beautiful.

And, as the arrogant one had said, the closer they came to the water, the cooler the air became. Ferren's brown cloak was wrapped tightly around her, her hood drawn low. Extra socks helped her feet, and a blanket was atop all of this. This was what the people of Espri would have called deep winter, yet this was, apparently, just the beginning ...

They were all shivering by the time the sun began to make its downward journey. Ferren was finding it difficult to keep her teeth from constantly chattering. It was true -- she must find warmer clothing if she was to continue. And continue she must – she'd wipe that smirk from the arrogant one's face! *Captain Zann* was their leader – not this arrogant man with his perpetual sneer who loved to tell everyone what to do!

Finally, Nico turned in his saddle to face those behind him. He was grinning very broadly now. "All right," he shouted, his breath escaping as a sudden mist. "Turning Point is only a couple of leagues from here!"

CHAPTER NINE

The Icetombs

The lights of the little town beckoned to them. And, as they came closer, the lights brightened as though offering them welcome. Although it was small, Turning Point boasted three inns – two large and one smaller. It was said to be an important place for travelers to pause – for some, to reconsider their plans once they had been informed of the extreme weather awaiting them should they continue further north, and for a few, to ensure that they had gathered enough of what they would need to take nature's dare and see how they'd fare against the harsher elements beyond.

Creda felt a stab of fatigued dismay when they passed the first inn. They hadn't even paused to see if the place was full. She called over to Nico, wondering aloud why he hadn't stopped here.

"Why, Sister Creda," he said dramatically with a wide grin, "surely you don't think I'd consider anything less than the *best* inn for my friends!"

But this explanation didn't seem to be the only one, for when they were just past the first inn, a figure stepped into the street beside Nico's mount. The figure reached up towards Thunder's bridle, as though to bring the stallion to a halt.

"So you're back," said the man's voice as Nico pulled on the reins, urging his mount to a stop.

"Mac!" Nico spoke jovially, as though he and the man were old friends.

Mac wasn't smiling. "No doubt you've come to pay me back my money," he said evenly. His hand was holding the rein, just upward from Thunder's mouth.

"Pay you back?" Nico looked blank, as though the man was speaking some unknown language. "Pay you *back*? I think not, old man. That money was won in a fair game!"

Mac didn't agree, and something resembling a growl escaped him. Nico moved as though to pull the rein from his grasp, but Mac resisted. "Mac," Nico said firmly. "I'm not about to pay you any money that you seem to think I might owe you. Now, out of my way. I wouldn't want Thunder to step on you." Nico was no longer smiling.

Mac hesitated, raising his eyes to return Nico's cold stare.

"Out of my way, Mac." Nico's voice was very firm, his entire expression very serious.

After a moment, Mac stepped back, into the shadows, and Nico clucked to Thunder to continue. He leaned forward, stroking the horse near where Mac had touched him, as though wanting to erase any trace of that man's touch upon his beast.

Creda had watched the exchange, and now urged the mare to hasten so that they rode side by side. "What was *that* all about?" Her voice was concerned. Creda had been rather alarmed by the icy tone of Nico's voice and the seriousness of his stare, but now his usual grin once more occupied his face.

Nico laughed loudly. "Let's just say that I know well some of these townspeople –and some of them *think* they know me!" He laughed again, apparently finding this to be quite humorous. He looked at her face, his broad smile showing his white teeth. "Don't be concerned, Sister! Surely your training has taught you how folk can develop disagreements when they're playing games and putting back a few mugs!"

Of course, that was quite true. In case Creda was to sometime live and work among townspeople or country folk, using her enchantments to help them when necessary, the Tower Superiors had taught her about such. Yet part of her wanted to ask Nico to explain further about this particular situation. She still wasn't sure just what sort of man this Nico was. There seemed to be two conflicting sides to him. She felt that she knew him to some degree, yet there seemed to be much of him hidden away –

When they arrived at the smaller inn, a few other men recognized Nico as well, although the name which they called him was a rather different one. A serving woman knew him, too, and said that she *owed* him something. Then she slapped him soundly across the face. Nico's old acquaintances banged their hands upon the wooden tables and laughed uproariously. Nico simply grinned.

Yes, wondered Creda as they headed to the stairs which would lead them up to their rooms, what sort of man *are* you, Nico? At the bottom of the staircase, Nico paused, and courteously motioned to her to go first. As their eyes met, he rubbed at his cheek. Creda gazed at him, shaking her head slightly.

His dark eyes gazed into her pale blue ones. Was she going to ask him about the story behind that encounter as well? "A northern custom, Sister," he grinned, "to welcome back one's conquering hero!"

Creda shook her head once more, and headed up the staircase. Veras was behind her. She, too, had heard Nico's comments, and returned his look when his eyes met hers.

"Sister," he said respectfully, and extended a hand to assist her with the first step. She accepted his hand and held it for an instant before making her way up the stairs. He watched her, but then Vander was making his way behind her, and he was not so interesting to watch.

The night seemed to pass quickly, although they were not disturbed by early morning street noises as they might have been in more southern areas. Here, the heavy shutters were closed and bolted in an effort to keep out the cold. All during the night the wind had howled like a hungry wolf seeking a way inside. And despite the small blaze in the fireplace, the chill had never left the room.

They mounted their horses and headed toward the marketplace, Nico once more leading the way. The air was very cool, crisp, and the sky was blue, decorated by a few cottony clouds. The smell of fish drifted towards them, becoming stronger as they came closer to the market. And, as they came closer, the *sounds* of the market became stronger too. There were many open stalls where the fish were sold, each merchant shouting that his or hers was the freshest, the biggest and the best value. Many of their words were unfamiliar to the travelers, as these northerners had their own dialect. The shops which offered clothing and supplies, though, were indoors.

Nico was in his element. He knew these people, and he knew that he was skilled in haggling to ensure the best value for his little group. Even Ferren found herself admiring his skill here, for on several occasions the party ended up paying a fair bit less for supplies than the shopkeepers had originally requested.

Finally, after one more hot meal at the inn, they were on their way.

They'd ridden for some time when Nico glanced over his shoulder and noticed that Creda had paused. He motioned for Zann to pass him. Veras, too, had noticed that Creda tarried, and Nico reassured her as he turned back to check on the Sister. When Nico joined her, she was gazing toward the lake ...

"What is it, Nico? The water no longer flows at all!" Her breath became mist as she spoke.

Nico smiled, but an icicle of concern touched him inside, as this was a reminder of how dangerous the cold could become. "Have you not seen ice before, Creda?"

Her gaze was still on the frozen water. "Not in so great a quantity," she replied, her eyes still taking in the shimmer of the sun's rays where they hit a surface that looked like a mirror.

The big man sighed. He had sweet memories of sliding on ice such as that, what seemed like many years ago. "Ice can be treacherous," he said, "but it can be good fun too! If only we had time to stop ..."

Creda's gaze left the lake to focus on ... something inside of herself. *Fun.* When had she lost her appreciation for it? Nico was certainly older than she was, yet he still seemed to understand the concept.

But onward they moved, all now clad in thicker, heavier cloaks. A good thing, too, for after a time the winds began to pick up a bit, and then even more a little later. Ferren had her cloak gathered snuggly around her, her hands gloved and that smaller bit of warm material that Nico had called a *scarf* pulled up to cover her nose and mouth.

Yet still the shivers reached out to seize her and shake her. Then, up ahead, there appeared to be a very thick mist or fog of some sort. The winds seemed to cause this to swirl constantly –

She'd never seen anything like it. Ahead of them, she could make out Nico's broad shoulders, now covered by a thick, grey cloak, disappearing into the mists. She urged her mount forward, then paused beside Sister Creda, who seemed to be slowing her mare. "We must keep up and follow," she shouted over the wind to the Sister. "I've not seen the like of that either, but we must not fall far behind Nico." It seemed odd to say that, when not long ago she'd have been only pleased to lose sight of the braggart.

After Creda had urged her mare to a faster pace, Ferren followed, her eyes narrowed against the blast. She strained, anxious not to fall too far behind. Little droplets of ice continually fell into her eyelashes, threatening to obscure her vision even more.

But then she could see them. The little group was stopped just ahead. Nico had said something to the others, and, speaking loudly over the winds, the captain turned to share this with Ferren and Creda. "A shelter just ahead, with a lean-to for the horses."

Welcome news, indeed! They forced their way through the blast and to the small structures, settled the horses with some of the hay they'd brought in sacks. And the beasts certainly seemed to welcome the dried apples which Veras had brought with her.

Most of this weather was not new to Nico, yet even he was anxious to get out of the cold and this wind that never seemed to end. A bit of concern nagged at him, as one could never know in what condition the previous occupants might have left the shelter … But he shoved firmly against the heavy wooden door, Zann offering his shoulder to assist. Darkness greeted them, as the shutters were tightly fastened. They ventured inside, and Nico hastened to find the candles – hoping that they weren't burned completely. Most travelers followed the accepted courtesy and replenished what they had used, but not everyone did.

With Zann's help, they managed to get the candles lit, and set Sohn and Tavis to lighting the fire. With the help of the flames, the group could get a look at their surroundings. It was one large room, empty except for a large table in the middle. The wall had a long bench built into it, which continued around the entire room, except for the one door.

Creda pulled off her scarf and let her hood fall back, grateful to be free of the wind's cruelty. She sat down on the bench –

And watched as what looked like five years' collection of dust floated upward. She coughed. Veras, nearby, sneezed.

"It looks like you northerners don't use these shelters all that much," Veras said.

Nico's teeth looked very white in the candlelight. "No one has come this way in a long while."

"Why is that?" Veras asked while she used her scarf to clean off a section of the bench.

Nico had claimed a section of the bench for himself, and began to remove some of his outer clothing. "Because the truly frigid weather seems to be moving closer to Turning Point over the years. What we've yet to come to is the *real* winter weather."

"Then what was that we just came through!" Creda said.

"Just the beginning," he said, his voice softer than usual. Suddenly he turned away.

Exhausted, it was not difficult for the group to fall asleep once they had supped. They rode the next day and were pleased when Nico saw another shelter ahead. Again, it was easy to fall asleep.

A single ray of sunshine somehow managed to find a tiny slit in the shutter, and shone its beauty into the room. Creda watched it, sighing. If sunshine could find its way through, then certainly there could not be the *snow*, as Nico had called it, blowing about anymore.

Rising, she wrapped herself in her winter robe. Three of the others were seated at the table, supping on the breads and cheeses, dried meats and fruits they'd brought. But it was soon time to move on again, and again they prepared to leave.

When they opened the door, this time the sight was a truly beautiful one. Creda had never been so close to snow before, having thought of it as something which only settled on mountain peaks.

All around them were stillness and quiet. And everything seemed to have been covered snuggly by a huge, endless blanket of white – albeit a cold one. The sun's rays seemed to dance where they struck the surface of this, sending almost blinding light everywhere. The snow made crunching sounds under their boots.

Creda removed her glove and reached downward. She looked at the little frosty bits upon her fingers, watching how the tiny crystals mirrored the light of the sun, and how they slowly changed to droplets as they were warmed by her body's heat. Curious, she licked them from her fingers –

"Don't ever do that in earnest!" Nico almost shouted from behind her.

She whirled, startled, eyes wide.

He looked down at his own gloved hands, and took a deep breath to collect himself. His harsh reaction had been automatic. Always, from when very young, the northern children were warned against filling their bodies with the frigid stuff. "Creda," he said, much more softly," should you become separated from the rest of us and become thirsty, do *not* fill yourself with snow. It'll only turn your insides cold."

He turned his head so that his eyes met hers. There seemed to be a sadness about his face. "Promise me," he said gently.

"I – I promise," she stammered, still startled by his reaction.

But his smile returned now and he extended his hand to help her to her feet. "Today will be colder," he advised, "so we can be thankful that the winds have died. It'll be important, though, that we stay together, in case another storm arrives." He grinned broadly, touched a hand lightly against her cheek, and moved away.

They rode onward, admiring the tremendous beauty of this frozen land. But they did not forget, even for an instant, the dangers of the cold. They had covered themselves almost completely in their warm clothing, each one leaving only his or her eyes exposed.

Then, off in the distance, a huge white mountain seemed almost to grow from the alabaster surface, stretching – so it seemed – almost to the sky. As they rode more closely, they could see that at least part of it was covered with a glistening, smooth coat of ice.

They came to the foot of the thing and now rode slowly and carefully upward, ever upward through the snow. It was a gradual incline thus far, and not difficult. But now they had come to a stop, for the way became much steeper here – and, not far away, the crunchy snow became a smooth glistening surface of ice.

"What is the way to find a route around this thing?" Captain Zann asked Nico.

Nico's dark eyes were fixed on the huge, white mound before them. "We don't," he said softly.

"What do you mean?"

"That, Captain Zann, good Sisters of the Tower and members of the escort, is the Mountain of the Icetombs," he said loudly, glancing at everyone around him.

The Sisters exchanged looks, for inside of this thing was the section of the talisman which the warlock had managed to conceal from the Witches – the section of the talisman which they must now find in order to defeat him. The section of the talisman which the Great Seer had indicated was – somehow – not visible to the human eye.

Veras sighed, turning her gaze to Nico. "Where is the entrance?"

"Who knows?"

Her blue-green eyes studied his face. "Do you have any idea how one is to enter?"

"There is a narrow ledge. If you look there," he pointed with his gloved finger, "you might see that it looks to continue from the bottom, winding around the mountain, to somewhere near the top. This is the closest that I have even been to it."

Veras looked carefully at the strange, huge mound of white, and found that she could, indeed, see a graceful bluish path which began not far from where they were, and wound around the high, white glistening thing, around and around, although where it ended high above she could not see.

Veras dismounted, and Vander took the reins for her. She could see where the path began, and gazed in that direction. Nico and Creda joined them, Nico offering them sacks to wear on their backs which contained tools to help them.

"You must take some of the escort to help you, Sisters, but I fear that I might be too big for places where the path might narrow –"

"If you stay here, Nico, it would be appropriate for me to accompany the Sisters," offered Zann.

"I'll go with you," said Ferren quickly.

With Nico assuming command of the remaining escort, the others made their way, step by step, along the icy ledge. The going was not difficult at first, but as the ledge angled to a steeper incline, they were grateful that Nico had provided them with metal toothed objects which helped them to grip the icy wall of the Icetombs as they kept as far from the ledge's brink as they could. They had just made their way around a turn when an icy wind blast caught the captain by surprise –

Ferren turned at the sound of a yelp, saw the captain as he lost his footing, his body now sliding downward toward the lower section of the ledge. But the ledge was too narrow here –

It took only a second. Ferren strained forward, a hand stretched in his direction, but he was already gone. "Captain!" For a heartbeat of time, Ferren wondered if she could somehow use her metal toothed thing to claw her way to the edge and do something –

But a whispering sound took her attention. She turned. Sister Creda was grasping her amulet in one hand while her other held the wall with the gripper. She was speaking softly, her eyes closed. And then Ferren could hear Captain Zann's voice shouting, incredulously, that he was all right –

Ferren took her metal gripper from its place in the wall of the mountain and moved it down onto the icy surface of the ledge. She lay flat and used the gripper to pull herself along to the edge –

She could see him! He was just below the level of the ledge, atop something which she couldn't see. He was spread out on his stomach, much as she was, but his arms and legs were outstretched. He was staring upward, and seemed very pleased to see her.

Ferren looked back toward the Sisters. Creda was blinking, still cradling her amulet. Veras touched her shoulder. "I shall bring him back," she said.

Creda nodded, and blinking, came free of the spell. Veras's hand disappeared beneath the neck of her robe, reappearing with her golden, circular amulet. She closed her eyes, and her lips began moving. Creda watched in fascination, for this was an advanced spell which she did not have the knowledge of.

Ferren gasped, and she and Creda stared. Veras pointed a finger in Zann's direction, and he floated upward, then slowly back over the lip of the ledge where Ferren was now sitting. She reached a hand to help him, and pulled herself, and him with her, back to the support offered by the Icetombs' wall. He sat here, back against the wall, grateful for the chance to catch his breath, while Ferren retrieved his ice gripper and returned it to him.

"Thank you, Sisters," breathed the captain, as the Sisters approached.

"Let us be more careful," said Veras. "We cannot be certain what might await us inside. We must not use our energies more than necessary before we arrive there."

The captain nodded, and they returned to their task.

Finally they arrived at something which looked like it might be a cave entrance, but it had a transparent wall of ice covering it. Could this be the way in? If it was, how would they get through?

Veras studied the thing intently. There were various possibilities, but which choice would be best in this situation? They still had no idea what challenges might await them inside. "The *Heat Spell* might suffice," she suggested to Creda, "if we use the energies we can create through working together."

And so each extended a hand toward the ice covering, each closing her eyes to enhance her concentration …

Ferren watched in fascination. The Sisters seemed to be in some sort of deep trance. It was almost as though their spirits had left their bodies entirely. All that she could see were moving lips, hands clasping amulets, fingers touching the ice barrier.

But then she gasped. The ice was becoming less bright, less shiny –

And the Sisters' hands seemed to be sinking inside of it. She wondered if she should grasp Creda's robe to stop her –

73

But before she had a chance to do anything, both Sisters were gone –

She looked at the captain, and he, too, stared. Mindful of her mission, Ferren stepped quickly to follow --

CHAPTER TEN

The First Missing Segment

Creda wasn't sure how long she'd lain there. She wasn't sure if she'd gone into a faint, or simply lain there catching her breath.

Light gleamed into the ice-palace from somewhere above. Not much was needed to enable her to see, as the beams bounced from one reflective wall to another. All around seemed to be shiny, whitish/bluish walls, extending up, up, up ...

It was all very beautiful, very still –

And all very, very dangerous.

Creda managed to climb to her feet, as her eyes drank in the sights around her. She could see no sign of Veras, though, and that, combined with the eerie silence, left her feeling quite uneasy. A sigh escaped her – a long mist which seemed to hang in the frigid air after leaving her mouth –

Somewhere inside the strange ice-palace was a segment of the talisman. And, although it was not visible to the human eye, they had to find it.

But first –

"Veras!" She'd meant to call loudly, yet only a hoarse whisper found its way from her lips. In the stillness, even that seemed more than enough.

"Veras?" Still silence greeted her ears, other than a faint echo.

She knew that she should conserve her energy as much as possible, and not utilize spells any more than absolutely necessary ... yet she also had to find Veras. What could have become of her? Surely the Superior had come inside, too. For Creda, the thought that she might be *alone* in here was far from comforting!

She sank down upon the icy floor, her fingers seeking her amulet, wondering if she could send out her awareness to the Superior. It wouldn't use a great deal of energy, but it could alert Veras to her whereabouts ...

Yet no. The warlock's talisman segment was here somewhere. She *must* conserve her energy for whatever might lie ahead –

"Veras! Are you here?" *Please say yes!*

Silence.

Creda moved carefully along the ice-floor, one hand seeking the cold security of the wall. Her eyes scanned the icy projections which rose here and there from the floor, and the smooth ledges which appeared almost to be fastened to the walls. There were various walls through the large interior, some higher than others – behind which something ... or some*one* ... might hide –

Then she heard it.

A sound. A small one, but a sound. A skittering. A scraping. Something was moving, somewhere here inside.

Creda was *not* alone in here. A little shiver, which had nothing to do with the cold, made its way along her spine, from the top of her head and downward. She turned, trying to determine from where the sound had come. But it was difficult in this strange place, for any sound seemed to fill the silent space completely.

Again. *Skitter. Scrape.*

And then she saw it – at least, she saw its movement. It was very difficult to see *it*, as it was as white as snow. It was as though a section of this vast whiteness had somehow found life, separated itself from the surroundings and had escaped.

Creda blinked. She could see it more clearly now. A small creature, white, scurrying along to disappear behind an icy ridge –

How many more creatures might there be in here? And might there be any *large* ones?

Another sound. She jumped, her hand on her heart as though it needed help to stay inside of her –

"Oooooh."

A low moan. Creda turned, trying to find the source –

"Veras!" She could see reddish hair now, just beyond one of the ice mounds which seemed as though it might have grown from the floor. As quickly as she could, she slid her feet along the floor of the place, grasped an icy rock, and pulled herself around it.

Veras was attempting to gain her feet, one hand holding her head. Quickly Creda moved to assist, putting an arm around her teacher and helping her to sit on one of the ice mounds.

"I – I'll be all right, Creda. But oh, my head! I must have hit it against something when we came in – and no wonder! Look!" She pointed back at what must have been the way they'd come. There was the transparent covering at the top of a smooth incline, which must have afforded a quick slide downward, once they'd fallen past the entrance.

"Have you – thank you, Creda – I'll be all right to sit here. Have you seen anything inside of this place?"

"Not really."

"Well, we must find some answers, Creda. Let's set to work." Veras began to scan the inside of the ice-palace, yet all she seemed to see was white and blue, white and blue, shadow and light. "There! What was that?" Veras pointed. She'd seen some kind of movement –

"Probably a creature. I saw one, too. A small thing, like a ferret. As white as the snow –"

Veras shook her head, eyes still fixed in the same direction. "No. There. That's no creature." She was pointing toward the very centre of the place. High above they could see the place's peak where a thin tendril of sunlight gleamed through, almost as though pointing to that centre. Together they moved carefully in that direction, the sight becoming clearer – yet at the same time more puzzling – as they came nearer.

Creda gasped. Beneath the surface of the ice, there were –

Faces. Somehow there were faces, with something resembling bodies in tattered clothing attached. But these were not ordinary faces. No indeed! The features were indistinct and distorted, as though being viewed through a slight fog, or slowly moving water.

Creda felt suddenly very cold, indeed.

"Are they –are they *dead*?" Yet even as she asked this, it seemed that, somehow, she knew that wasn't the explanation. There still seemed to be some spark of life in the eyes.

Veras shook her head as she pulled her hood down lower to ward off the chill. She had not moved her eyes from the sight beneath and before her. "They *should* be, Creda. Look at the misery upon those faces!"

"Have you – have you heard of the like of this before?"

"No, not in reality. But I have heard of the possibility of such. Something sought to drain them of their spirits, then stored their bodies here."

"But – but why? What could be the purpose?"

Veras sighed, still gazing upon the faces before them. She reached out a hand to the surface, wishing she could somehow bring these poor ones comfort. "If the bodies are free to accept death, then their spirits will seek the final ascension into the afterworlds. And no longer be the prisoners of – of the warlock." She was silent a moment, touching her gloved fingers to one of the distorted faces. "Perhaps he has another purpose which we simply don't understand just yet …"

A cold panic gripped Creda's heart. Hastily she peered into the icy depths, scanning the faces, the horrible distorted features, praying that she would find Carlida – no, hoping that she would *not*! She did not see her anywhere amid the misery below. *Was this a good thing or bad?*

"The warlock may be even more powerful than we've thought," breathed Veras.

"Why do you say so?"

"Well, we know that there have not been any reports of his raiders coming this far north. But he managed to conceal his talisman segment here when he was banished, and now he somehow stores these bodies here …"

For a few moments there was only silence. They *must* find the talisman segment! If ever those below the icy floor might be re-united with their spirits, they must complete the talisman and defeat the warlock.

Veras rose to her feet, smoothed her robe. Her face seemed devoid of expression. "We must complete our task," she said firmly. "We must find the talisman segment." She scanned their surroundings again, wondering where the thing could possibly be. "I had hoped that we might use a *Seeking Spell*. After all, even if we couldn't see the segment itself, the spell would reveal its location. But we shall have to wait until moonrise for that. Do you have suggestions which we might try before night comes?"

Creda, too, had been considering alternatives. "What of your *Spell of Undoing*?" This was an advanced spell, only used by Superiors, which could reverse some enchantments enacted by other sorcerers.

But Veras shook her head. "If the warlock's power is great, he may sense the use of my magic if it is used against his own spell. And if he senses our presence, well, that could well be *our* undoing."

After a moment, she continued. "So, it seems that we must await the moon. We may not receive enough moonlight in here. We'll likely have to initiate the procedure outside, and hope that there is no magic about this place which might interfere ..." She sank down upon a rocklike piece of ice, chin in hand.

"No. There's one more thing."

Veras raised her eyes to meet those of her student, surprised by the tone of great confidence in her voice. It was true that Creda had shown confidence in her skills from time to time ... but, in *here*? In the Icetombs? "Creda?"

"The creature," Creda said with a slight grin.

Veras still looked confused. "But what of it?"

Creda's smile grew broader. "Already I can sense its presence."

Veras rose, putting a hand on each of Creda's shoulders. She gazed deeply into Creda's eyes, wishing that this was something she could easily understand. "This – this special skill of yours is so unfamiliar to the rest of us! What if something goes wrong –Creda, you've had very little experience with this skill. How can you be certain that you'll be able to manage it?"

Yet, even while she'd been speaking, she could see that Creda's consciousness had already gone to the creature, for the pale blue eyes were blank, concentration now elsewhere.

And, just as the winged creature of the Witch had received Creda's thought and ceased his attack on Vander, so this one raised its little, squarish white head, seemingly in wonder at its sudden urge. It stretched its long, thin body out of the little burrow where it had been curled amid shed fur, and climbed higher, higher still, until it reached the section which was icier. It was not difficult for it to climb, for its possessed strong, sharp claws for pulling itself along the slippery walls, upward, downward or sideways. Finally, it emerged into the great empty space of the Icetombs, tiny pale pink nose twitching. It did not understand *why*, but it must seek, seek …

Under edges of the ice projections, it searched. Around the edges of the icy interior, it searched. It climbed high, higher along the ledges which lined the walls, seeking, seeking, searching. But its eyes were not sharp. It relied upon scent. And it had no idea as to how this thing might smell –

In sudden understanding, Creda came back to herself, seized the red pouch with the talisman segment. She opened it, pulled it to her nose, hoping desperately that the scent of this segment would be similar enough to the one being sought.

Veras watched her student in awe. This was the first time that Creda had moved at all since beginning her rapport with the creature. And now her eyes were blank again --

The little white beast was beginning to tire. And hunger was competing with Creda's urgings, fighting for its attention. It would need to go a long way down, beneath the ice in order to find something suitable for its dinner …

The little creature sat down upon its haunches.

No, thought Creda. She sent forth another urging, a prod of energy to poke this animal into action –

It rose, and returned to its search. Finally, its tender nostrils found something bearing resemblance to what it knew it must find. It seized the metallic bit between its jaws ...

"Yes!"

Veras's blue-green eyes were wide. "Creda?"

"Yes! It has it! Up there!" Seeing once more with her *own* eyes, she pointed to a tiny, narrow section of icy ledge which wound its way high up the inside wall.

They could both see it now, a little slithering of white as it wormed its way along the ledge. But, now that Creda had pulled her consciousness back into herself, the little beast was moving on its *own* initiative, and it was moving quickly –

The burrow! Suddenly Creda realized that this was likely where the creature was heading. She didn't know exactly where the burrow was, but she remembered that it was back in the direction of the transparent entrance -- and the little beast was *fast!*

"Veras! Try to stop it! It's headed there!"

Veras opened her mouth to speak – to bade Creda to return to the beast's consciousness, but she could see that Creda was already attempting to do so. Veras watched the little creature for a moment, then moved in its direction. Creda tried to push her mind inside of the little white head once more. But she was tired from the first time she'd done so, and anxious. She seemed unable to control her own mind anymore.

Veras slipped, grasped at the edge of an icy projection. Now she had to strain to see where the creature had gone. Her head, still sore from hitting the ice earlier, now pounded, pounded. But she had to ignore it and find the creature! How much further could it have gone in such a short time? If it had the talisman, she *must* be successful in finding it!

Creda once more took a deep breath, forced the panic, the fear, the fatigue from her mind –

Finally, Veras spied it. Thankfully, it wasn't heading high up on the wall. She could see it scurrying along toward a little, barely visible hole at the bottom of the wall on the far side. She made her way as quickly as she possibly could. She saw it heading toward the little opening – *no!*

She threw herself forward, belly on the ice, slid after the thing, straining towards it, seized its tail –

Creda concentrated every bit of energy she possessed. She must stop the little creature, must! *Stop, stop, stop –*

Veras stared, incredulous! *Its tail had come off in her hand!* She dropped it, slid forward, half-crawling, moved as fast as the slipperiness would let her. *Keep going!* It was almost at the burrow!

There was screaming inside of Creda's mind. It was herself, trying desperately to get the creature to STOP! STOP!

But it leapt forward, dived into the hole, Veras's hands grasping behind it –

STOP!

Veras sat, staring down at the hole. NO! The thing had gotten away! All was lost!

STOP!

The Superior leaned over, peered inside. *It was there!* Two little eyes shone up at her. She reached in a hand, barely able to squeeze it in. She gasped in pain. The thing had bitten her! There was another sensation too. Veras withdrew her fingers from the hole. One was bleeding –

But her fingertips clutched the talisman piece, for when the creature had bitten her, it had released it.

And Creda's message had finally gotten through. A little white head poked its way out of the hole, gazing at Veras as though to ask what she wanted.

Then Veras heard Creda moan, and the sound of something falling –

The creature retreated to its burrow.

Ferren and Captain Zann sat, huddled tightly together against the wall of the Icetombs, bodies curled in an attempt to thwart the winds. Their scarves covered their noses and mouths, warm winter hides their bodies, yet Ferren felt as though they'd been waiting days and nights for the Sisters to reappear. But no complaints would leave her lips. After all, the captain never seemed to complain, and she would follow him to the end of the world if need be. Snow had been falling for the last while, and clouds had begun to blot out the sun. The temperature was falling. And the increasing gloom of the sky did nothing to help their spirits.

"Zann!" Nico called from below.

The captain attempted to peer in that direction, although he was not able to see Nico from here. He pulled his scarf away from his mouth to reply: "Yes, Nico!"

"We could change the guard now, if you wish," came the voice from below.

The captain tried to exchange looks with Ferren, but so little of their faces was visible that nothing was revealed. Zann ignored the fact that Ferren had been visibly shivering. She would feel that she had disappointed him if he appeared to have noticed.

Ferren sighed, preparing to rise. The solidity of the ice when she'd tried to follow the Sisters had been like a door slammed in her face. She had a role to play in protecting the Sisters – how could she do anything if she was shut out? She managed to get to her feet, grasping the icy wall for support, prepared to begin the descent. She cast one more glance toward the spot where she'd seen the Sisters disappear – curse it all! *She should be with them!*

Suddenly her jaw dropped. "Captain!"

Quickly he followed the direction of her gaze. The icy covering was melting once more! He reached a hand inward, a grimace on his face as he reached into he knew not what. But a hand seized his own, and he pulled its owner through.

"Sister!"

"Captain Zann, thank you!" Veras reached behind to assist Creda, who appeared paler than usual, despite the brisk temperature. "She fell faint from her exertions. We must assist her."

Ferren moved to assist Creda, while the captain turned to Veras. "Did all go well?"

Veras beamed. "We have it! Thanks to Creda! I will explain to everyone when we get down from here."

The way down the ledge was difficult. Not only was Creda weak, but the fading of the sun's light had left opportunity for the shadows to steal into their path, and these hid some slipperier sections from view. Creda lost her footing and would have fallen had not Ferren caught her from behind, and held her until the Sister's feet had found a bit of security once more.

Ferren was deep in contemplation. According to the Superior, this small Sister had somehow been heroic. Ferren had always assumed that *Veras* would be the important one …

Veras had said that the *One* would not be a 'man'. Could it possibly be that she, Ferren, might be the *One*? Surely if this small Sister, who hadn't even completed her final tests yet, could be heroic –

Surely there was a chance that Ferren's role might be greater than had been assumed …

Finally, they reached the bottom of the icy downslope. Nico and Tavis had been about to begin the uphill trek, but once aware that the group was on its way down, they'd begun preparing the horses for leaving, instead. As usual, when they were all back together, Nico took over the entire situation, or so it seemed to Ferren. The large man easily set Creda atop her mare, passed her something to drink and dried fruit to replenish her. But the winds had risen once more. Despite the eagerness of the escort for details, and Veras's desire to share them, talking above the noise of the wind was simply too difficult. Nico motioned to them to follow him.

They made their way back along the roadway in the direction of the nearest travellers' shelter. Part of the way back, though, they reached an impasse. The snow had fallen heavily enough down here that it had filled in sections of the roadway completely.

Nico uttered an expletive, but the wind caught it and held it, and the others didn't hear. There had been a time when he had thought that those of sorcery only needed to snap their fingers in order to deal with a situation such as this. But a glance in the Sisters' direction said clearly that their energy levels were too low – especially Creda's –for them to undertake the business of magic just now.

He turned Thunder back toward the others. "Don't worry," he shouted over the wind. "There'll be another way out of the area." He urged Thunder in the other direction, his teeth clenched, hoping that what he had just told them was right.

They wandered around the base of the icy mountain, finally finding a pathway between some rocks. They had to dismount here and walk, the descent somewhat steeper than the horses were comfortable with. Nico slipped along carefully, sliding a bit of the way, slowly encouraging Thunder. He tried to keep an eye on the others as well, for this was tough going, indeed.

Then he heard it.

He knew immediately what it was. But he hesitated, part of his mind wanting desperately to deny it –

It was only a heartbeat of time. But it was too much –

"Seek shelter! Seek shelter – *now!*" He shouted as loudly as he could, while he pulled Thunder's reins –

But suddenly a huge dumping of snow fell –

Veras had just looked in his direction. And then she was gone.

All was deathly quiet. It was as though there was no sound anywhere. The entire world was nothing but silence.

Was this the afterworld? Or would she awaken to find herself preserved beneath the frigid floor inside the Icetombs? She tried to move, but she couldn't ...

She took a breath. It was difficult, for there was just a bit of air, a pocket of sorts around her nose and mouth –

She started to gasp, then stopped herself. She remembered Nico's warning. He'd told them all of the dangers of falling snow from high above –

You are a Superior of the Tower of Giefen. Use your skills.

Veras could not breathe deeply, but she managed to get a bit of air into her lungs. Now she urged herself to relax, to calm herself into complete and total relaxation. She slowed her breathing, her heart, her mind, so that she asked as little as possible from her body. There was no thought, no concern, as though she was floating effortlessly on a soft cloud. She opened herself completely, so that Creda could have easy access to assist her ...

And then she felt Creda's presence. It was warm, and good, and seemed to envelop her in a lovely shade of pale blue. Now she could hear the dim sounds above as her companions struggled to reach her – and voices ...

Nico's heart was pounding. He dug his gloves into the snow, took a deep breath, and *heaved* a large mass of the heavy stuff out of the way. Vander and Tavis were nearby, digging like dogs in dirt, while Ferren, Sohn and Zann tried to use their blades to carefully dig away the surface.

"Look, Tavis! There's her hood!" Nico sounded jubilant, and he thrust his fingers quickly around the brown material, anxiously trying to clear the snow from her nose and mouth –

Her head was free now, and the others worked quickly around her shoulders. Nico crouched before her, pulled off a glove and put a hand upon her cheek –

Her face was barely chilled at all! He glanced back at Creda who sat atop her mare. She was just opening her eyes after using a spell to keep her Superior safe ... and, apparently, warm ...

Veras, in turn, had reached up to touch *his* cheek. He pulled off his other glove with his teeth and put his own hand atop hers. His heart sang at the sight of those blue-green eyes. She smiled. And so did he.

CHAPTER ELEVEN

The Wolf

He stood before her. He was very tall and possessed an extremely powerful appearance. His robe was black with silvery designs upon it which seemed to be constantly moving and changing in pattern. His beard was long and flaming red in colour, long strands of white winding their ways through it.

As he stood before her, arms crossed, she could see the many golden rings which decorated his long fingers.

And his eyes –

His eyes were of a strange shade of brown. They almost glowed bright red as the light from the fire gave them life …

And the fires were all around them. The two of them were on some sort of island floating upon a sea of flames.

She lay on her stomach, elbows propping her up just enough for her to see this monster before her. He smiled then, and a sickening leer of a grin it was.

"And so, little Sister, you think you are the *One* to defeat me! You think that you alone possess the power to defeat the Great Warlock! Ha! I can suck the life energy from you even as you try to make your spells. And then I'll use them as my own. Defeat me, Sister. Go on. Let me see you try."

As he spoke, the section of the island behind her feet suddenly began to split away. With a gasp, she moved forward, gathering her feet beneath her –

Just as another chunk fell into the world of flame beneath her left foot –

She moved forward, quickly –

Not much space separated her from the enemy now. She had no further options. She was the *One*. She had to defeat him, even though she would die in the process. Her fingers travelled toward her amulet …

She grasped it. But it came away with its chain. This could not happen. The chain itself was bewitched.

She held the amulet in her hand. Something was wrong –

It was turning to dust as she watched. She looked up at him as he stared at her with that awful leer. She had to defeat him! But how? There was only one chance.

"Veras! Veras!" She wailed the name as loudly as she could.

But the sound of her cry was lost in the deep tones of the enemy's loud laughter, rumbling forth like an earthquake.

And then she could see Veras's face where it gazed out from behind the frigid sheet in the ice-prison –

"Veras!"

Ferren held the cool, limp wrist, squeezed and massaged the cold hand. "Come, Sister Creda. Wake now. You're all right."

And pale blue eyes blinked up at her from the wan face.

Ferren gave the Sister an encouraging smile, tucking the blankets around her more snuggly. At last, Sister Creda might be waking, and strong enough to help! Ferren stepped away, toward the fire.

Creda closed her eyes, trying to fight the dizziness that seized her. She breathed deeply to calm herself, then opened her eyes to study the welcome sight of the inside of the travellers' shelter. Her gaze stayed on the pleasant vision of the crackling fire, not far from her feet. With a sigh, she gave into the fatigue that was seducing her back into sleep, but suddenly Ferren was speaking to her once again –

Ferren eased her into a sitting position, supporting the Sister with an arm around her shoulders. "Drink this," she encouraged, and held a cup of warm tea to Creda's lips. She watched as the Sister sipped carefully, then accepted the entire contents of the mug eagerly.

"Thank you," Creda said softly, sitting without support now. She turned at the sight of the apparently sleeping figure of Veras, lying not far from her. But the usually pinkish tone of the Superior's face now seemed alarmingly ashen –

"Veras," murmured Creda.

"Sister," said Ferren, "I am so glad that you have regained your strength! Veras was extremely weak, but conscious when we recovered her. We have done everything we could for her. I put her into dry clothing, and we have kept her warm … but we have no idea what more we should do. She remains very pale, and we cannot wake her!"

Creda was silent as she took in all the information which the sight of the Superior might give her. She knew what she must do … yet the fatigue still pulled at her, enticing her to lie back down, to float away to wherever her dreams might take her. But the dream she'd had of the warlock was still fresh in her mind. And that gave her the strength to do what she must.

She was still a bit dizzy, but she moved carefully, closer to where Veras lay. Nico had moved in their direction and now stood nearby, watching. Creda reached for her amulet. She would do whatever she needed to for the Superior. One hand on her amulet, and the other on Veras's cheek, she closed her eyes, seeking contact with Veras's internal world –

But she felt no sensation of welcoming contact. Cold, cold it was. The others had managed to warm the body, but the Superior's energies were not strong enough to maintain her spirit. Creda grimaced, concentrated *harder*. Although she herself was weak from assisting Veras when the Superior had been buried, she *must* provide for Veras the energy which she now lacked. She sent some of her pale blue power inside of Veras's spirit, seeking the deep blue of Veras's energy. Creda would bolster these in a similar manner to what she had done when Veras had been buried.

But there was so little! Veras's power was at a low ebb, indeed! Even with Creda's support, there might not be enough – not sufficient to allow her to recover as a Superior, nor perhaps even as a Sister. There was barely enough to allow her physical recovery alone!

Slowly, gently, not wishing to shock the Superior's system further, Creda pulled back into herself once more …

The others watched, their reactions a mixture of fascination and concern. Although there appeared to be no change in the Superior, Creda now swayed dizzily as she kneeled. Quickly, Nico placed his arm around her shoulders, supporting her. Creda's hand moved from her amulet to her aching head, her other fingers still touching Veras's pale cheek.

"Creda," Nico said softly, trying to control his impatience to give her time to respond. When she nodded, he asked: "Veras … is she – will she …?"

The Sister could only shrug her shoulders, and turn her pale eyes to gaze into Nico's deep brown ones. "Her energies have sunk so low. I – I," she muttered, shaking her head.

Nico exhaled sharply. "There *must* be something you can do!"

Creda shrugged again.

"Creda!" He spoke harshly, turned her to face him. He did not hold her gently now – his fingers gripped her shoulders hard enough that they hurt –

"Nico!" Zann now stood behind Nico and placed his hand firmly on Nico's shoulder.

"Hush!" Nico returned his full attention to the Sister. *"Creda."* Her eyes were wide now as they returned his stare. "In the Tower they must have taught you something that you can use!"

"But I already –"

"We *need* her, Creda! Or do you want to face two more challenges and the warlock himself with only the magic that you, yourself, can create!" He shook her, his actions tempered somewhat by Captain Zann's grip on his shoulder.

Creda focused on the importance of those words. She managed to nod, placing her hands on his thick forearms, and took a moment …

There had to be something …

She fingered her amulet, reassured by the power of her own energies which she could feel there.

And she thought of Veras's amulet, which the Superior did not even have the strength to touch, in order to help herself focus. A sorcerer's (or sorceress's) amulet was keyed to respond to the inner powers of its wearer only (unless its magic had been affected by someone whose power was greater). It was a matter of courtesy that one of the Tower would not touch the amulet of another, other than by accident –

But, in a dire emergency, it was possible for a sorcerer or sorceress to hold his or her amulet, thus focusing their own power, and *also* that of another. This was a very dangerous procedure, however, and most of the world of magic passed through their entire lives without experiencing it.

It might be their only chance.

Creda took her amulet in her left hand and closed her eyes until she could feel, see, hear, smell and taste the power as it stirred within her, preparing itself for whatever might occur next.

She reached downward, the fingers of her free hand feeling the softness of the blanket, the edge of it. Then, as she sought further, the cool hardness of Veras's amulet. Creda focused the energy swirling beneath the fingertips of her left hand, and willed it to leave her amulet and to enter her being. She felt a sudden surge of warmth as what her spirit saw as pale blue tendrils made their way inside of her. She concentrated deeply, with her mind pushing those tendrils down, down to her other arm ...

Toward Veras's amulet.

This was quite an unusual action to take – unusual enough that Creda's own instincts against it gave her difficulty. She could see her pale blue tendrils as they made their way down through her arm and into her fingers – but stopped there, resisting the command to violate the sanctity of another's amulet.

Creda could now feel how empty that other amulet was. There was not even a spark of Veras's natural defences against intrusion. Just nothing ... except for the faintest glimmer of deep blue that Creda hadn't noticed at first.

The fingers on her right hand felt like they were burning with all the energy now focused there. It was almost as though she was holding them over a candle flame. She had to concentrate every bit of strength she still had on that tingling energy in her fingers. She counted silently, willing her power to its strongest –

At the count of ten, with an enormous effort, she gave a huge push against that hot energy –

It resisted! But she struggled, pushed again, blackness now threatening her consciousness –

She was through –

But she was thrown back, the force jolting her away, dimly felt Nico's strong arm as it braced her. She opened her eyes, and once the dizziness had passed, she saw Veras's amulet as it regained its life. It was glowing brightly – a brilliant, deep shade of blue. The silence was broken by gasps and sudden intakes of breath from the others around them –

As they watched, faint sparkles of sapphire blue began to glitter, more and more until the amulet resembled a ball of light shining its bluish brilliance so that it seemed to fill the entire room of the shelter.

Creda let her breath go in a long sigh, and relaxed against Nico's shoulder.

"I *can* travel. I'm really quite all right now. And I really would prefer that everyone stop fussing. Really."

Yet Veras's redundancy seemed a signal to Creda, for Veras always considered her words carefully before speaking. The Superior fastened her blankets and supply sacks to her horse's saddle, perhaps a bit more roughly than necessary.

Veras turned to the others, giving a little sigh. "I *am* grateful for your concern. But we must hasten. We've lost too much time already! I'm all right, Nico. I *don't* need your help!" She pushed his hand away, thrust her foot into the stirrup –

And slipped, falling backward into his arms. He was grinning broadly, as was usual, now with his arm around her waist.

"Well. Then, let's *go!*" Creda was suddenly impatient to see Veras in the saddle, where she should be –

She urged Gem forward and was quickly followed by Captain Zann. Indeed, they were *all* eager to head away from this cold place, knowing that warmer climes awaited them.

Ferren followed Nico and Veras, who rode for a time side by side, the joviality between them continuing. At first, he'd been teasing her about her insistence that she needed no help. But after this, Ferren had been unable to grasp snatches of their conversation. Nico's low voice, followed by light-hearted laughter from the Superior, aroused Ferren's curiosity. And she wondered, too, about the response from Sister Creda, for she had turned a frowning face in their direction.

These were Sisters of the Tower, after all. Ferren had been under the impression that, as such, they would never marry, for such a relationship would take a sorceress's focus away from her powers. Although Ferren had known that some sorceresses who acted as healers or other helpers to communities married, it was certainly rather unheard of for Superiors in the Tower. Such an arrangement simply added unwelcome complications to one's life.

She sniffed, turned her attentions elsewhere. Certainly, the arrogant big man didn't merit her interest. She found her gaze turning in Creda's direction and watched her awhile.

One of the young townsmen had ridden up to travel beside her. "Ferren," he said in a quiet tone, "Sister Veras said that next we'll journey to the Noble Mountains –"

She turned to him. "Yes, Tavis."

"Isn't it true that we'll be entering the territory of the Large Dragon and the Mountain King? You've lived in our area much of your life – surely you've heard the tales!"

Ferren studied the grey eyes of the young man, whose fair hair always seemed hopelessly disheveled, reminding her vaguely of a bird's nest. "Tavis," she said, "I have served our King and Queen for some years and have been proud to have Joul Zann as my superior officer on more than one assignment. If there is one thing which I've learned as a soldier, it's that some things which one hears prove true, while others are falsehoods, rumours and simple fairy tales with no basis in fact at all."

She continued, raising a hand to silence the young man's attempt at interruption. "I have journeyed through the area of the Noble Mountains before and have not seen any indications that any dragon or Mountain King ever existed. It may be that they were simply hidden away when I was there, or that the stories about them are stories only. Or perhaps they *did* exist at one time, but that was long, long ago. You may believe whatever you wish."

Captain Zann shouted something to her, though, and after a brief nod to Tavis, she urged her mount to join the captain's up ahead.

Tavis looked morose, indeed. This warrior woman had said nothing to ease his mind. Certainly she, herself, did not seem concerned. He tried to take solace from that.

They entered Turning Point just as the sun was beginning to set. Nico was grinning like a madman, so it seemed to Ferren, as he held his hand high in greeting. Several onlookers were shouting what must have been congratulations, Nico nodding triumphantly in return, replying in the northern dialect.

How she wished she knew this tongue! She would love to hear what Nico might be telling them. Certainly nothing about their specific quest, but she'd be willing to wager that he boasted of their having reached the Icetombs. Perhaps he was adding his own fabrications, telling them that he'd ventured inside. Ferren wouldn't be surprised if he had. She shook her head at the thought.

Well, *he* wouldn't be the *One* to defeat the warlock, at any rate. At least he wouldn't be able to gloat over *that*! And Ferren let her imagination play with a fantasy —of this fearsome sorcerer being felled by *her* blade, which proudly bore upon its hilt the crest of the Royal Family —

They supped well at the inn – the larger one, this time – and tankards of ale were eagerly emptied by the escort, while Nico gave exaggerated and sometimes rather fabricated accounts of their experiences. He translated for the escort and enjoyed the merry laughter of the men.

But then he rose, as though to offer a toast. "Sisters, escort, our task is yet far from complete. We will not have more to drink until it is. Let us take to our beds, as tomorrow awaits us."

Ferren was once more a bit irritated. Who did he think he was? Ferren never drank more than an occasional mug of ale while on a quest. She didn't need to be told to be responsible, as though she was a child. But, then again, perhaps some did –

She put out a hand to steady Tavis, who'd evidently already quaffed more than his fair share. She eased him in the direction of the staircase.

Something like an icicle suddenly ran through Veras's insides. *Creda.* Since the energies of their amulets had been shared, they seemed to be much more sensitive to each other. She turned to Creda, who had followed her up the stairs. She studied the Sister's expression as her fingers turned the key to open the door to their room.

Creda let the door bang shut behind her. "Veras," she said irritably, "we haven't shared any details of the truth with these townspeople. If the warlock has the power to use the Icetombs as a sort of prison for people's bodies, shouldn't these people be told what is going on? If the warlock can make use of the tombs, he may well be aware of this town, and intend to lay waste to it as he did poor Carlida's encampment!"

Veras took Creda's hand in her own, feeling her distress. "Creda, no matter how the warlock has managed to make use of the Icetombs, his raiders have *not* appeared up here. Considering that he has elected to remain in the south, they would likely not choose to venture into the chill of this northland. There must certainly be some powerful magic, enchantment, which has enabled him to imprison the bodies in the Icetombs. We have seen no indication of anything further. So it just doesn't make sense to me to alarm these people with details of an attack which seems highly unlikely to occur."

Creda sighed, turning away from her Superior to examine the basis of these emotions. Her sorrow for Carlida had grown into anger, as well as a strong desire to keep others from losing loved ones as she and Joul had.

"Unfortunately, Creda," Veras continued, "it seems more likely that his raiders would attack Espri than this little town. There would certainly be more people for him to take, as well as it being less further north."

"We must hurry, Veras!" Once again she faced Veras. "Perhaps we should find more volunteers to help before we continue ..."

Veras shook her head. "I'm certain that Nico would have told us of suitable warriors here if he thought it necessary. And, anyway, a small group – rather than a large one --might well have an advantage in approaching the warlock. Our band will need to be small enough that we'll not arouse suspicion as we travel. So I think we should let it be as it is, Creda. Let these people believe that Nico is a braggart who has travelled to the Icetombs on some sort of dare. Let them be relaxed in their ignorance. Allow them to have the peace which we cannot. Should there be any indication of danger before we leave, then we will tell them all there is to tell."

Most of the group were quite happy to exchange their heavier winter clothing for supplies which would suit their next trek to the mountainous regions, south of Turning Point yet still north of Espri. It was on a cloudy and windy morning that they headed southwest.

They travelled quietly that day, the howling of the wind making conversation a bit difficult. They were headed away from the colder areas into large fields of grasses and trees where various types of grazing animals nibbled peacefully. A tremendously relaxed feeling came over Creda as she watched a bull not far from the fence along the roadway. His jaws moved rhythmically, and she found herself sharing his contentment as he returned her eye contact ...

So, here it came again. This strange rapport which sometimes seemed to spring at her from the beasts, and which she could also initiate as she had with the Witch's guardian and the tiny white creature of the Icetombs. She still felt far from understanding this strange skill, yet well she knew that without it they might not have found the important talisman segment! If only she could think of some way that she might make use of it against the warlock ...

The next day Joul was pleased to tell Creda that it appeared they might be within a day's ride now of the mountains.

As night began to fall, they stopped in a forested area where a grove of trees offered some protection from the gusty winds. Quietly they sat around the fire, each absorbed in his or her own thoughts.

The Sisters had been sharing more details of their quest as they came closer to the mountains. It was thus that poor Tavis's concerns were aroused when the more precise location of the next talisman segment was announced. Thus far he had spoken no more about it, and Ferren had offered no comments. But his unrest nibbled away at his insides, and continually disturbed his peace.

As most of them took to what would serve as their beds, the sky was very clear, and bright starlight lit the blackness. Although the winds blew, the trees offered adequate shelter, and the winds seemed nothing more than rushing sounds as they toyed with the tree branches high above.

OOOOOOOOWWWWOOOOOOOOOOO

That had *not* been the wind! Those who had been sleeping were instantly awake, sitting up or standing quickly, grasping blankets or thrusting them aside, scanning the area for intruders. It was quiet once more, but Nico stood very still, clutching his blade as it glinted in the firelight. Joul was on his feet and moving quietly in his direction. Ferren stepped to the Sisters, her own blade in her hand and ready. Sohn joined them.

"Wh-what was that?" Creda managed to whisper, her mind conjuring up images of the warlock's army.

"Maybe a wolf," Ferren said evenly. Her face was devoid of expression as her eyes scanned the area for any sign of intrusion.

Nico crossed over to them, while Joul went to speak with Vander and Tavis.

"Sounded like a wolf," Nico said softly. "And –" But he stopped, his eyes now more quickly checking the area as though he'd heard something more –

"And?" Veras prompted.

"It's likely to be more than one, seeing that they're pack animals."

Prompted by Joul and Nico, they all moved closer to the fire, and brought the horses closer as well. The escort would remain on watch three at a time now, rather than one, with Joul or Nico acting as leader during each shift.

Veras lay on her back and sighed. She could hear Creda beside her, moving about as though unable to find a comfortable position.

"Creda," she said softly, extending a hand to touch her, "we must try to relax ... somehow –"

O O O O O W W W O O O O O W W W O O O O O W W W OOOOOWWWWOOO

The awful cry seemed to fill the whole area. Tavis suddenly shouted, "*The Large Dragon!*" Vander tried to reassure his companion, but still Tavis muttered and trembled. His hand on his sword, Nico crossed to the young man and said something quickly to him. Tavis remained quiet, but the look of terror on his face now seemed more due to Nico than anything else.

Nico, Ferren and Sohn now moved quietly about the area, alert for any movement. An icy sensation of fear made its way up Creda's spine. But as she watched Gem's restless tossing of her head and snorting, Creda realized that it was the horse's fright which she was feeling, not her own ...

Veras watched, puzzled, as Creda rose to her feet and, pulling her brown robe more tightly around herself, moved to the mare. She touched the beast's long nose, and appeared to faint, but suddenly grasped the horse around the neck. Now Creda, like her horse, was sniffing the air ...

OOOOOOWWWWWWWOOOOO

The horses all appeared to be getting quite agitated. Some of the escort had moved to the beasts to calm them. Veras rose and reached beneath her clothing for her amulet, her lips already moving to produce a *Spell of Relaxation* to help the horses to quiet.

Creda had felt the icy terror course through Gem, and, touching her amulet, pushed the terror aside to leave a deep sense of peace in its place. She could *feel* Gem's breathing begin to even out, her fear slipping away into mild anxiety. And she felt, too, gratitude and enjoyment of the closeness with her human ...

When she had pulled back into herself, Creda could see and hear how much calmer all of the horses now were. Indeed, everything seemed quite fine again.

But again came the cry –

And this time, Creda could feel the *pain*. She grasped her left wrist. Then she looked at it. It seemed all right. *What?* The creature again howled, and Creda's hand ached horribly, as though it had been stretched from her wrist – and she felt fear … and horrible, horrible loneliness and sorrow …

Veras watched her, fascinated. She knew that Creda was in some sort of rapport with the beast which had howled. This was something that no other Sister or Brother she'd ever met had been capable of. Joul moved in Creda's direction, but Veras stopped him with a word. "No one is to interfere with Sister Creda without word from me," she said firmly, looking at each of them.

Creda was moving away. Veras followed, but kept a few paces behind, and encouraged the others to stay behind *her*.

Creda's mind was flitting back and forth between images from her own eyes and· the beast's sensations as she made her way to the edge of the clearing. She was dimly aware of Veras behind her, whispering to the escort. Into the wood Creda ventured, *knowing* that she was headed in the right direction, *feeling* the presence of the animal and its need for help.

No conscious thought entered her mind. She was a creature of sensation, nothing more. And so it was that she felt no element of surprise nor fear at what she came upon. The grey beast eyed her, yet seemed to know that she was somehow different, special. He stood still, tongue protruding, misery evident both outside and in. Creda reached a hand toward him, half-seeing through *his* eyes and half through her own. She felt the pain in the left forepaw as vividly as though it was her own. She took the rope in her fingers –

And saw his memory. A rabbit had been caught in a snare, and when he'd approached to investigate, he'd caught the human scent too late, for a second trap had been set, and he'd wandered into it. He'd pulled away, and part of the rope had torn loose. He was free, but he could not gain release from the awful rope which was strangling the life from his paw.

Lost in the wolf's memories, Creda had not seen Nico extend his small knife to her, but when she was once more herself, she seized it. She entered the wolf's mind again, asserting her influence as she did. She sent soothing messages down and into the wolf's trembling body.

Her fingers sought the rope – and she watched through *his* eyes as her fingers took the dagger and began to saw through.

It fell away in two pieces. Still inside the mind of the wolf, she watched as her fingers reached inside of her robe to her amulet. She sent a *Spell of Relaxation* to aid in the healing process. This was quite easy to do, her rapport with the wolf's mind so complete …

And, as she began to withdraw, the beast's consciousness was once more active –and he sent her a sensation of gratitude … and devotion … and love. So beautiful were his gratitude and the tremendous sense of sharing that Creda's eyes were wet with tears.

A furry muzzle sought physical contact with her hand, and with it, the warm wetness of a tongue.

CHAPTER TWELVE

The Cave

The birds twittered pleasantly, and a ray of sunshine managed to find its way through the leaves and needles of the greenery high above. This, in itself, was ample reason to feel good. The *other* sensation left Creda feeling especially at peace.

She'd always enjoyed animals, even stubborn old Portar, although he'd been difficult at times. She supposed that she had always known that she had some sort of rapport with creatures, although she had never considered it as anything serious. So it was not contrary to her nature to enjoy being with the animals wherever they were housed or fed. It was as natural for her as drawing another breath.

She reached over to stroke the wolf again where he lay stretched out by her side, his back to her as though a long-time lover with whom she shared her bed. How wonderful it was to feel the coarser hair and then to dig her fingers more deeply into the ruff to find the softer undercoat. Although she'd never experienced anything quite like this before, she knew that she now had a loyal companion the like of which she never would again ...

She even knew his *name*. Her total rapport with him had told her what that was. There was only one problem –

It was in the form of a *scent*. But she was human, and needed something which could be spoken. So she considered something which might relate to his cry – his particular howl which would be used to tell others of his kind his identity when too far apart for a sharing of scents.

She decided on *Baru*, which she would pronounce as BaROO, as this vaguely resembled the first phase of his call. Her fingers caressing his ear, she sent her message through her fingertips and into his consciousness. She felt his agreement – and his determination to agree with anything from her now that she'd rescued him.

And, as she sat up, so did he.

She draped an arm around his neck and murmured to him, "you don't have to come with me, you know. Feel free to return to your pack, my friend!"

But, as he had each time that she'd suggested this, he lay back down determinedly, head on forepaws, as though his mind was quite made up.

Nico poked at the fire, trying to stir the embers to a longer life. He gazed in Creda's direction, shaking his head. What an odd situation! The Sister had befriended a *wolf*, of all things! Somehow, she seemed able to speak with the beasts, to understand them. Sorcery he'd heard of, but not this. He chuckled. The unusual and new suited him just fine, to an extent.

She walked over to him, the wolf choosing to keep his distance from the fire. Nico gazed at it as it stared at him alertly, as though cautioning him not to threaten Creda.

Nico switched his gaze from the wolf to the Sister –

She was looking toward the mountaintops which were visible off in the distance. The morning sunlight caught her cheeks, and her face seemed more colourful, healthier. It struck Nico that she appeared more confident than before, more capable. She looked down at him where he sat on a rock near the fire.

He smiled broadly. "Well now, good Sister! So you are one with the beasts, too. I did not know that they taught *that* skill in the Tower of Giefan!"

She chuckled. "I can assure you that they do *not*, Nico."

"So, then. How did you come to have such an ability?" His eyes twinkled with merriment, but his curiosity was quite genuine as he awaited her explanation.

Creda's mouth opened, but she could think of no response. She returned her attention to the mountain peaks that beckoned through the treetops. "And so we'll reach our next destination before nightfall."

"So it seems," he replied. Still he smiled up at her, wondering at her lack of response to his question. "Tell me, Sister, do you believe in the tales of the Large Dragon and the Mountain King?"

Creda sighed. "Tavis certainly does. We'll have to bear in mind his fear as we move closer to our destination …"

"And do *you* believe in these tales? You're from the Espri area, too, after all. Surely you heard the tales, too, that the others have spoken of."

"Has the north no legends, then? No exciting tales born of overactive imaginations and children's dreams of conquest, Nico?"

"You haven't answered my questions, Creda." His voice was very soft, yet firm.

"I was not *born* in Espri, Nico. And what I think of such legends matters not at all.

I have a destiny. And I shall face whatever is in the mountain which houses the talisman segment."

There was silence a moment, Creda still gazing at the mountaintops while Nico sat. The fire seemed to growl and spit at Nico, as though it resented his prodding.

When Nico spoke once more, he did so in a quiet voice. "Do you believe that you are the *One*, Creda?"

His question caught her by surprise. Her mouth opened, but at first, she could not express her thoughts. "It – it does not matter. All that matters is the defeat of the warlock before he can cause more destruction. That's all, Nico. That's all there is." Her vehemence surprised her. Was she frightened of the thought of being the *One*? She'd been assuming that it must be Veras who would have to bear the awesome responsibility.

Nico said nothing more, but at a nod from Captain Zann, began preparations to depart. Soon they had all completed their morning meals and secured their belongings once more to the horses' saddles. Creda was atop Gem's back, eyes still focused on the mountain peaks which awaited them. She was anxious to get there. No matter what else they might be called upon to face, all that mattered for now was that next talisman segment. The warlock was ahead of them – and hopefully, so was Carlida. They *would* defeat the warlock. The taking of Carlida and Joul's wife must not be in vain!

"Creda!" The forcefulness with which her name had been shouted told Creda that she must have been so involved in her musings that Veras had had to repeat herself.

"What of Baru?" Veras nodded toward the wolf, where he sat still nibbling on some of the dried meat which Nico had shared with him.

Creda gazed at him – her new-found friend! He seemed to feel her look, and turned to gaze back, alert eyes ready to share with her any part of his spirit that she might wish. How easy it would be to take advantage of his loyal friendship! But then she thought suddenly of the warlock, who would take anything of anyone's should he wish to …

"Baru," Creda said softly, more to herself than to Veras, "will do as he pleases. I wish no hold over him." But even as she spoke so quietly, he heard her voice and seemed to feel her intent. He walked toward her, his eyes seeking contact with hers. She allowed herself to drift inside of his spirit, just for an instant. It was as it had been last night. The sensation of his friendship and loyalty was almost overwhelming. She sent him a flash of her own friendship, adding an element of respect for his freedom –She heard Joul's voice – strange through Baru's ears – and drifted back into herself.

"Are you ready, Creda?"

She nodded, and, as he urged his mount forward, she encouraged Gem forth as well. They trotted quietly along in the cool morning breeze and, as they came back to the main roadway, she caught a glimpse of movement off to the right.

She knew immediately who it was that was making his way stealthily through the underbrush at the side of the road. She smiled.

They came to a section where the mountain path separated from the main route. The path narrow, they would need to ride in single file through the bushier area.

It had been a long time since Ferren had last been in this area. She had not forgotten the beauty -- the rolling hills, the steep mountain slopes with their misty peaks high above, looking as though they touched the clouds in the sky. The narrow trail picked its way between rocks and crevices, winding slowly but continuously upward.

Finally, the captain stopped his horse, turning in his saddle to grin, moustache twitching in Ferren's direction. He leaned to one side, so that she could see past him the wonder of the scene ahead. The valley was like a smooth, green sea, light breezes sending some longer grasses dancing in one direction, and some in another, almost like gentle waves. And there were, too, the Three Great Peaks, no less majestic than the crown of the King himself.

"What is it?" Veras asked from behind, unable to see for herself.

"The valley, Sister," offered Ferren, "and, with it, the Three Great Peaks which you seek."

"Good!" exclaimed Veras. "Let's continue then!"

And, ah! The scent! The fields around Espri boasted freshness, but not the like of this! It was so sweet, so clear –

Ferren's mother had been nomadic. And when Ferren had proven a sickly child, her mother had left her to live with an aunt, just outside the limits of Espri. After a time, they had moved inside of the city gates. Ferren had lived in the area long enough to have heard the old stories ...

It was said that many ancestors of those born in Espri had come from this valley. It was said that the valley had been tremendously picturesque and fertile –

So why, one might ask, would the people who eventually built Espri have left such perfection? The answer was that the *Large Dragon* and the *Mountain King* had constantly feuded over ownership of the surrounding mountain peaks. Their battles had made life in the centre of these quite uncomfortable and at times terrifying.

Or so the stories said.

As a child, Ferren had been fascinated by the old stories. Yet she'd always felt she'd been a disappointment to her mother because of her weakness. In her determination to prove her worth, she'd sought training with the Royal Army. She would certainly not allow any stories of old to keep her from serving well! Her hand was on her sword. She felt quite ready. The Royal family would have reason to be proud …

Closer, ever closer they were coming to their destination, the third highest mountain. The highest was closest, and the veiled sight of its peak was quite overwhelming to some of the escort. Its highest point was misted in a low hanging cloud and decorated in snow.

Finally, the path led through the trees at the base of the highest mountain. Once through here, they'd be at the base of the third. Hunger was gnawing at some stomachs, but they'd not stop their progress until they'd reached the base of the third highest peak. They could eat while they contemplated their next move …

At last, warm sunshine greeted them as they emerged from the little wood. Zann suggested that they move ahead, where there was a little grove. They could tether the mounts there and replenish themselves.

Those of the escort suddenly found themselves to be quite famished, and it seemed that some of the food was devoured as soon as it was seen. Baru disappeared into the undergrowth to do whatever it was that wolves did when on their own. Suddenly, though, raised voices split the peace

"No! We can't take such a risk!" Tavis's voice was a hoarse whisper. Evidently, he'd hoped to keep this discussion at a quieter level.

"Oh, come on!" The other voice was impatient – and it was Nico's.

"Captain Zann? You were designated captain of this group – what do *you* say?" Tavis asked.

The captain stroked his moustache. His gaze moved from the youthful intensity of Tavis's stare to the usual cool confidence of Nico, who stood taller than both of them.

But Tavis didn't wait for a response. "Captain, this man doesn't *know*! He's not from around here or Espri. He might've been helpful when we were in the north, but here he's just a – just a bastard foreigner!"

Nico's face betrayed no emotion as he calmly reached over to Tavis and lifted the smaller man up into the air, until Tavis's face was looking downward into his own, almost nose to nose.

The captain cleared his throat. "Nico, please put him down. That will be quite enough, gentlemen. No, Tavis! Not one word! You've said more than enough. We had best consult the true captains of our little army.

He turned to Veras and Creda. "Sisters, do you know of any risk in starting a fire in this area? We've all heard the rumours of the Large Dragon and the Mountain King. Do you of the Tower know of truth to them? Might some flying thing come swooping down upon us should it see our smoke?"

A titter from Nico had Tavis opening his mouth to speak. Zann raised a hand, demanding silence. "After all," he advised, "we *were* surprised by a flying beast at the Witch's cave."

The smirk disappeared from Nico's face. He sighed, turning his attention to the Sisters.

"Escort," said Veras, first to Nico, Joul and Tavis, and then including the others, "if you look above, you will see the opening into the mountain. That is our destination. I would suggest that those of you who wish to accompany Creda and me complete your meals and prepare for the journey. The rest of you should see or not to the care and comfort of the horses. It will certainly make no difference to me whether you light a fire or not. Whatever is in that cave – if anything at all – will be facing us soon, at any rate."

Then she added: "We can never know how much of the old stories are exaggerations, and how much might be based on truth. Perhaps we'll find some answers up in the mountain cave. I would suggest that those of you whose motives might be related to fear or awe or even curiosity remain behind. We have a task to perform and all concentration must be properly focused."

Silence fell upon the little group as Veras turned away, nibbling on honey-dipped bread. Nico's dark eyes followed her, a small smile lighting his face.

Creda saw his look of admiration, and it disturbed her for some reason. She sank down in the grass beside Gem, happy to be away from the others for the moment –

Suddenly the stench of something dead struck her nostrils, and she was about to call to the others in alarm –

But then she noticed that another companion had joined her for their meal.

She would have preferred, though, if Baru had chosen to share Nico's dried meat, rather than deposit a bloody rabbit by her side.

Creda had no memories of a father. Her mother had told her that her father had been a palace sorcerer for a queen from another realm to the southeast. He had not amounted to much, according to Creda's mother, as he was relegated to assisting the queen's household, and protecting the palace on the rare occasions when it was under siege. According to her mother, her father had never risen to the point of being responsible for advising the king in battle strategy, or assisting him while out on missions. And, according to her mother, her father's greatest skill in sorcery was apparently his ability to seduce women with his power – women like Creda's mother.

How much of all this was true, Creda had no way of knowing. But when Creda had shown ability in enchantment, her mother began to have high hopes for this younger daughter, and they moved to Espri, her mother's birthplace. Her mother was quite determined that Creda should succeed where her father had not. Creda must serve as Chief Sorceress of the Palace. Nothing less would suffice.

Yet Creda's conscience bade her to think of the people, the common people, for why should magic be used only to help royalty? She hated the thought of disappointing her mother, but after all, her mother had been one of the common people. Wouldn't helping them be of a higher value?

Perhaps this was one reason that she wished so very much to use her magic to defeat the warlock – to perform some service for all of the people …

Nico paused in his slow progress, his bulk and his big feet making the ledge seem narrower for him than it was for the others. He glanced at those behind him. Creda had paused, too, and stood on the ledge, one hand gripping the growth that covered the mountainside. Her face was a blank – she seemed quite lost in thought. But, although the breeze was refreshingly cool, their exertions had them sweating, and the Sister licked her lips repeatedly. Nico freed a hand to grasp his waterskin, which he thrust in Creda's direction.

"My thanks, Nico," she breathed.

"Not too much farther now, Creda," he said gently, maintaining a light tone to his voice.

As she passed back the waterskin, she cast him a glance which stated that he'd said those same words more than a few times now. He shrugged his broad shoulders, gave his white-toothed grin, and edged his way along. Creda followed carefully, with Veras, Zann and Ferren behind her.

Finally, they arrived at a sheltered area amid boulders, just to the east and below the cave entrance. They stopped here, muscles complaining about the long climb. They sat for a time, contented just to sip from the waterskins and stretch out, the rocks offering support for their backs. It was very quiet. Only the mountain birds could be heard as they screeched and called somewhere in the distance. The pale blue sky was wonderful to behold, the clouds looking like soft cotton spread across the azure.

It seemed hard to believe that all of this could change in just an instant.

Ferren gazed at Sister Creda, whose fingers caressed the segments of the talisman in the pouch which hung with her amulet around her neck. Her forehead puckered in a frown, though, and she raised her pale blue eyes to scan the sky, then the ledge around them, and then she stared in the direction of the cave. Her eyes were narrowed as she focused …

"What is it, Sister?" Ferren asked.

Veras overheard, and her attention too was now focused on Creda. "What is it?"

"I – I'm all right. I just … sensed something –"

"What?" Veras had moved closer. *Was this Creda's skill in rapport with the creatures once more?* They must be alert to this special talent of hers!

"I don't know," she said softly. Her eyes were wide. "It's something different ..."

"Well then," Veras said, rising. "Let's not waste time. Let's go and do whatever we must."

They left their little shelter and headed once more toward the mouth of the cave, where it was partially hidden from view by the rocky outcropping before it. One by one they clambered onto the outcropping, each extending a hand to assist another. Ferren reached up to grasp the captain's hand, and was soon with the rest.

From below, the rocks appeared almost to cover the cave opening, but they could now see that the mouth was set back, and most of the rocks were on the outcropping. Once past the rocks, the entrance was actually ... *large.*

Large enough for almost anything to enter.

They stepped inside a dark, dank and forbidding place, decorated with ominous shadows. The escort drew their blades, prepared themselves, though not certain whether they might find the Mountain King, a dragon, something else entirely, or, perhaps, nothing really to speak of at all. It was cool in the shadowy place ...

Veras had taken in all that she could of their surroundings, but her mind continued to be occupied with questions ... and no answers. She eyed Creda. "Do you sense anything further?"

But the Sister shook her head. She had a vague, nagging feeling about this sensation. It was *almost* familiar, yet not quite.

It was not exactly an enjoyable trek as they pushed further into the tunnel, especially as the light became dimmer and dimmer as they followed the twists and turns.

I am a soldier of the King and Queen, Ferren reminded herself as she felt her way gingerly along in the darkness. *I am a soldier and the dark is only ... darkness ...* "What about a torch?"

"Would we be announcing our presence to ... anything?" asked the captain.

Veras shrugged her shoulders. "We do not know for certain that anything is here!"

Nico reached into his pack and began to rummage –

"Look!" Creda said softly, pointing ahead.

Somewhere before them was a glimmer of light. And so, like moths before a flame, they drifted toward it. The light promised relief from the blackness, yet also an invitation to ... the unknown.

And, as they edged ever forward, the increasing light revealed characteristics of the huge tunnel which they'd not seen before. There were furred things which hung upside-down from the high ceiling of the place, and things which looked vaguely like torn cloth which seemed to grow from the corners and crevices. There was something about these strange things which made Creda all the happier to be moving more quickly toward the light –

They walked in silence, their progress easier now that they had no need to feel their way along the wall. It felt as though they'd never reach that light, as though it had been put there by magic, to frustrate them, draw them in and defeat them ...

But they turned once more, following the twisty tunnel, and suddenly the light was much brighter indeed! They'd reached the source ... and whatever was housed therein.

They stood at the entrance to the colossal cavern, blinking in resistance as the brilliance sought to invade the depths of their eyes. It was *very* bright. Finally, adjusted to the glare, they stepped inside.

The light came from several small openings far above. Evidently there were many, many cracks and holes directly overhead which allowed the sunshine to penetrate the area. It wasn't really as bright as it had first seemed. The contrast to the blackness before this had made it seem so.

The huge open area was quite empty, save for a few old-looking bones in the middle of the place. To the back, furthest from where they stood, there appeared to be several huge rocks, all arranged together in some sort of cluster. There were clumps of long grass here and there too – mostly at the back where the rocks were.

And nothing else. Rocks and grass and an empty, rocky floor.

The two from the Tower saw nothing of particular interest or concern. Nothing which seemed a suitable place to find the talisman segment ...

It was almost a disappointment. Were they to simply look among the small rocks or through the grasses for the segment?

Zann wandered over to study the bones, Ferren following. "A grazing animal, perhaps?"

"But how would it get up *here*?" Ferren responded.

Nico was studying Creda's face. She was staring in the direction of the rock cluster. As she moved toward it, he followed immediately, nodding to Veras. He put his hand on the hilt of his sword. Veras following, they eyed the strange rocks, which seemed to be arranged in a crude circle – five of them.

Creda gasped. The feeling was stronger. *Creatures* -- her heart was beginning to pound –

She reached toward the nearest rock, noting with a bit of dread how its surface seemed *awfully* smooth for a rock, and its design *awfully* similar to that of the others behind and beside it.

She touched her fingers to its surface and felt the life inside.

"Eggs." That was all she could say.

But it was enough.

Nico gave a low whistle. Curious, Zann and Ferren joined them.

"Eggs." Nico repeated for the others, a vaguely troubled look upon his face.

"Eggs?" Zann looked from one face to another. He, too, did not particularly want to accept this as fact.

"But what kind of eggs would be so – so *large*?" The colour faded from Ferren's face as realization hit her –

And, almost as though to confirm their suspicions, in *it* came …

CHAPTER THIRTEEN

Joul's Sacrifice

"What was *that*?" Tavis leaped to his feet, his dagger in his hand, eyes moving quickly to check the sky above, then the trees, then the mountain, and back to the sky. He ran a trembling hand through his already mussed thatch of hair.

"'Twas nothing. Relax, man," advised Sohn, his ruddy complexion bright in the firelight. "Come, have your tea. It was the wind, just the wind."

Tavis remained unconvinced. It hadn't sounded like the wind to *him*! He continued to gaze upward, turning to see Vander returning from relieving himself among the trees. *His* face was calm, too.

"Did you hear something?" Tavis asked.

Vander shrugged. His hands trembled as he recalled being attacked by the Witch's protective beast – but he wasn't about to let his companions know. "Just the rushing winds, high above."

But Tavis was insistent. "It *wasn't* just the wind! Mark my words! Did you see nothing?"

Vander shrugged again, then grinned. "I had to watch what I was doing."

"Tavis, relax," said Sohn once more, and extended a mug of hot, herbal tea in his direction.

Tavis passed a hand through his hair again, sighing. He accepted the mug –

But Vander sneezed just as Tavis raised it to his lips – Tavis jumped, the tea cascading from the mug like a tiny waterfall.

Vander laughed while Tavis muttered expletives. Sohn shook his head, wishing he could have climbed the mountain instead of staying with these two.

Those in the cave heard it too, and Tavis had been right. It was *not* the wind. It was a tremendous rushing noise as something hurled itself through the winding corridors and then burst into the cavern upon them –

Suddenly the space seemed filled with brilliant bluish green. Huge teeth dripped saliva as it roared, its flaming breath from everywhere at once, it seemed! A colossal creature, as tall as three men standing one atop another –

And it was angry. Very, very much so. Its roar was louder than a thunderclap, which seemed to shake the whole mountain. It gazed at them through huge, yellow eyes that had vertical slits for pupils, like a cat's. It was quiet now, at last, smoke still emanating from its nostrils.

Nico stood in front of the Sisters, his blade raised, his concentration focused on the creature. He could feel Creda's hand upon his arm, and he jerked away from her touch, wanting no distractions. He'd faced beasts before, but how one so enormous could move so quickly was beyond his understanding. Like a flash, its talons split the air, slicing downward. Nico ducked to the side, put one arm behind him to urge the Sisters back. And his hand bade them to stay there …

He moved slowly off to the side, away from the two women. But he never took his eyes from those of the great creature. "Come on, you," he shouted at it, brandishing his blade. "You want me? Come and get me! Come on, you big empty-headed beast!" He waved his sword towards the thing's face as it lowered its head to return Nico's stare. The dragon's eyes followed Nico's movements, as the Sisters stepped off to the side.

The dragon lunged again, talons itching for the blood of Nico's face –

But Zann's sword jabbed at it from the other side, and the dragon missed its mark. Now Nico moved in, sword held by both hands, ready to thrust it into the side of the great neck as the beast turned toward the captain –

Veras was prepared to enact a *Spell of Protection*, as she had for Vander when the Witch's protective creature had attacked him. She had had it ready for Nico, but now it was Joul Zann who was under attack. She'd have to make an adjustment -- yet again the creature surprised them with its speed. As it turned its attention to Zann and Ferren, it moved swiftly –

And caught Nico with its great tail. Veras's attention was once more on him, as he gasped, his shoulder feeling as though it had exploded, then he moaned as he hit the wall, banging his back and losing the air from his lungs.

Veras could no longer enact the *Spell of Protection*, as she'd lost sight of the others, and her concentration had been torn. Zann moved away from Ferren now, tried to taunt the thing and tire it with pokes and threats. Ferren stepped to the other side, shouted her own mock threats and brandished her blade. Perhaps there would be a chance, now, for the others to slip past the thing to safety –

And the creature *did* begin to tire, although not as they had wished for it to do …

Impatient, it gave a quick swipe with its clawed front foot, catching one of the irritating trespassers –

Ferren yelped, fell back upon the ground, her sword bouncing away from her. She clutched at the red-hot agony of her shoulder, crimson oozing between her fingers. She gasped, tried to focus again on her task, managed to move forward to retrieve her blade.

Nico took a breath, prepared himself. *He was not done yet!* He stole in cautiously, watching what appeared to be the dragon's turn to taunt and tease, for it grasped at Zann, then withdrew, then frightened him back with a blast of fiery breath, then repeated the exercise.

No, you don't! Nico lunged quickly, wishing he could somehow reach the throat. He thrust as high as he could, hoping for the face that the beast teasingly thrust downward in their direction. But the speed of the thing was awesome, and it turned --

Nico's blade sank into the thick, scaly hide of the top of the creature's foot.

The great roar of the beast drowned out Creda's cry. But Veras saw all, watching in amazement as Creda grabbed at *her* foot in the ankle area. Veras stared at the dragon, then back to Creda, knowing already what must be happening –

Creda was leaving herself and entering the life of the beast. She could *feel* the dragon's agony and anger as if they were her own sensations. And now she felt, too, the fear the dragon felt when the intruders were so near to her young –

Creda opened her eyes. The dragon was staring at her – she, too, felt the rapport.

Gasping, Creda stepped away from Veras, hurrying toward the great beast. She cried, begged the dragon's forgiveness, and reached her hand to the wound. She touched it, sent a quick *Spell of Relaxation* – how much easier this was when in such close rapport! Now the wound would heal more quickly. Creda felt the warm stickiness of the magenta blood. She put her face against the wound, kissed it, tore a large part of her robe's sleeve and held it there until the oozing ceased.

She was inside of the dragon once more, feeling the creature's sorrows, joys, fears, love and anger. Then she shared her own. She withdrew, and they beheld one another, the contact now a slender thread between them which neither wished to break.

From the corner of her eye, she saw Joul step toward her, but stop at a sign from Veras.

The dragon knew, now, why they were there. But Creda wanted desperately to repay her for their horrid intrusion and for causing such pain when the dragon had only been seeking to keep her young safe. The thread of understanding still between them, Creda stepped back in the direction of the eggs. She gazed at the dragon's face, seeing their contact as a thin, light blue fibre reaching from one to the other.

She touched the nearest egg and felt the life inside against her hands. She sent this experience to the dragon, watching the yellow eyes widen in delight. She moved to the next, and the next. They were all alive and growing. Some were large enough to quite fill what room the egg offered. It might not be too much longer that the dragon would need to wait.

Creda's face was wet with the tears of the dragon's joy – the tears that dragons could not shed. She walked over to the creature once more and touched her fingers to the mouth, happy just to continue sharing the rapport for a moment longer …

But a touch from Veras brought part of her back to herself. Creda withdrew slowly from her rapport with the dragon, not wanting to add to the disorientation for either of them. And Creda stood, very much alone once more, aware of the sense of loneliness that this brought with it. But Veras was by her side, and the physical closeness was enough to enable her to sense the Superior's spirit now, too.

"Creda," Veras exclaimed. "This – this *skill* of yours is becoming so strong! We should no longer consider it a – an anomaly. You should bear it in mind for quick use, just as you do your spells."

Creda nodded. She, too, was rather amazed at this development.

They were distracted by another sudden movement from the dragon. She had turned toward a far corner of the cavern, behind a rocky outcropping. Here she dug at something with her claws. She paused suddenly, to gaze in Creda's direction.

Creda exchanged a look with Veras. Veras nodded, and managing a smile, urged Creda to move in that direction. Nico followed behind them as Captain Zann used a bandage from the sack on his back to bind Ferren's wound. The three stepped around the outcropping—

The dragon's gold! Here was a great mound of the stuff – goblets, coins, necklaces, rings, bracelets and items of gold whose identities were uncertain.

"The talisman segment must be in here," whispered Veras.

Creda nodded, after exchanging glances with the dragon, and they began to search. They sifted through items of great value as if they were nothing more than unwanted junk – except for Nico, who was obviously admiring some of the items. A puff of hot smoke from the dragon told him to behave himself. Nico looked up at the creature and let go a long breath. He kept searching but sat back after a time. How would they ever find the thing in this heap? Yet he did not want the Sisters to be disappointed in his efforts, so he returned his attention to the task. "There!" he shouted, pointing to a goblet which lay on its side. "Under that, Joul! I'm certain of it!" He was pointing to an item not far from the captain.

But, for what seemed like the hundredth time, something was moved only to reveal a simple coin beneath. Nico sighed, and turned his attention to the Sisters. Creda's forehead was puckered with concern, while Veras's face revealed nothing except grim determination. He gazed at her in admiration, and then returned once more to the task. He cast a glance over his shoulder at the dragon whose breath seemed awfully hot just behind him. For a moment, he was sure he saw anger in the thing's huge eyes.

And then, finally –

"It's here," said Veras, her hushed voice revealing something close to reverence. Creda hastened to peer into the Superior's palm. But Veras turned to allow each of them an opportunity to view the segment. Silently, Veras withdrew the other two segments from their pouch and arranged them on her open, flat hand. She placed the new one in its spot among them.

There was only one space left. One more missing segment –

The Sisters rose, preparing to begin their departure –

But a large, clawed foot had been placed in their way. On the top part was a wound which was already healing, fibres of Creda's robe still clinging to it. The dragon eyed them, and smoke puffed from her nostrils –

"Of course," said Nico quietly. "One can't simply take gold from a dragon's collection! Have you a solution for this problem, Sisters?"

Creda took a moment to prepare herself, then once more slipped into the dragon's mind. Here she found understanding, but that did not alter the facts. It was true. One simply did not remove gold from a dragon's collection, and, despite the rapport with Creda, despite the joy of the eggs which Creda had shared with her, the dragon did not view the taking of any gold as negotiable.

"A *trade*," suggested Captain Zann. "In that way, we will not be reducing her collection."

Creda's rapport with the dragon confirmed that such seemed acceptable. But there remained a problem. This group of people was not rich. The Sisters had only the gold of their amulets, which they were certain they must not sacrifice. And Nico and Ferren had none at all.

Sighing, Zann spoke again. "It seems that it's to be up to me, then. I have only one item, and I hope that the dragon finds it acceptable." With that, he removed the ring from his left hand. He held it a moment lovingly, turned it in the light to read the inscription just once more – *To my beloved, Joul. Amis*

"Your wedding ring," Creda murmured, hating to see him have to part with it.

He gazed at her. "Sister, if parting with it will help give us the means to recover my wife, this symbol of our love will be well worth the sacrifice."

The dragon eyed the two humans. She seemed to understand that this object was special somehow. She raised her clawed foot, and Zann slipped the ring over the tip of her claw. She raised it to her yellow eyes, peered at it, then added it to her collection.

"Good," breathed Veras, and carefully placed the talisman pieces into the little pouch, tucked this inside her robe, and patted it.

Creda bowed respectfully to the dragon, and made as though to move away, but the dragon shook her great head from side to side, as might a person. Creda hesitated, uncertain, as the dragon nodded toward her broad back. Creda moved closer, and the dragon moved her shoulder so that the Sister could easily reach her wing –

Creda's heart seemed to have jumped into her mouth – she was moving upward! She clung to the wing, fearful of falling to the rock floor. But then she was on the dragon's back, just behind the thick neck. Creda looked down to watch, as the dragon next extended her wing toward Veras.

"She's offering us a *ride!*" Creda shouted down to her friend, but she was half-laughing at the idea.

Soon Veras was beside her, then Ferren, then Joul.

The dragon turned toward Nico then, giving a little snort as she did. Nico looked doubtfully up at Creda, but the Sister nodded, her face serious.

Nico had to struggle to hang onto the wing, for the dragon didn't seem to feel that *his* lift upward should be as gentle as the lifts of the others had been. He cursed as she plopped him onto her scaly back, but Creda was laughing quite happily now.

Then they were quickly searching for something to hang onto as the huge body began to move. There were thick folds of skin at the back of her neck, the right size for them to grasp. And the scales of her back were peeling as new skin developed underneath. These loose scales offered adequate footholds. The great beast lumbered as she turned her bulk to face the entrance. She walked through as they clung to her back -- Zann with an arm around Ferren to support her, Creda still laughing happily and Nico still cursing ...

Then, the dragon stepped through the cavern entrance and back into the winding blackness of the tunnel, bursting forward as though flung from a catapult.

The rushing was incredible. It was like being inside a whirlwind! It took them several moments to adjust to the sudden change –

The beating of the powerful wings had them wondering if she might be trying to punish them, for the great winds these created seemed quite strong enough to cast them off her back and fling them against the rocky walls. But they had little opportunity for contemplation, so occupied were they with the task of staying where they were.

And the twists and turns of the black tunnel seemed even more so as they hurried through them. They seemed to be continuously turning left or right, sharply or slightly, again and again and again. At one point, Veras began to slip, and Nico quickly pushed his hips against hers to hold her securely until she'd adjusted her grip.

Then – and the sensation was breathtaking – they were suddenly free of the darkness and dankness once more. They were in the cool evening air, and the constant beating of the wings slowed, as they found the draught of air they needed for soaring.

It was beautiful! They grew brave enough to gaze at the moon and stars as these became more visible against the darkening sky. And the view of the mountains was splendid as the peaks seemed to reach upwards as far as the stars themselves.

Down below, if they moved very carefully closer to the dragon's shoulders, they could see the tops of the trees and the lovely, grassy fields in the valley below. These seemed to be getting closer and closer, until they could see the firelight of the escort waiting below ...

Then, suddenly, as they came closer still, they could see a flurry of quick activity below. The firelight was suddenly flickering and dimming as they could see someone stomping on it at great speed. Someone seemed to be rushing about in a panic as though not sure what to do. Eventually, they must have rushed into the rocky areas and bushes, for those above could no longer see any activity.

Then the dragon became almost motionless in the air as they approached the ground. Very slowly she dropped to the grasses, with her riders still clinging to keep from slipping off. She reached a wing back for each, depositing him or her gently to the grassy ground.

Perhaps she was fatigued. Perhaps there was something which distracted her concentration. Perhaps it had been completely planned ...

When she reached downward with her last human – who happened to be Nico –she didn't *quite* lower her wing entirely to the ground, as she had previously. And she wriggled suddenly, as though she had developed a sudden cramp in her wing –

And the sound of curses reached their ears once more as Nico rubbed his newly bruised back end.

Creda walked to the front of the dragon and thanked her, although she wasn't sure if the creature completely understood. But she touched a hand to the huge face once again, loving the glint of the bluish green scales in the moonlight.

She turned to rejoin the others. The sight which greeted her was quite a contrast to the vision of the beautiful dragon gleaming in the light of the moon on a still night. Nico was leaning against a tree, rubbing at sore spots and cursing quietly, staring angrily in the dragon's direction. The others were trying to persuade Sohn, Vander and Tavis to emerge from their hiding places. When the first two finally did, Tavis refused to come out of the rocks and back to the smoldering fire.

But then they heard the dragon as she flew upward. She was wonderful to behold as she soared away, the moonglow making her sparkle like a bright star …

Creda turned back to see Tavis's pale face peering from among the rocks.

But all Creda could think of to say was, "yes, she truly *is* a Large Dragon!"

They passed a pleasant evening – all except for poor Tavis. Now that the legendary Large Dragon had been proven to exist, he was terribly concerned that the Mountain King would descend upon them next.

Veras and Creda applied salves to Ferren's wound. Not as deep as first thought, it would heal well. Only a slight *Spell of Relaxation* had Ferren resting comfortably. As they put their medical supplies away – Nico having denied any need for such assistance – Creda asked Veras quietly if she had told the others where they would be headed next.

"Not yet," said Veras. "Let them have an evening to enjoy what's already been accomplished. And Creda …"

Creda paused in packing a satchel and gave Veras her full attention. "Yes?"

Veras sighed, shaking her head. "I was your *teacher*, responsible for sharing with you what *I* knew, yet now I see this – this strange skill of yours with the creatures, and it's quite beyond my understanding! I don't believe that our quest with the dragon could have been completed without it. Creda, we must always be prepared to make use of this skill whenever need be – perhaps, somehow, even against the warlock himself."

And, as though to remind her of this strange rapport with the beasts, a warm, furry head was suddenly thrust against her arm. She reached over to pat Baru, happy to welcome him back after his wanderings. Yet she had no idea how a skill with animals might be used against the warlock … unless he was some sort of animal himself …

It was a dull, grey, windy morning as they prepared to move on. And blustery coolness with gray skies didn't provide a very cheery atmosphere for explaining to the escort where they were headed next. That location, too, had its own legends, rumours and stories … some true, some not.

"We will be heading southwest," Veras explained as they were preparing to mount. "The final segment of the talisman is housed somewhere along the far north shore of the Sea of Extremes –"

"Sister Veras," began Tavis, as Veras had suspected he would. "Is – is the next segment housed somewhere – somewhere *magical*, or legendary? Like the last two?"

Veras sighed softly to herself. *Poor Tavis.* His voice held both awe and fear. "Yes, Tavis. It is."

There was silence a moment as he ran a hand through his bird's nest hair. He stared downward and let go a long breath. "There's a cave or a series of caves, or something that the old stories talk about. Oh, I know! You all thought I was being foolish when I was worried about the Large Dragon – but I was right, wasn't I? There sure *was* one!" He was looking up at the others, something like triumph on his face.

"But we saw *no* Mountain King, Tavis. So what does this prove about old stories? Maybe the dragon being there was just a coincidence—"

But Tavis was not to give up easily. "Oh sure, Sohn! Coincidence! How likely is it to be coincidence when almost all of the dragons died out decades ago –"

"Unless *that* is just an old story," offered Nico. This youth wearied him! Nico could feel the ice of Tavis's stare but showed no outward reaction.

Still Tavis continued, this time turning to Vander for support. "You know, Vander. The story about the She-Serpent!" He whirled then to face Veras and Creda. "Is it true?" He was whispering now, and his eyes became unfocused as he began to recite:

Beware the Sea of Extremes, my child
And never wander there.
For there lurks the powerful She-Serpent
With her seaweed hair!

Never go near the Sea of Extremes
Or the nearby caves –
Once you're with the She-Serpent
You can ne'er be saved!

Avoid the bewitching She-Serpent!
Child, heed my wish!
For she's only to stare into your eyes
And you'll become a fish!"

Silence. Just as Tavis ceased his dramatic speech, the silence suggested that they might all be wondering if there could be some element of truth to this after all. There had been something about the wild, unfocused look in the young man's grey eyes, his as-usual disheveled mop of hair – something about the way the wind was making whistling noises in the distance – something about the damp chill in the air which seemed to seep to their innards until it touched their souls ...

Then Nico laughed. Loudly. And heartily. The atmosphere had changed abruptly. And Tavis left, suddenly preferring the company of his horse.

Veras stepped after him, pausing beside Nico to lay a hand on his arm, bidding him to stop. He complied but looked away from her.

She continued to Tavis and touched his shoulder. "Tavis," she said softly. "What you have heard may well be true, entirely or partly. Then again, it may not. We have no way of knowing what stories to believe and what not to believe. All we know is that inside the caves we shall find the third segment of the talisman. And, no matter what we will face there, it simply cannot be anything that will stop us from defeating the warlock."

Tavis's grey eyes held her gaze for a few seconds. Then he blinked – and Veras could sense his readiness. "You speak truth, Sister Veras. We must defeat this warlock. We *shall*." He put a slender hand upon hers. His trembled, but he took a moment to steel himself. And when he squeezed her hand, she sensed an inner strength that he hadn't shown before.

She smiled. And when she glanced in Nico's direction, he was smiling too, just slightly. He nodded to her.

CHAPTER FOURTEEN

Nature's Challenge

The gusty winds had become stronger and steadier, making it more difficult now for them to make their way along the narrow mountain trails. Finally, though, the land became less steep, the mountains became rolling hills then gentle slopes and finally fields filled with green grasses and bushy growth. The trek was somewhat easier now, except for one thing –

The *wind*. There was little shelter from it now, and it was becoming even stronger. Now it was a fight for both beasts and humans for every step they gained against it. Shelter! They simply *had* to find some sort of shelter until it lessened. It howled now, whistled loudly. Frantically they struggled to keep their eyes open against the dust and dirt which constantly swirled into their faces, as they tried to find something to offer some kind of relief from the onslaught.

Finally, after trying valiantly to make her way through the gusts, Gem decided that she'd had quite enough. She managed to find a small tree, and stood with her long nose buried among the meager leaves, hoping to find a break from the relentless attack upon her poor eyes and face.

Creda slid from the mare's back and, one hand struggling to keep her hood fastened at the neck, reached up her other to pull on the reign –

"Gem, come *please*! This isn't enough shelter! Come, girl. Let's try to keep up with the others."

126

But through the battering of the winds, through the stinging of the dirt as it struck her cheeks, through the howling and screaming of the blasts, she could sense Gem's fear and weariness. Creda tried to send her messages of reassurance. She considered using a *Spell of Relaxation*, but concentration in the midst of all this would be pretty much impossible.

Leaving Gem at the tree, Creda moved away, hoping to somehow find someone or something that could help –

She peered through her fingers as she tried to shield her eyes from the vicious gales, but by now all she could make out were branches flying by, dust blowing and the tears which constantly filled her eyes.

In the distance she thought she saw a grove of trees, so she struggled in that direction. She had to try walking into the wind, though, which was extremely difficult. She turned her back to the terrible squall, but walking was horribly awkward when her robe seemed to want to serve as a sail! She didn't know how it could possibly become any worse, but suddenly she found herself struggling just to keep her place and not be forced who knew where by the gusts. She had hold of a small tree with one hand –

Gritting her teeth, she managed to force her other arm up to grab hold too. As she desperately managed to keep hanging on, she was continually assaulted by the many things being blown about – dirt, leaves, small sticks. Her fingers ached, and her whole body was beginning to feel rather numb …

And now she was awfully tired – tired of trying to keep her place, of being pelted with debris, of the achiness of her shoulders, arms, wrists, hands, neck –

So tired. It would feel good just to let go. To let the wind carry her wherever it wished. Perhaps she'd just float upon the clouds …

But a furious gust had her knocking her head against the little tree's trunk, and this brought her back to reality. *What had she been thinking! She had to hold on!*

She tried to adjust her grasp, to give her fingers and wrists a bit of a break … but when she opened her fingers on her right hand, she found that she could barely make them do her bidding anymore …

This was just … too … much …

Veras! Perhaps Veras could help!

Their rapport had become more powerful, even for those of the Tower. Creda tried to focus her energy, but the constant tumult around her kept destroying her concentration. *Veras! She must think of Veras!*

She tried to focus on the deep blue which characterized the Superior's spirit and inner powers. She tried to see in her mind the dark blue tendril wrapped with her own azure one …

Too hard, too hard. Her hands and fingers screamed for release, and her head ached from the continuous din and constant assaults –

It was *just too hard.*

She opened her mouth to shout to someone, but all that came out sounded like a pathetic whimper, against the awful screaming of the wind. How she longed for the touch of Nico's strong hands! It would even be worth seeing his teasing grin if only, only, he could help her now! She tried to focus on sending a message from her spirit to his, which would have a minimal chance of success anyway, but when she was fighting the onslaught of the furious winds, it was simply impossible.

And finally, she knew it.

She was beaten this time. She was *not* to battle the warlock. It must be that Veras would be the *One.*

Creda could struggle to maintain her position no longer. Her hands ached beyond belief, her face was raw from being beaten by the winds and the debris they carried, as well as from her own tears. There seemed no end to it. How long had she managed to cling here, expending every bit of energy simply to keep from being blown away? And it just didn't seem worth it anymore.

It wasn't really a conscious effort to let go, for her body had simply reached its limit. Her hands could no longer hold onto that tree, and her body's need for rest was becoming paramount.

As she struggled to hold on, she could feel her consciousness begin to slip away. Everything was becoming hazy – tiny twinkles like little stars upon a dark background. She dreamed of the warlock again. And a fearsome beast/man he was. He was big – bigger even than Nico. He was coming for her. He would imprison her spirit.

She knew it. Yet she couldn't move. She wanted to scream, but no sound would come –

Closer he came – he was almost upon her – and she tried, she tried – she did everything she could to raise her arm and defend herself, but her body just wouldn't respond –

She could feel his hot breath on her neck, her cheek. She could feel the ice-cold touch of those long-nailed fingers. She could feel the sharpness of his teeth against her throat – and a flash of red pain –

And, with a fury she never knew she had, she sent her *Spell of Protection* through her skin and into every aspect of him – or *it* – which touched her –

His cry of agony was long and loud. She watched in satisfaction as his body sailed away, away, away off into the sky –

Nico moaned. His head pounded – *all* of him seemed to hurt. He was grateful to his friend for providing him with shelter.

He sat up, one hand patting the black mound of horseflesh he'd been curled up against. Thunder snorted, was happy to get back onto his feet now that the wind's strength had died down somewhat. Gently, Nico led the stallion up the slope of the embankment and back to the roadway. Here they stood while Nico gazed first in one direction and then another. The wind still blew, but its strength was much less now. All around him he could see signs of the storm's damage. Tree limbs had been torn down, debris of all sorts was scattered about. There was even an uprooted tree not far away …

But he saw no sign of the others. No sign at all.

Clucking to Thunder to follow, he walked back down the road in the direction from which he thought they'd come. Then he heard it, above the continuing whistle of the winds.

A *moan* –

Quickly Nico looked in that direction –

Zann! He was half-lying, half-sitting at the base of a tree, his face a mask of pain. Nico hastened to his side, offered him his waterskin –

"Nico! By all gods and goddesses, what a wind! Thanks. That helps a bit. Ah!" He tried to adjust his position, but it caused him too much pain.

"What are your injuries, Joul?"

"It – it's my back, Nico. I fear I've done something to the muscles. Gad, it hurts!"

"Rest, captain," Nico said gently, and eased him back into a lying position. He retrieved his own blanket from Thunder's back and placed it over the captain.

"The others?" Zann asked weakly.

Nico shook his head. "You're the first I've found," he said softly. *This was not the sort of news he liked to bring!* He was here to *protect* the others! He rose to his feet, his teeth clenched as he scanned the area. He *had* to find the rest –

Then, just a way off, he saw Zann's brown horse. He whistled to it, but it was still nervous, and pranced a bit but didn't want to come closer. Cautiously Nico approached, clucking and talking softly to the beast, and wishing he had some of Creda's strange ability to relate to the animals.

Finally, the horse allowed him to approach, and he stroked the beast's nose and neck reassuringly. As he did, something caught his eye –

There! Between two bushes, off to the side. He hurried to it, knelt beside it –

A brown robe. He pushed the hood from the face ...

Veras! His heart pounded as he spoke her name, patted her cheeks, but there was no response. He poured water onto a bit of cloth, bathed her face, her hands, her wrists. And again, he called her name.

But she did not respond. He sighed deeply, and gently kissed her forehead.

The silence was delicious. Creda feasted her ears upon the peacefulness of birdsong and the gentle swishing sounds as the breezes toyed with the treetops.

And, in her memories, she was with friends again. Back atop the dragon's back, watching in amusement as the dragon deposited Nico in less than gentle fashion upon the hard ground. She was standing in front of Portar again, tugging uselessly on those reins, then looking into the dark eyes of this stranger who was to become a friend …

But then something was pulling at her, tugging at her, something far away. Through the blackness in her mind, she saw something. It was a faint glimmer of light, like a star off in the distance –

And it felt wonderfully warm, and comfortable beyond measure.

"*Come,*" it seemed to say. "*Come with me and I'll bring you peace. Come, Sister. You have earned a chance to rest at last.*"

So warm did it feel, so wonderful, that she could feel her spirit stretching to its limits, trying to get closer to this tremendous feeling. But she was still too far …

She could feel her spirit as it sought to leave her body behind entirely –

But then she heard voices, and she began to see images once again …

Her sister. Playing with her by the stream when they'd been young girls – and later, visiting her among her husband's people …

The remains of that group. The sensation of death which had filled the area, even though no human remains were found.

She saw herself once more as she sought contact through that bloodstain in the ruins. And she saw the warlock's raiders –

And she felt once again the horror.

What right did she have to seek rest and warmth? How could her spirit even imagine freedom from this world when the likes of the *warlock* wandered, taking prisoners and ruining families? How could she ever leave Veras, the Superior, behind to face the warlock and his armies all alone?

Oh, how she wanted to go! How she longed for the rest promised by that gleaming whiteness! It was so inviting – and her soul was already seeking to leave and let her body die …

"But I cannot," she found herself murmuring, over and over, again. "I cannot leave them behind. I simply can*not* …"

Finally, Nico was making some progress. He'd found most of the others, and they had gathered the horses together. They would stay here for a while and regain their strength.

But Nico's spirits were low. He ached in places, although he knew that he would recover. Tavis, too, had been fortunate. Ferren had added a few bruises to her collection, but that was all, which was fortunate for she was still recovering from the dragon's slash. She had splinted Vander's broken finger. Sohn's condition worried Nico, for he'd broken an arm, and, although Nico and Ferren had splinted it and prepared a sling for him, still Sohn was in great discomfort.

Weary, Nico sat beside the Superior, who continued to lie as though asleep. His gaze was on her pale face. "What are we to do," he murmured softly. "What *are* we to do?" For the first time in a long while, Nico felt at a complete loss. Veras looked too much like death itself – Veras who might be the *One* to defeat the warlock! And that thought set him trembling a bit, for Nico's very heart ached when he looked at her in this state. He leaned over her, putting his hand against her cheek. "Please Veras. *Please.*"

Straightening back to a sitting position, he rubbed his throbbing forehead, letting a long sigh escape –

And *Creda*! He hadn't even *found* poor Creda!

For someone who had pledged his protection to these Sisters, he certainly did not feel as though he'd done very well in keeping his promise.

She felt warmth upon her face, and the sensation was nothing short of wonderful. She could hear the breezes again but couldn't feel them. She tried to open her eyes, but something within her resisted. And so, she just lay there, happy to feel the sunshine as it bathed her in its glow …

When she awoke again, it was her vision which sought information about her whereabouts. She opened her eyes and had to close them quickly to shield them from the brightness surrounding her. Now her head felt like it was spinning around and around on her neck, determined to confuse and disorient her. She shielded her eyes this time and opened them very slowly.

Between narrowed lids she could make out a bit of her surroundings. She was in a little clearing around which was a growth of trees and bushes. It was quite beautiful as the greenery caught the sunlight's glow. She managed to sit up, very slowly, her hand on her head in an effort to keep it from spinning completely off of her neck, or so it seemed.

And, when she moved her left hand, a stab of agony rewarded her. The smallest finger on her left hand appeared to be twice its normal size. It was bluish in colour and stiff enough that she couldn't move it at all. Nor did she wish to. Her ring and middle fingers were rather swollen too, but she could move them about at least a bit without the awful pain.

But her wrists! Both ached horribly. Although she could move them, they seemed agonizingly weak and sore – and her neck and her back did not seem much better.

She took a deep breath, but bruised ribs cautioned her that this, too, was not a good idea. She scanned the area, seeking something that might help her. She passed her right hand through her hair – or, at least, *tried* to – but found tangles and stickiness. When she looked at her fingers, she was not surprised to see blood. She tried to think, but could remember only very little – wind and rain, wind and weariness …

Not far away were fallen branches. She managed to break off some small bits and use some torn pieces from her robe so that she could bind these to her injured fingers. Then she ripped the hem from her robe and wrapped the material around her wrists for some support. The main part of the branch would serve as a walking stick. She leaned her back against the tree's trunk and placed both hands on her walking stick. Finally, she was standing … or at least, leaning.

Water. That was definitely the next priority. She had to find water.

And the others! Surely, they must be somewhere around the area.

She listened carefully but could hear no sound of any living thing save for the rustling of the tree branches, and the songs of the birds. She tried to call out, but all that came from her parched throat was a frog-like croak. And so, leaning heavily upon her walking stick, she moved unsteadily forward to find what she could …

How weary she'd become! She'd tried to search the area but had found no sign of the others. And she was simply too weak and bruised for very much physical activity. She could see a cliff above which might give a better view of the area, but she could see no way of reaching it. She wondered if she might be able to sense Veras's presence nearby. Creda managed to touch her amulet, but the pain from her fingers and wrists kept her from the concentration which she needed. And so she moved on.

Presently she found herself at the top of a hill. Slowly and carefully, she eased herself down the slope a bit –

And gasped. *Cottages!* Two – no, three – were visible from here. Comfortable, cozy they appeared, with sheep grazing and nursing their lambs in the fenced areas, and chickens clucking contentedly as they wandered about. The barns looked large, and newer wood suggested that additions had been built to them recently.

Very inviting, indeed! With a sigh, she set about the task of finding a way downward. There did not seem to be as much damage from the storm down here as there'd been above, and she eagerly kept her eyes on the vision of that cozy picture ahead of her. She *should* have been focused more on her footing as she made her way down the slope –

Suddenly she was on her backside -- and sliding downward at a much more rapid pace than she would have preferred. She managed to grab hold of a gnarled root which protruded from the ground, and she came to a welcome stop. Breathing heavily, despite the complaints from her ribs, she hurriedly tried to push her robe back down into place. At the same time, she was frantically pleading with the fates not to have permitted anyone to have seen her lying there with her clothing pushed up, displaying her knees … and more.

Fortunately, though, she was only halfway down, and still sheltered by bushes and undergrowth …

Fortunate, too, she reflected, that Nico wasn't standing at the bottom of the hill to laugh at her indignity! Part of her, though, wished mightily that he could be here, laughter or no …

More carefully now, she eased herself down the rest of the hill. She'd lost her walking stick, and now had to settle for one which was much too short for her. Leaning over in a posture which made her feel much, much older, she made her way slowly from the shelter of the trees and into the more open grasslands.

Few enough lived in this little area that the roadway was really nothing more than grasses pressed flat by hoofs and wagon wheels. She watched the sun as it began its downward journey, silently begging it to stay aloft a little longer. Finally, she arrived at a wooden fence surrounding the front yard of a little dwelling. She reached over, fumbling for the latch on the low gate –

She saw a shadowed figure. She couldn't see much of what she now knew was a man, except for his silhouette as he carried a bit of firewood under one arm – but she could hear him breathe, rather loudly and heavily.

Thinking that he might be in pain, she opened her mouth to ask him what was amiss –

But the raspy sound greeting her ears did not sound like her at all!

The figure responded quickly, turning in his place, eyes wide as he looked in her direction. "Mother," he shouted in the direction of the side of the house. "Go inside and bolt the door! The woods-demon is here!"

Quickly, despite the agony of her neck and back, Creda managed to look over her shoulder, searching the area for any sign of a demon … or *warlock*. But she saw nothing.

Confused, she turned back toward the young man –

And gasped. He held the block of wood aloft now, and was stepping quickly towards her –

"You don't frighten me, demon! Get away! Get away or I'll bring this down on you!"

"Baaa -- but I'm not a demon!" Creda raised an arm to shield her head.

Still the block of wood circled over her like a bird of prey planning its kill. And she was too weak even to stop it with a spell –

"Please," she said softly. "Please, sir. I am a Sister of the Tower of Giefan. The storm caught me and I am injured. Please, kind sir." Although unable to reach her amulet, Creda knew how to use her voice to calm others, and – despite the roughness of her voice – she used her tone to send a soothing message to the young man.

Her plea gave him pause. Creda did not know whether or not the young man's mother, too, believed that a demon was in the area, but it was she who now moved toward them. She held a lantern aloft, apparently intending to gain a better view of this intruder in the waning light of the sun.

CHAPTER FIFTEEN

The Creature at the Door

They'd managed to put together an encampment of sorts, most of the party having been found, and some whose injuries were only minor. Most of the horses, too, had been found, and all had escaped serious injury.

Nico ran a hand across the back of his neck, moved his shoulders this way and that to ease the aches that continued to plague him. He sighed. His heart, too, ached. The Sisters were his responsibility, yet here lay Veras like death itself – again – and as for Creda, he wouldn't let himself think about her at all.

What were they to do? Should they fashion something to carry Veras and Zann, and find them help at the nearest town? Sohn, too, would need more assistance than the rest of the escort could give him …

What was that? Something on the other side of the bushes …

He'd seen something move – something a different colour from the greenery which partly hid it –

He moved quickly but quietly in that direction, drawing his blade. He stopped, silently. Listening and watching –

With a deep sigh of relief, he sheathed his sword, pushing aside the branches to make way for the restless beast –

"Gem," he murmured, stroking her long nose, her flank. "There's a good girl. It's all right now."

He ran his hands over her reddish-brown neck and flanks, checked her thin legs, but found nothing more than a few minor cuts and scrapes. Holding her reins, he stepped back in the direction from which she appeared to have come. It was early evening, and there was not much light, but he searched this way and that eagerly. The horse following, he continued his hunt, peering beneath bushy growth, both hoping and not hoping that he'd find another unconscious sorceress ...

But nothing. He called her name softly, then more loudly, but there was no reply. He was not really surprised, for he'd searched this area before. If only *he* had that special rapport with the creatures! If only Gem could tell him –

"Where *is* she, Gem?" He sighed. "Where *are* you, Creda?" This time he spoke to the night itself.

The only reply was silence, and a few quiet voices and the crackling of the fire from the encampment a little distance away. Sighing, he led the mare back to the camp. Silently he led her around the perimeter to tether her with the other horses. He removed her saddle and bags, brushed her coat and black mane, and gave her water.

"Sister Creda?" It was Ferren's voice. He hadn't heard her approach.

Nico just shook his head and continued brushing the mare.

"No sign?"

"No."

Ferren raised an eyebrow. *No Creda*. Without the little sorceress ... perhaps, just perhaps, it could be true that *she* was the *One*.

But she returned her attention to Nico as he continued to care for the mare. "It isn't your fault, Nico," she said softly.

He paused in his brushing, but his eyes were still focused on the horse. "I gave the Sisters my oath," he said, very quietly, and continued his brush strokes.

"Nico," Ferren continued, still from behind him. "We're all here to help. We all took the oath. There's no need for you to shoulder this burden yourself!"

The man's hands stopped moving once more. He let them rest upon the horse's back while his eyes seemed to study the ground.

Then, suddenly, he stepped back and turned to flash a broad grin in Ferren's direction. He gripped her upper arm as one might an old friend, leaning in to speak closely to her. "Indeed, you're quite right, Ferren. Quite right. It'll all work out quite well, you'll see! Things are getting better steadily. Now we've Gem here, and she's in fine shape. Yes, it'll be quite all right."

And, almost as though to prove his words correct, Tavis called them from not too far away. "Nico! Ferren! Sister Veras – she's waking!"

The woman looked Creda up and down, and the fear in her grey eyes was unmistakable.

These people were not cruel – just very frightened of something. Creda pulled her amulet into the lantern light, her injured fingers and wrists complaining strongly about the action. Creda turned the thing so that the woman could see the outline of the Tower of Giefan upon the underside.

The woman nodded, but her frown did not lessen. "Whatever are you doing *here*, then?"

"I – I was caught in the storm last night and I've lost my way. I'm injured and I need help so that I can rejoin my companions."

There was silence as the woman and the young man exchanged looks. When the woman spoke again, her voice was much gentler. "Well, injured you must be, Sister – or you're lying and you're not a Sister at all! That storm was *three* nights ago! What say you to that?"

Creda was shocked. She knew she'd lain on the ground for some time – but *three* nights? Evidently, her look of surprise was a blessing –

For suddenly the woman smiled slightly. When she spoke, it was to her tall son. "I'll not doubt the words of one whose face bears *that* look! Giever, you'll not mind giving up your bed for a night or two, now will you?"

Her son chose not to reply at first, but his eyes sought the sky as the sun began to disappear entirely, leaving an eerie ribbon of golden red along the horizon. "Whatever we do, mother, we'd best hasten! There's not much time left!"

The two exchanged meaningful glances once more, then Giever rushed off in the direction of the barn. The sense of urgency was obvious in his movements as he hurried the livestock into their shelter.

The woman took Creda's arm and muttered something about her name being Kemi, but Creda's mind wasn't focused on her words. She was scanning the skies for what she assumed must be an incoming storm which was causing these people alarm --

The cottage was small but quite comfortable. Indeed, almost anything indoors would seem like a haven now!

Creda was led into a tiny room which was off the cooking area. It might have been intended as a storage room but was obviously used for sleeping now. All it contained was a bed, a wooden table beside it, and a small chest which Creda assumed must contain Giever's clothing.

She undressed as best she could. Her hands seemed to be a frightful mess. Even those fingers not splinted were bloodstained and scraped. Her wrists and forearms were spotted with bruises. She gave a deep sigh – and instantly offered silent apologies to her injured ribs. Suddenly the weariness, the aches, the anxieties and loneliness became overwhelming and, in the shelter and comfort of the little cottage, she felt free to weep. And Kemi returned to reassure her as she gently cared for Creda's wounds. A sense of peace came to the sorceress's spirit once again.

But suddenly Kemi paused in her bandaging, apparently thinking that she'd heard something outside. "Anything?" She was calling to Giever, who was in the other room.

"Nothing yet, mother. I'll stay alert."

She nodded, although he couldn't see her response.

"What is it you fear?" Creda studied Kemi's face while the woman bandaged the injured fingers of Creda's left hand.

Kemi paused in her task and met Creda's eyes. "You said you came from up the hill," she stated, seeking confirmation.

"Yes."

"You saw nothing? Oh, forgive me, Sister. I'd forgotten. Of course, your injuries would have prevented you from making sense of anything. Well, don't worry, Sister." She tried to smile, but it seemed to fall from her face.

"What is it, Kemi?" Creda wanted somehow to return this woman's kindness. She would use what little energy she had for a spell, if that might help.

"I – I just wish Giever's father was home. That's all. He went to the town early this morning to find some people to help. I'd really hoped he might've gotten back before nightfall …" The faraway look in her eyes touched Creda's spirit. The woman's heart was with her husband.

"To help with *what*, Kemi?"

The woman looked at Creda's face once more, smiling slightly. Creda could feel an ongoing battle between two parts of Kemi. One side wanted to share her concerns, while the other struggled to present the face of someone who had everything under control.

Kemi tucked a strand of greying hair back behind her ear. She adjusted the rest of her dark brown hair where it was tied at the nape of her neck. "Here," she said. "This is likely to be a bit large for you, being mine – but I'm certain it'll do while I fetch you some warm food."

Creda thanked her, and carefully donned the nightdress. She could hear the woman moving about in the kitchen, and overheard lowered voices as the woman and her son discussed the possibility of something returning. They sounded concerned for the safety of their stock, and even wondered if the doors and shutters of the cottage could keep them safe.

Creda rose and pushed aside the curtain separating the sleeping room from the large cooking area. But she moved a bit too quickly, and dizziness attacked her senses.

Giever was there quickly, assisting her to sit upon one of the wooden chairs at the table. Hastily Creda reassured Kemi that she was fine there – she had no need to eat food in the bed.

In the lamplight she could appreciate how very much Giever resembled his mother, with his dark brown hair and grey eyes. He looked to be about fifteen, although perhaps tall for that age …

Both seemed almost like forest creatures as they moved about the large room, stopping every now and then to listen for possible goings-on outdoors. Not a moment seemed to pass when they were not totally and completely alert to every noise, every*thing* they might hear outside ...

Creda sipped the broth which Kemi had brought her, but her eyes were on the two and their obvious anxiety. "What are you listening for?" Creda tried to sound politely concerned, and not as though she might be prying ...

Kemi returned her look, and Creda could see once again the inner struggle. Finally, with a sigh, Kemi decided to share her concerns, sitting down on a chair across the table from the sorceress. Giever joined them.

"Sister," she sighed, shaking her head. "You must be blessed. I don't know how you managed to escape detection by those beasts! For the past two nights – since the storm – terrible beasts have been descending upon us! Horrible, growling things. We heard of them from our neighbours. And how grateful we are that we didn't actually set eyes upon them ourselves!"

Her hand crept across the table and seized her son's larger one. Not embarrassed as some sons his age might be, Giever responded.

"Wh – what did your neighbours say of these things?"

"That – that one came lumbering toward their daughter and they – and they barely had enough time to pull her inside to safety! Fanged beasts, they said –

"So we built up our barns and chicken houses as best we could," put in Giever, his eyes faraway in recollection. "That's worked all right – at least, none of the things have killed our stock. But still they come, like they're searching for something to eat ...."

A chill slithered up Creda's spine despite the warmth of the broth. The sudden silence was shattered by the clatter of her spoon as it dropped onto the table. "Ex – excuse me! I'm sorry."

But it was easy for Giever, with his long limbs, to retrieve a cloth and help to wipe up the spill.

Quiet returned – but Creda's stomach was aching as she tried to still her suspicions. Surely not! She didn't want to believe that the warlock's raiders had made their way over to this area too! "Please. Tell me. Were these men – or creatures of some kind – on horseback?"

Kemi and Giever exchanged curious glances.

"On *horseback*, Sister?" Kemi blinked.

"Our neighbours didn't say anything like that, Sister," Giever replied. "We assume them to be four-footed beasts."

Suddenly Kemi was gripping Giever's hand again – this time very hard. Creda strained her ears, could hear no sound of hoofbeats –

Soon, though, the sounds of beasts snuffling about was audible through the gaps in the closed shutters. And growling, yes …

The three couldn't move. It was as though they were all spellbound. They sat, listening, as the beasts lumbered about outside of the cottage –

The sounds of growling became louder and louder, and now they could hear what seemed to be bodies banging against the doors.

"Wa -- was it always like this?" Creda managed to sputter.

But Kemi shook her head. Her grey eyes were very wide as she watched Giever seize a long knife. "N- never before has there been such a sound! Usually they just growl, snuff about and leave!"

The pounding was becoming louder at the back door, which entered into the very area where they sat, trembling. Giever rose and stepped quietly closer to the door, knife positioned in his large hand.

"Geiver, no!" Kemi motioned to him to come back to the table, further from the door, but he ignored her, obviously intending to protect his mother. The snuffling, growling and pounding were all becoming even more intense. It seemed like tonight might be the last one for all of them –

And Giever, brave young man that he was, stood by that door as though prepared to take on anything at all which might make its way through to them –

The way that the door bolts appeared to be weakening from all of the abuse, they had to consider the possibility of attack now. Kemi handed Creda a knife, and they prepared to move the table so that it would be on its side across the door –

Then Creda felt it.

For one, brief heartbeat, she'd freed her mind from her fear …
and *it* had found its way in.

"Wait!"

Kemi regarded her, eyes wide with terror.

But Creda could only babble. "It – it –"

And then a howl filled the air, and she was sure. She looked
toward her benefactors to see that their faces were as white as flour.
Her heart now filled with peace and joy, Creda made her way
awkwardly to the door.

"Sister, what are you doing?" Giever moved in front of her,
blocking her path.

She let go a long breath, her face a picture of peace and
contentment. "You need not fear," she said softly.

"Magic, Sister?" asked Kemi as she gripped Creda's arm, seeking
reassurance.

Creda thought for just a moment. "Yes, Kemi. Yes, in a way, it
definitely is."

But still Giever moved from her path only with great reluctance,
his forehead puckered in a doubtful frown.

The door handle felt cool in Creda's hand …

There was a rush of air from outside as she pulled the door open –

A half dozen of the things were there, moving purposefully
about. All looked quite formidable, except one …

Tears found their way down her cheeks as she moved in that
direction. But these were quickly wiped away for her as she sank to
the ground. "Baru," she murmured, "my dear friend. You gathered
your companions to search for me! I should have known!"

When the licking had ceased enough for her to look about once
more, she saw that the other wolves now seemed rather bored by this
business. With what little strength she still had, she sent her spirit out
to each of them, sending them gratitude and friendship. Still grasping
Baru's thick neck, she turned back to her human friends.

And here was another sight which she'd never forget, for both
mouths were quite open in astonishment.

Creda began to laugh. And it felt wonderful. Here she was with
humans to care for her injuries, Baru and his friends looking for her,

and no sign of anything to do with the warlock. Tremendous! But then her ribs reminded her that she still needed rest.

"I – I," she stammered, trying to regain some sort of control as Baru assumed she was requesting further face-licking. "I – I'm quite certain that you need have no further fear of any beasts. Baru here is my dear friend. He and his companions have been searching for me. I know it sounds incredible, but it *is* true!"

And, as though to prove her story to the humans, the other wolves began to wander off into the shadows of the night. Their help was no longer needed. At Creda's request, and obviously not certain as to what was happening, Kemi fetched a bowl of water and a bit of chicken. Baru was quite grateful to receive them.

So they sat, contented, enjoying the quiet of the starlit night. Suddenly a hand was upon Creda's shoulder.

"Sister Creda," came Kemi's gentle voice. She'd apparently recovered her composure to some degree. "Sister, you've fallen asleep. Do come inside now."

And Kemi was quite correct. A couple of times, Creda had dozed off, only to awaken when her head had fallen forward. She hadn't wanted to be separated from Baru, yet now she could see no sign of him. "Baru," she murmured, scanning the night with weary eyes.

She sighed as Kemi helped her back inside.

Veras was quite awake now. Although her head ached, she was recovering her strength. Nico knelt beside her. In his hand he held a mug of warm vegetable soup, which he extended to her. Her hands trembling, she reached for it. Nico placed it in her hands and held his own atop hers until she was holding the mug steadily. "Thank you," she murmured, turning to smile at him.

Nico didn't respond. He was scanning the night. Suddenly he was crouching, alert, ready to stand and move should the need arise …

"What is it?" asked the Superior.

"I'm not sure," he replied in a quiet voice, "but something's out there." A bit more loudly, he called across the little clearing. "Ferren! Tavis, Vander." He motioned to them to join him. The three made their way swiftly to his side, Ferren sensing the urgency in his face and voice, already pulling her sword.

"What?" she whispered.

Nico was standing now, his eyes steadily scanning their surroundings. "There's something out there. I heard something moving in the bushes, and I think it's coming closer ..."

There was silence, as their ears strained for whatever it was. Ferren looked up sharply, gripped her sword anew, grateful that her shoulder was mostly recovered from the dragon's slash. She was ready – oh, so ready – to face this warlock and let him taste her blade.

Suddenly there was a restless snorting from one of the horses. *They sense it too,* she thought.

Then it entered the camp area, some of the horses pawing the ground and snorting–

A wolf! Vander was holding the captain's sword, and moved as though to use it –

A large, strong hand was on his arm, though, and pushed the blade away.

What a wonderful dream! Creda saw herself as a beautiful princess, asleep in the forest and awaiting her true love's arrival. She awoke to the warmth of sunlight as it gleamed downward through the trees –

And when she woke, she looked into the eyes of her own true love, just as the legend had said that she would.

His eyes were grey, and his hair was light brown. His eyebrows and his moustache were shaggy, and he was older than Creda. He did not have the overpowering good looks of Prince Yurmar, it was true. But her love had a wonderfully kind, gentle and intelligent look about him. There was a warmth in the way his eyes crinkled at the corners when he smiled that left her feeling as though the deepest recesses of her soul were filled with joy.

"My own true love," she murmured to him –

And he threw back his head and *laughed*! Loudly! As he did, somehow he seemed to change – his hair was suddenly dark, his eyes now such a deep brown that they were almost black –

And he laughed at her! She was insulted! How could her own true love scorn her so? This was not part of any legend!

But no – it wasn't his laughter in her dream that she heard. It was someone else's.

And then her entire world began to fall apart – at least, her *dream* world – and once more reality beckoned to her.

CHAPTER SIXTEEN

Injuries

Gazing down at her, Nico chuckled happily. He watched as she opened her eyes – a welcome sight, indeed! She ceased blinking, and fixed those pale blue orbs on his face–

"*'My own true love'*, Creda? Ha! So you were dreaming of *me*, then!"

Creda's pale face began to pout, almost as a child might. "No! Not you – not you at all!"

Nico continued grinning, and laughed, bending lower to pat her shoulder. The woman who stood in the doorway cleared her throat, as though to remind him that she was still there – and that she saw all.

"Is it – is it morning?" asked Creda, frowning at the blackness which she saw beyond the shutters

"No, dear," said Kemi, stepping closer to the bed, and extending an arm to help Creda to sit up. "Apparently," she said, her voice icy with disapproval as she eyed Nico, "your *friends* were concerned enough about your welfare that they felt a need to come for you in the darkness of the night!"

Nico grabbed a chair from the eating area and deposited it just inside the doorway. He sat down backwards on it, with his arms crossed on the chair's back. "Baru came to us quite eagerly, Creda. He seemed very pleased that he'd found you. How were we to know that you were being so well cared-for? For all we knew, you might have been in danger! Baru had no way of explaining these things to us. And so, here we are."

"'We', Nico?"

Nico nodded over his shoulder back toward the other room. "Tavis is in the kitchen –"

"Where all gentlemen should be, rather than coming right into a lady's bedroom –especially a *Sister's*," put in Kemi coldly.

This was the most fun that Nico'd had in a while! Imagine the woman being concerned about such things – if only she knew what he and Creda and the others had been through together. All that mattered was that Creda was all right. He smiled broadly.

In response to Kemi's loud sigh, Creda said: "He – he's quite harmless, Kemi, I assure you."

Harmless? Nico raised his eyebrows at this, while Kemi pushed past him to enter the cooking area.

"Well," said Creda as she smoothed the blankets around her, "what are your plans now, Nico?"

"'Twould be good if we could all set out tomorrow. If you're able, that is."

A look of steely determination gave the Sister's face a look of gravity. "I *must* be, Nico. I will be."

There was silence for a moment. Although she was not looking directly at him, she knew that Nico was gazing at her, assessing how ready she was to move on.

"Well," said Nico. He rose from the chair and stepped to the side of the bed, taking Creda's hand in his. He studied the splints on her other hand, frowning. He patted her good hand. "We'd better all get some rest, then."

The floor creaked as Kemi stepped into the doorway. Her arms were crossed.

Nico turned to her. "We'll rest tonight, and set out tomorrow, good woman." He spoke with great courtesy, bowing to Kemi respectfully.

She returned this with a grudging nod of the head. "And just where do *you* intend to rest tonight?"

Nico grinned. "Oh," he began with mock seriousness, "perhaps the floor right here—"

Kemi was shaking her head.

"Perhaps on some chairs pushed together."

Kemi was shaking her head.

Nico had a wry smile on his face now. "Or," he said, looking at Kemi's face as he patted the bed, "maybe I'll just tuck myself in with Creda here!"

Kemi turned her back and moved away as Nico's laughter filled the room. In a moment she returned, carrying blankets which she thrust in Nico's direction. "The *barn*," she said firmly.

Nico winked at Creda and headed away. Creda could hear Tavis's laughter outside as he followed Nico.

Creda awoke to wonderful smells the next morning. The scents of teas, eggs and rolls – and even chicken stew – assailed her nostrils delightfully. The odours alone seemed to bring her the strength she needed, and she shoved the blanket away, easing herself to the side of the bed. Even her hands seemed steadier as she donned the robe which Kemi had repaired and cleaned for her. Carefully she stepped to the window, gently shoving the shutters open.

How beautiful the world looked! Sunlight bathed the surroundings and lessened the morning's chill, while the grasses in the distance gleamed like emeralds. The livestock in the yards seemed thrilled by all of it, too, as they guzzled their water and nibbled at morning meals …

Two young goats were gamboling gaily, not far from the window. Creda watched as they leaped and scurried, then turned toward each other to butt heads once again.

She was not the only one enjoying the sights. Nico paused in assisting with the barn-cleaning, and dragged a large forearm through the sweat on his face. He, too, grinned as he watched the innocent play of the young creatures -- and grinned even more when he saw Creda's face. He'd thought he'd never see her smile again! He waved to her, and she returned it.

Nico mounted Thunder, then reached an arm down to pull Creda up behind him. The Sister gazed down at her new friends, wondering how she could ever repay Kemi's and Giever's kindness. They'd cared for her, prepared breakfast for all of them, repaired her robe, tolerated the terrifying presence of wolves … and contended with Nico.

Kemi and Giever had been asked if they'd seen any signs of something which might threaten their way of life (other than the wolves' visit), but they'd responded negatively. Creda had told them no details about the warlock and his armies. They hadn't been here yet, and – hopefully – the Sisters and the escort would prevent that from ever happening. They had shared only that there was some sort of threat from the south, and that their group was on a quest to defeat this threat, in order to preserve the freedom of people like Kemi and Giever and Kemi's husband and neighbours.

Creda glanced at Tavis, who was sharing his chicken with Baru by the roadway. She wondered how Kemi would feel about such use of the breakfast she'd cooked!

"Kemi, Giever," she said softly. "I cannot thank you enough for your care and kindness! I truly do not know what I would have done if not for you. I would like to leave you with something – something to repay you somehow. But I am still weak, and my powers are limited. Please ask, though, and I'll gladly do what I can. What can I do to repay your kindness?"

Kemi and Giever exchanged looks. "Sister, there is one thing which we'd most appreciate," said Kemi with a hesitant smile. "My husband – I'd hoped to see him home yesterday before darkness fell. You took away the threat from the beasts, and for that we're grateful … even though, it seems, you were also responsible for bringing them here! But still I can't help but wonder after Giever's father and why he's not returned. Sister, can you tell us? Is there any power you possess that can tell us whether he's run into some sort of danger or trouble?"

Creda hesitated. A *Seeking Spell* could definitely help. She eyed the sky, but the moon wasn't to be seen at all, and its shadow was an essential aspect of this spell …

As she considered, she caught another glimpse of Baru, who was gazing in her direction. She smiled. Yes!

"I – I'm not certain if this will work. It's … it's something I've yet to develop fully. But if they're not too far away, I might be able to find them." She reached for her amulet, caressed it, hoping that it could help her –

And she relaxed, opening her mind, her senses to the creatures …

Yes! She could sense them, certainly. But such a confusion! For she could sense clearly the spirit of Baru, and Thunder, and then the gaiety of the young goats, and the other livestock in the area – it was rather overwhelming!

She clenched her teeth, tried to direct her power, tried to shut these out –

And, opening her mind once more, she reached outward, and away from the area --

Horses. Yes. She eased her spirit through them, separating all the sensations, until she could determine how many there were. She could not afford to stay with them long – this was tiring her –

She pulled back into herself, drawing a long breath. Suddenly she was aware that Nico had turned sideways to support her with a strong arm. She managed to mutter her thanks.

Kemi was staring at Creda with distress on her face.

"I – I'm all right. There are – there are horses not far from here, heading in this direction. I – I'm not –"

She stopped. Now that she was back to herself, she could remember some of the sensations more clearly. Yes. She couldn't determine this at the time, but it was clear to her now. "One of the horses – I can feel it now – one of them belongs to your family, for I could feel his eagerness to be with both of you again!"

Giever's eyes widened. "He's coming, and he'd bringing others with him! Then I *can* go!"

The slight grin which had lit up Kemi's face disappeared. "No, son –"

"But mother! Father will be here, soon, and he's bringing others! One's likely to be Uncle Jack, you know that! And he likes to stay here, to help out –"

"Giever," said Kemi, very firmly. "Giever, how can you speak of going off with these people when they haven't even told us exactly who or what they're after? You heard them, son. It's most likely that whoever it is will never venture over here anyway. So why do you want to fight them?"

"A *quest*, mother! A quest!" His eyes wide, he turned to Creda and Nico atop Thunder, and Tavis on his mount. "Let me come with you! Oh, how I've dreamed of this! And I can handle a sword! My father's cousin left me his!"

But Kemi was clinging to his arm. "It's not the work here that concerns me, Giever – it's you! Yes, Jack is good with the animals. But you're my only son!"

Giever turned to her, and smoothed her hair with his hand, then put his arms around his mother and hugged her to him. Although he spoke to *her*, his words were heard by the others. "Mother, theirs is an honourable quest – an important quest. A quest which could have great consequences for all life in the area. The seriousness is in their eyes, their words. Can't you see it? They'll need all the help they can find! They need me. I *must* go!"

Nico exchanged glances with Creda and Tavis. More help would be welcome, but this boy knew nothing, really, of the quest. They'd have to tell him all that the Sisters had shared. And, if they did this and Giever changed his mind, might he panic his neighbours by sharing this knowledge?

Nico drew a long breath. "We have told you very little of this 'quest'. And we will not, either. But you're right. It *is* important. It may save many from fear and horror, perhaps even death. And it may result in *our* deaths.

They left, then, Giever and Kemi still embracing. They spoke not. Nico's heart felt heavy again as the awesome feeling of responsibility came pressing down on him once more –

He shook his head against it, shoved it aside. And he turned his attention to the fact that Creda was with them once again. He smiled broadly, and, after checking that the Sister was securely positioned on Thunder's back, urged his mount into a gallop. Soon the group would be reunited!

She was willing all the strength that she could into the strained muscles of the captain. Her eyes were closed, and she felt her energy intertwine with that of her amulet, to send comfort and relaxation to him. It was like climbing part way up a hill, then losing one's footing to slide back down again. Not all the way down, though. With each effort brought a bit more progress up the slope.

But progress was slow. Veras realized that she had been drifting, somewhere between concentration and nothingness. She simply didn't have enough energy.

Sounds interrupted. With a sigh, she opened her eyes. Captain Zann was grinning, looking in the direction of the noises. He sat up higher, leaning his back against the trunk of the tree. Veras was a bit disoriented at first, having just come back to herself. But then she was smiling too.

They had returned! Tavis and Creda were greeting Ferren and Vander. Nico was still on Thunder's back. He gazed in her direction, a frown on his face. But when his eyes met hers, he smiled.

Nico was not pleased to see the Superior already striving to help the others. Surely she needed more rest! But he did not want her to sense his disapproval. He dismounted, assisted Creda down, and turned to Ferren. "How goes it?"

"Veras is stronger. She claims that she has sufficient power to assist the others. But ..." Ferren shook her head, nodding in Sohn's direction where he sat a little distance away, beneath a tree with the captain. "I fear there's not much we can do for him. None of Veras's spells can mend broken bones." She was, indeed, concerned about Sohn. She hadn't known him well at the beginning of their journey, but he'd revealed himself to be stoic, determined to try to ignore his constant pain, and not cause concern to the others. "I don't think he can continue with us, Nico."

Nico nodded, and passed his eyes over the little group. Weakened or no, somehow they must go on. A sound from the side attracted his attention, and he turned to see Veras approach, watched as she and Creda embraced. He was pleased to see the Superior moving about and smiling, but it would be better if she could rest until the pinkness returned to her cheeks.

"Another day or so of rest would seem needed," he said to the group around him. "We'll all certainly need to be prepared when we meet the evil that awaits us. I'd best take Sohn to the nearest town for some help. Ferren, Tavis, Vander – you have the responsibility of protecting the Sisters ... and Captain Zann. Maybe I should take him into town, too."

But Veras shook her head. "He'd not agree, Nico. And I believe that he is recovering. He has made improvements."

Nico eyed her, nodding after a moment. "I'll leave with Sohn then. Take care."

Ferren felt strange as she watched the two head away. How often she'd wished that the arrogant Nico wasn't with them. How often she had wished that he would just leave. And now that he *was* leaving again, this time with poor Sohn, she was left with a vague uneasiness. And now Creda was back, with her fingers and wrists bandaged. What could *she* do to save the country from a heinous fiend? Could she really be the *One*? She watched as the Sister went to join Veras where she was once more enacting some sort of spell to help the captain.

They had been without Nico for a night, and this was the first morning that they prepared to move on without him. Everything seemed ... quieter ...

Veras and Creda combined their strength to aid the captain, and he insisted that he was much improved – although he required assistance to mount his horse.

Creda adjusted the sacks which hung from Gem's saddle, and found herself missing Nico's sarcasm. Gem gave a snort and tossed her head, as though she was anxious to go. "Shh," Creda murmured to her as she patted the mare's neck. "It's all right, Gem. It just seems so odd that, for years, Veras and I have been careful about use of our magic. For so long, it seems, we discussed use of our powers before enacting spells, yet now we seem constantly to be draining our energies." She gave a bitter laugh. "Perhaps that's to be our secret! Perhaps there'll be nothing left of our energies for the warlock to take from us! Then he won't see us as a threat!"

She climbed awkwardly onto Gem's back, her fingers and ribs reminding her that not everything was healed. Her mind was filled with images of what they might face next. Veras wore the little pouch containing the talisman segments, and so Creda did not have it to toy with while she pondered.

They headed across flatter lands now, which made their journey easier for a time. How they hoped that the weather would not cause them more difficulties!

The climate was becoming warmer, too – a reminder that they were heading southward as well as in a westerly direction. How far south were they to venture before seeing any signs of the warlock's raiders?

Ferren rode beside the captain. He still experienced discomfort in his back. And Ferren was the one who would assist him with anything should he require help. She glanced at him from time to time, wondering how he fared. And she knew that, each time she looked his way, he tried to sit a bit straighter in the saddle so that she would not worry or fuss.

Onward they continued, and still they saw no sign of the warlock nor any raiders, nor any violence nor danger. The day's ride had been uneventful.

Creda was grateful for Baru's friendship, for he seemed to sense her moods and emotions, and was very responsive to them. This night, although Creda could see his nostrils quivering as he read something in the air, he lay close to her while she attempted to sleep. It wasn't until she awakened during the night that she knew he'd gone. She wasn't concerned, though, for she knew that he would return before the grey of early day was lit by the rising sun.

Without Sohn and Nico, they were a quieter group. As they broke their fast by the fire, Tavis talked again of the old tales of the She-Serpent, and Veras wondered about this next challenge they were to face. If it was true that a person could not look upon the She-Serpent without becoming *One with the Sea*, then how could they approach her? And they were getting so close now. One more talisman segment.

They had ridden for most of the morning with Ferren leading. She paused just over the crest of a hill. There was something in the air –

Yes! Now she could see it, off ahead –

The sea! A tingle ran down her spine when she thought of arriving at their next destination. She pulled on the reins, heading the horse back to the others so she could share the news.

On the other side of the hill, though, something else became apparent. The group had stopped, all listening and looking back in the direction they had come. Hoofbeats –Tavis had been the first to hear them. Initially, Veras's spirit had become joyful at the thought of Nico returning. But the sound told her ears that there was more than one horse –

Suddenly, Creda urged Gem to leave the group, and Veras watched as they headed at a gallop toward a grove of trees not far away. Obviously – for some reason – Creda felt a need to hide from something.

Veras pondered this. Although she heard more than one horse, she did not perceive any threats nearby, but Creda had her rapport with the creatures to give her information which the others did not receive. Could there be danger approaching?

Veras turned to the others. "Perhaps Sister Creda has perceived some danger that I have not. Let us all go to the shelter of the grove until we see who it is that approaches us."

And so they all made their way over to the grove.

"Creda?" Veras looked closely at her. The younger Sister was trembling and pale. "Creda, what do you sense? Are there beasts approaching?"

Creda swallowed hard. Sudden memories of the warlock's raiders flooded her mind. But now that Veras was asking her, she felt foolish. She had sensed nothing. It had been a memory, then panic. "I- I'm sorry," she stammered to the others. "I had no sense of anything in particular – just the memory of the warlock's raiders."

Veras frowned. There was no place for overreaction at this stage of their quest. Creda should be better-prepared than this. Creda was still breathing heavily. Veras pulled her amulet from beneath her robe, preparing to use it to sense what she could of the advancing riders.

But there was no need, for the group could now be seen, and the riders approached them.

"So, Creda! So happy to see me that you're breathless!" Nico grinned broadly at her. He was about to say something about being her *One True Love*, but the group had turned their attention to the other rider.

"Giever," said Creda with a smile. "This is a pleasant surprise!"

"Yes, Sister! And glad you'll be that I'm here!"

Creda and the others groaned. Already he was sounding too much like Nico!

As they headed away from the little grove, Veras rode beside Creda. Creda opened her mouth to speak, then changed her mind and closed it again. Veras reached a hand across to touch Creda's arm.

"Creda, I know how anxious you are. I am, too. Please don't feel embarrassed. On one hand, it was not good that you took such hasty action without any need. That could, in another situation, be dangerous to us all. You *must* control your actions no matter what is happening to you on the inside. On the other hand, though, I could feel the strength of your energy. So this was not a useless exercise. It told both of us that you possess the power inside of you that you need. You are ready for whatever awaits us."

Despite feeling foolish, Creda had to smile. "Ah, Veras. Is it the mark of a true Superior, then, to be able to change what seems bad into something good?"

Their eyes met, and both knew that, between the two of them, they would meet whatever was ahead with strength.

The warm air had begun to have a cool aspect to it now. Ferren sniffed it, felt the saltiness that seemed to travel in the breezes themselves. The sea! And she could hear it now, too, the splashing of the waves against the rocks –

It brought back memories from her childhood of visits to the lakes and streams in the area. But these had been much, much smaller bodies of water, where one could stand on one side and easily see, or swim or wade to, the other.

Now Ferren pulled up on the reins, brought the horse to a stop. For there it was. As far as she could see, there was blue-green water, stretching along the horizon, seemingly forever. There were bushes around her here, and beyond, near the water, the sandy shore. This became rocky as she gazed to the west, building to a large rocky cliff the end of which she could not see from here.

The splashing sounds, the back and forth movement of the waters, were almost mesmerizing. She felt as if she, too, was moving rhythmically, soothingly …

She was grateful that the captain and his horse had moved up beside her, distracting her – *waking* her, almost.

Was this a sample of the strange power possessed by what they sought here?

She trembled.

CHAPTER SEVENTEEN

The Talisman

Up a little hill, in the direction of the rocky cliff, they found a clearing among the bushes, where they tethered the horses and prepared themselves. Veras had been watching the others, wanting to ensure that no one was overly anxious. It would not be helpful if Tavis was getting stirred up by the old tales he knew so well. She looked over at Creda who was standing by her mare, finishing a snack from one of the bags near her saddle. Veras watched her. Creda had finished her snack and yet stood beside the mare, unmoving, as though lost in thought. Veras approached her and placed what she hoped was a reassuring hand on the Sister's shoulder.

Creda jerked a bit, startled. "Yes, Veras," she said. "I'm ready. Sorry."

Veras could easily sense the feeling of dread that coursed through the Sister. "What is it, Creda?"

She sighed. "We've heard so much about what awaits us, yet we have no way of knowing how much might be truth, and how much simply stories. When we got the last segment of the talisman, we were told stories about The Mountain King and The Large Dragon, yet we found that only one of these appears to exist. We really have no way of knowing what to expect. Should we bring something with us to defend ourselves? Baru, perhaps?"

Veras was silent. She, too, was finding it difficult to deal with the unknown. But they had no choice. And it was *her* responsibility to do all that she could to ensure that their venture was a success. "Creda," she said firmly, one hand still on the Sister's shoulder. "We must remember that we are here as friends. No matter what awaits us, we have been directed here by the Witch of the Great East Wood for the purpose of retrieving the third talisman segment. We want the She-Serpent to see us not as a threat, but as an ally against evil. We shall take nothing except ourselves."

They and the escort headed to the rocks and cliffs. There were several places where the She-Serpent's cave might be hidden, and, although they approached these hesitantly (especially Tavis), they found nothing of particular interest nor concern.

Then, finally, past the rocks at the base of the cliff, they found an enormous cavern, half-hidden by shadows. It was filled with rocks and water, and at first glance seemed that it might be impassable.

"Is there anything here at all?" wondered Vander.

"We'll determine that soon," declared Nico. He removed his boots and socks, and rolled his pants part way up his legs. He came to the cavern and ducked beneath the low-hanging rock above –

He cast a glance at those behind him, keeping his face impassive, then turned back to the cavern. Yet he hesitated, and he wasn't certain why. He swallowed, steeled himself, and glanced back at the others once more. This time his usual broad smile broke the tension – for himself, as well as the others –

"Well then," he chuckled, "nothing like a bit of dip, eh?" With that, he slipped downward and into the water. It wasn't deep at all, the others could see, for the water did not rise past his knees. He gazed ahead and off to the side, though, and saw where some of the water began a downward rush –

And, just ahead, he could see what it was which the Sisters sought …

Creda paused to kneel beside Baru. How she wished she could take him with her! The feel of the soft fur beneath her fingers never failed to bring her a wonderful sensation of comfort. She wondered if he was consciously wanting to share this with her. She put her arms around his great neck, hugged him closely. Then she moved to join Veras, who had already removed her shoes and left them with the escort. As they prepared to step beneath the overhanging rocks, a voice gave them pause –

"All the best, Sisters."

They looked over their shoulders. "Thank you, Nico," said Veras.

He flashed his bright smiled and winked.

Veras held her robe at knee level with one hand and braced herself with her other hand on the rock above. Carefully she bent and stepped through. Here, although she stood in knee-deep water, she could rise to her full height. To the left was a steep downward grade, which the water rushed over as though eager for excitement. To the right was the narrow ledge which Nico had mentioned. With a bit of effort, she managed to pull herself upon it.

"Creda!" She motioned to the Sister to join her and reached a hand to help her step onto the ledge.

They could see a shadowy opening into the rocks. This was what Nico had seen. Just above the opening were letters engraved into the rock. The sun found enough of an opening among the rocks to shine a glimmer of light upon the inscription. "There," said Veras in a breathless voice, and pointed to it.

> *Be it know to all who enter*
> *You had best say your goodbyes.*
> *What you are now will be lost forever*
> *Should I gaze into your eyes.*

> *If you venture inside my cavern*
> *And I decide that it should be,*
> *You will dwell in my world forever*
> *As one with the Goddess and sea.*

Creda turned to Veras, blinking. *"Goddess?"*

Veras shrugged. "So she says. Remember what I told you about her gaze, Creda. The stories say that there was such a one with snakes for hair long ago, who would turn men into stone if she looked upon them. Men would try to use their shields as mirrors to defeat her.

We have no shields. But we are Sisters of the Tower, and we have the self-discipline to avoid her gaze, and that we must do." Taking a moment to steel herself, Veras stepped through the opening, Creda following closely.

They crawled along a dank tunnel for a time, the wet rock making progress awkward, and knees sore. It was with relief that they were finally able to rise to their full heights once again. Veras put both of her hands at the small of her back and stretched and arched. They waited as their eyes began to adjust to the darkness, then studied their surroundings.

They could hear the trickling of water upon water. It seemed to emanate from a few different places, although it was not possible to be certain, as the sound echoed from one rocky wall to another. Tiny pinpricks of light gleamed downward from above, although they were too small to offer much illumination. The cavern was damp and chilly. They could hear the waves splashing against the rocks outside. Now they could see other entrances, one close to the left, and another further off. Veras stepped in the direction of the closer one –

And stopped. *Movement* – she'd seen *movement* –

Careful not to look in that direction, she reached a hand back to hold Creda's. "Creda," she whispered. "Don't look!"

Once again, the water stirred where something was moving through it. *So difficult not to look!* In her peripheral vision, Veras saw what might have been a tail. It was greyish-green, and eased along through the shallow water like a huge snake.

They heard a strange voice, different from any voice either of them had ever heard before. It came slowly, as though the speaker savoured each sound, each word. And it did not keep to the same pitch. Instead, it wavered from high notes to low to middle and back.

"What isss it you ssseek? Sssissstersss of sssorcccery would not intrude upon my home sssimply for adventure."

Creda's mouth fell open in surprise. She almost looked up –

The serpent had recognized them as Sisters! Had she, then, more knowledge of the outside world than one might think possible for a being who lived in a cavern?

Veras's heart was pounding. She took a moment to calm herself. There was no need, after all, for alarm. The serpent had already acknowledged that they must have a good reason for coming here. "Please excuse our interruption, She-Serpent. We have been advised by the Witch of the Great East Wood …" She paused. How much should she say? How much did she *need* to say?

"Ah, the Witch of the Great Eassst Wood. Ssso, tell me. What isss it that you ssseek? *Tell* me. It isss my right to do with you asss I wish, consssidering that you have tressspasssed."

Again, Veras felt her heart and it seemed to be beating extremely hard. But surely it was safe to tell everything. And it would not be easy to get away with a half-truth. "We seek the third missing segment of the talisman, She-Serpent." She spoke softly and with respect.

There was a bit of silence as the serpent made little splashing sounds as she moved through the water. When she spoke once more, her voice was closer than before. "Now why would I give sssomething like that to you, Sssistersss?" Her voice was very calm —almost bored, as though she had heard all this before.

Could she be toying with them?

Veras licked her lips, tasting the salt of the water. "It is needed if the warlock is to be stopped and, hopefully, destroyed." She hoped that her voice sounded confident.

"Ah. Interesssting. And how isss it that you know sssuch?"

The Superior took a deep breath. "We of the Tower of Giefan called upon the Great Seer to find the Way – and the Witch explained that the talisman, once having belonged to the warlock, holds the power to stop and destroy him. We must find the final segment to make the talisman whole. Will you help us, She-Serpent?"

There was a long silence now, broken only by the sounds of water trickling somewhere, and the slithering noise as the serpent – at least part of her – moved along the rocks. With the constant echoes inside the cavern, where the serpent was bound could not be determined – at times she seemed to be everywhere at once …

Finally, she spoke again – and Veras inhaled sharply, for the creature seemed to be directly in front of her. She closed her eyes as the serpent spoke.

"You have the other sssegmentsss with you, then?" Her voice seemed very soft and gentle, now ...

"Yes," Veras whispered, her eyes still firmly closed.

"Give to me the talisssman sssegmentsss," said the gentle, yet now very firm, command.

Veras kept her eyes closed, shook her head. "With all respect, She-Serpent! We cannot! We have been instructed by the Witch to collect *all* of the segments! We must have them if we are to stop the warlock!"

The She-Serpent was directly in front of her now for certain. Veras could smell the creature's fishy breath, feel light splashes of seawater as the serpent moved near her. She did not know if the thing had arms to reach out and touch her – and she dared not open her eyes to see. Her hand was on the pouch which hung around her neck. Her fingers felt the talisman segments through the material.

Over and over, continually now, the She-Serpent was saying again and again, to give her the pouch, give her the pouch ...

The voice was mesmerizing, pulling Veras, lulling her ... until she began to *want* to give the talisman segments to the She-Serpent. Her fingers were moving, were reaching to pull the cord up over her neck – and to open her eyes –

Creda could sense that something was happening between Veras and that – that *thing*. Quickly she fingered her amulet and sent her own spirit to bolster her companion's. And now Creda could *hear* it, too. The breathy voice asking, demanding, that Veras look at her face, give her the pouch ...

The voice was as sweet as peppermint to a child. Its tones rose and fell rhythmically now, so relaxing, soothing, like a mother's arms as they rocked her infant –back and forth, so gently, gently, gently ...

Such wonder, such delight. Sheer joy and pleasure could be theirs if they would only find the courage to thrust all concerns aside and let her have the talisman segments. They would share everything!

All her knowledge, all her skill. Everything and anything – whatever they desired ... yes, yes, it would be true, true ...

Come, come my darlingsss. Give the pouch to me. Come now. All that I have I possssessss only to share with you, my lovesss ...

Creda could feel Veras being pulled, pulled. And she was moving closer, too, closer to losing all control. Suddenly Creda realized that if she separated from Veras, she might be able to use her power with the creatures to influence the serpent –

But she couldn't pull away! It was as though she and Veras were locked together as one in their power. Creda could see it now – a great chain of light and dark blue, melded it seemed ...

Then if felt like the terrible windstorm had returned! They shouted, gasped, clung to each other physically as well as spiritually. They were being shaken with tremendous force, powerless to help themselves –

Lightning flashed everywhere at once – it seemed as though their heads were spinning – gold and blue flashes burst around them, inside them –

Helpless. Helpless.

It wasn't a sensation of pain. Not really. But the feeling of complete exhaustion was overpowering. They felt like they were completely empty. They'd given all that they could, and were now simply empty shells ...

They were still inextricably bound together. All that Veras felt, Creda felt too. Neither could determine whether she felt the ache of her own body or that of the other. It was as though they were, together, one complete being. Each of them could see their chain as it sought to cease its spinning and turning and come to some sort of stop. They each concentrated on this, until their chain began to feel stronger. How strange it was. As Veras gripped Creda's hand, she could feel both herself holding Creda's hand, and Creda's hand holding hers.

They could not see clearly. Everything was shrouded in mists. Instinctively they turned in the direction of the light. Painfully they managed to move toward it, hands grasped as though they'd never let each other go. Back through the low entrances they moved, barely conscious of where they were headed. Their bodies were moving without direct instruction from their weary minds.

As the water bounced from the rocks, the spray helped to revive them just a bit. They could look at each other's face now, and actually see this with their own eyes. But they dared not break the spiritual link between them. Such would need to be done with great care.

Still clasping hands, they lowered themselves beneath the edge of the outcropping and onto the beach. Creda moaned as a wet tongue quickly greeted her –

Voices surrounded them. They were being lifted – their fingers almost separated –but someone noted the importance of this, and they were carried together without their contact severed.

It happened very slowly. In Creda's mind, the primary image was that of the dark and light blue chain. She felt an inquiring touch from Veras's spirit, and responded. Eyes closed, they watched their chain as they carefully unbound themselves. Veras first pulled her spirit from where it touched Creda's at one end. Slowly, slowly. Gently, Veras unbound her dark blue thread while Creda focused simply on remaining still. Then, she too unbound and moved back into herself ...

"Veras?"

Wearily, she opened her eyes. She took a moment to just lie still and breathe. Gently, but firmly, she was being eased into a sitting position. Nico held a warm mug of tea to her lips, and helped her to drink. When she had had enough for now, he took the mug from her, but continued to sit beside her and hold her hand.

"Can you speak, Veras?"

She managed to smile at his concerned face. "I am – I am so very weary, Nico."

"Then rest, Veras. Rest."

Ferren looked down at him. "There's so much we need to know!"

Nico snapped at her angrily. "I *know*, but we don't dare push the Sisters too hard too soon. We can't afford to place them in any risk! We're nothing without them."

Ferren headed away, impatience gnawing at her. She glanced back to see Nico stroking the Superior's face and hair.

Veras awoke the next morning from a dreamless sleep which felt almost as though her spirit was suspended in nothingness. But memories returned of a dark, dank cave —and the creature – *goddess?* – within. And what had been done to them was very unclear and confusing. She turned to see Creda watching her.

"Sit up slowly, Veras," Creda suggested. "I was almost ill the first time I tried."

Veras nodded and followed her advice. Once she could sit up, she took a deep breath, then another. There was sunlight glinting down from the treetops above. They were still near the sea, for she could smell it in the crisp air.

"What – what happened, Veras?"

"I – I'm not entirely sure, Creda. Our energy levels are extremely low. We wouldn't even be able to *begin* a spell now. Yet we seem free of injury. She did not directly harm us, Creda. But she *did* do something which has cost us a great deal of strength. What, exactly, I don't know."

"Veras," Creda whispered, "do you suppose she might be allied with the warlock somehow? Might she be draining our energies for him – or to protect him?"

A terrible sadness had settled inside Veras's heart as she considered everything. "Creda." She spoke very softly, not wanting to say what she knew she must.

The melancholy in Veras's voice was touching Creda's heart – which began to pound, as she considered what might be coming next. "Veras, what is it?"

The Superior sighed. 'We – we were never given the talisman segment."

Creda gasped. It couldn't be! After all they'd been through, how could that be? "No," she said, shaking her head. She swallowed. "Then we must confront her again!" Her voice was filled with determination at first, but that faded to dread.

Veras put her hand on Creda's shoulder. "That's not the worst of it." If her voice had been any softer, Creda might not have heard her at all. Veras had been looking downward. Now she raised her eyes to meet Creda's. There were tears on the verge of escaping. Veras passed her sleeve across her eyes. "Creda, the talisman segments and the pouch are not here."

Suddenly the sea breeze was no longer cool and crisp. Now it stung like ice pellets.

The Sisters, Vander and Tavis sat around the fire. Quietly. It would take them all some time to absorb the shock of what they had been told. The others had been too restless to stay at the fire while pondering what to do. Without the talisman, how could they continue? What would be the *point* of continuing, if they needed the talisman to complete their mission?

"We've got to try to find it! Surely it's still here somewhere!" As much as Creda hated the thought of confronting the serpent again, they *must* have the talisman – for her sister, for Joul's wife … and the many others he'd taken.

"I know, Creda. I know," Veras was saying, "but if the pouch is anywhere inside that cave, we will need to face the serpent again. And we're still too weak to consider confronting her."

It was a sad sight which greeted the two who approached on horseback, for Creda stood, twisting her hands, her continuing anguish evident on her drawn face. The Superior sat by the fire, looking tired and distraught.

Anxiety nibbled at Ferren as she dismounted. Nico was already down, and stepped toward the Sisters. Anger edged his voice as he spoke. "Do you still insist that none of us enter the thing's cave?"

"Yes," answered Veras, wearily yet firmly.

There was silence. Veras was staring downward again while Nico gazed off into the distance, as though hoping to find an answer somewhere. Ferren gave voice to her anxiety: "What will we do, then? You said that we *must* have the segments to defeat him! What can we do?"

Veras sighed. It was true – they must think of something. "Well – together, Creda and I might attempt a Seeking Spell. I think we might be able to manage this –"

"*No!*" It was Nico. He swallowed, then continued in a softer tone. "No, Sisters. You need to recover and save your energies. We'll just have to defeat him with*out* the thing –"

"But Nico," Ferren cut in. "They were told that they *must* have it –"

"I'll not risk them or their health!"

"Please!" Veras raised a hand to stop their words. "We can manage this, Nico."

Nico stared at her, but, once again, she gazed downward. Nico sighed and looked away.

Creda and Veras sat close together on a log near the fire. Kneeling close to them were Nico and Ferren, as instructed should one of the Sisters require physical assistance. They gazed in fascination as the Sisters produced the spell needed to give them the vital information …

Evidently, they had finished, for they appeared to be coming back to themselves. Nico moved to sit on the log beside Veras, who was swaying unsteadily. The Sisters were blinking as they attempted to orient themselves –

"Sisters?" prompted Ferren.

Creda drew a hand across her mouth, saying nothing. Shakily she rose and began to walk away. Ferren stood, wondering if she should follow. She looked to Veras, who shook her head.

Veras gazed up at Ferren, then at Nico who sat with an arm around her shoulders. "We could not locate it," she said softly. "In fact, it might be nowhere near here. The only place that our spell could not penetrate was inside that cave. It is either inside of it, or somewhere far from here. We have no way of knowing which."

Hoofbeats distracted them. Zann and Giever arrived on their mounts, urgency evident on their faces. Nico rose to his feet, as the captain slid from his saddle, hastening to join them. "The time has come! The evil one's raiders have spread their destruction further west! Come!"

CHAPTER EIGHTEEN

Capture

They urged their horses to fast gallops as they followed the captain and Giever. Onward they rode, away from the sea. They went up a hill to find themselves on a grassy ledge overlooking a green valley – what had once been a beautiful, fertile valley, it would seem –

It had been the home of a number of villagers. Now it lay lifeless, save for a few chickens and a horse or two which had ventured back after fleeing the attack. A few carrion eaters found remnants of meat amid the destruction and screamed now and then as they fought over the feast.

The silent group urged their horses carefully down the other side of the hill, looking for a less-steep descent. At the bottom, Zann tethered his horse to a tree branch, the others following suit. Creda's heart was pounding as she fought the awful memories which threatened to come crashing down upon her. Already her spirit was calling out *Carlida, Carlida …*

It wasn't exactly as Carlida's village had appeared, for these villagers had not been nomadic. These homes which had been destroyed had been small, wooden cottages. Although most of the doors and shutters had been torn away, the dwellings themselves still stood.

How strange it seemed to the captain and Ferren – and Nico – for they had seen battles before. They had seen the results and the effects upon surrounding areas. Yet here, amid the destruction and wreckage, there were no signs of actual *killing*, except for the few creatures which must have found themselves in the attackers' way. There were no signs of any dead humans anywhere.

Zann knelt, examined a bloody cloth. He turned to see Creda observing him, reaching forth her hand to touch it. He shook his head and put it back down. "Neither of you is yet strong enough," he said.

He was correct, Creda knew. They must not use their energies just now for that purpose. She had learned what she could at Carlida's village, and all evidence here suggested that the people of this village had met a similar fate.

Zann rose and stood beside the Sister, as he eyed the damage. When he spoke, his voice was very quiet. "Do – do you suppose there's any chance – any chance at all – that I might see my wife again?" He averted his eyes. The question had been difficult for him to ask.

But Creda could offer no comfort. "I just don't know, Joul."

Veras stood, her heart very heavy as her eyes took in the sight of what remained of the village. Vividly she recalled Creda's reports of the destruction of her sister's village. But to see it for herself …

This was terrible magic indeed. In her memory, she repeated the words of the Great Seer and the Witch of the Great East Wood. It must be *magic* that would defeat this ruthless warlock. The Witch had, after all, alerted the others of her kind to tell them that the Sisters were coming. So, in a way, she and Creda might not be completely on their own. And, anyway, the purpose of the escort had been to get them safely to where the warlock might be. This recent destruction suggested that he might not be that far away, or at least, his armies might not.

And so, her mind was made up. Her heart ached with despair, but she must rely on what her mind told her now.

She watched Creda and the captain, and stepped in their direction. She stopped and spoke briefly to Nico, who nodded, and turned to say something to Tavis, then continued to the others. In a few moments, they were all standing together … a rather solemn gathering amid the destruction.

Veras studied the faces surrounding her. "Let us leave this place," she said hoarsely. "My heart hears the villagers crying out for help." Resolutely she walked to the horses. All could see that her mind was quite made up. Talisman or no, she had said that she would do whatever she could to defeat the warlock. She was about to mount when Nico stopped her.

"Dear Veras," he said softly, gently placing one of his large hands upon hers. "Let us all replenish ourselves. We can go to the grove at the foot of the hill."

"Very well," she replied. "We should talk further, at any rate."

The sights they had seen sickened them, but, at the same time they found themselves famished and very thirsty. They talked of the destruction, and what might lie ahead of them, then sat quietly for a time around the fire, grateful for the food and warm tea.

"As I have already said," Veras reminded them in a soft voice, "you are all free to go. Creda and I will continue."

"But without the talisman?" Ferren couldn't imagine being the *One* without the mysterious help of the thing.

Veras sighed. This was not the first time that someone had questioned their chances of completing the task without the talisman. "Someone must oppose the warlock, talisman or no. The Prophecy stated that there was a *One*. We have every reason to believe that the *One* is myself or Creda. We shall continue whether or not we have the talisman."

"But Sister Veras," Ferren continued, "what is the point of confronting him if we don't have the talisman, and it is necessary?"

Veras studied the woman's face. "We interpret the Prophecy as a promise that the *One* will be a female – and it seems most sensible that this must be a woman who knows the magic arts. It was the Witch who said that we needed the talisman. Perhaps she was in error … or we may have misinterpreted her, somehow."

Ferren returned her gaze. "Perhaps you'll be surprised. After all, it could be that *I'm* the *One*." In the silence that followed, Ferren felt breathless, felt the warmth of pink in her cheeks. *There. She had said it!*

Veras smiled slightly. "You may be right, Ferren. After all, nobody knows for certain who it might be. But the way ahead of us will be difficult and fraught with danger –"

"I am a warrior, Veras. I am a representative of the Prince, and therefore also the King and Queen. I have served proudly in the Royal Army and am ready to face this thing." Her thin face was set, her jaws clenched.

Nico watched the woman as she spoke. Could it be that she *was* the *One*? He frowned. The thought unsettled him, for some reason –

Vander then offered his continuing services, too, and Giever responded with his usual enthusiasm, despite being unsettled by the wreckage they'd all seen. Tavis gave a look of uncertainty for a moment, then nodded his tousled head. Joul simply smiled at the Sisters, his thick brown moustache edging upward at the corners.

Veras looked beside her at Nico. "We have no hold on you. You have performed wonderfully for us and we will be forever grateful. Please do not feel any responsibility or need to continue –"

Nico was shaking his head. He did not agree with her words. *Performed wonderfully* – if only he believed that could be true! But he said: "I pledged my service to you both. And I do *not* break my word. So long as you and Creda have any need of protection, you shall have mine." He drew in a long breath, steeling himself, determined that he'd serve them better from now on.

As they had shared their thoughts and their meals, the sun had begun to make its downward journey. The warlock's army having already been through this area, it seemed reasonable that the group might stay in the grove to rest for the night. Rest seemed especially important when they considered that they really had no idea whatsoever might await them on the morrow.

Ferren lay quietly, hoping that sleep would come soon so that she'd be rested for her shift on watch duty. She drifted into a light doze, her mind filled with images of herself confronting the warlock, her blade running him through while the Sisters held him captive with their spells. Then there would be a hero's welcome upon her return ... with Prince Yurmar himself kissing her hand in gratitude.

A smile appeared on her sleeping face as the pleasant dream lifted her spirits.

Creda's eyes flashed open, and she was sure she was still dreaming –

But a hand was across her mouth – a *real* hand, a rough hand. There were men –but *not* men – everywhere, or so it seemed –

To the right she saw Tavis staring, wide-eyed as one of them injected something into his body. Giever raised his sword and swung –

But somehow the attacker managed to disappear, only to reappear a short distance away. Giever, too, then sank to the ground, senseless.

Creda could feel Gem's distress, and the sorceress hoped desperately that the intruders would not harm her, or Baru. But then, with relief she realized that he had gone on his nightly explorations.

She kept expecting to feel a jab that would render her senseless, but so far the thing that held her was simply shoving her in the direction of something like a large cart, just visible on the other side of the trees. She had a little bit of an idea what was to happen, and she was becoming filled with determination –

Somehow, she was going to avoid being drugged. That might be her only hope of escape. The intruders seemed especially likely to jab those of the escort who were actively trying to defend themselves. Perhaps, if Creda appeared to co-operate, she could avoid or at least postpone being jabbed by the little knife-thing which apparently held the potion.

So she let the man/not man push her in the direction of the cart, which she could now see had a large cage-like thing filling the space behind the drivers' seats. Inside it were some people – senseless, lying on the floor of the thing.

The intruder did *not* intend to leave her conscious. That much seemed certain –

Could she do it? Did she have enough energy and presence of mind? Could she defend herself as a Sister of the Tower? She closed her eyes and whispered the words of the *Spell of Protection*. She had to do so without touching her fingers to her amulet, as the man/not man held her arms from behind. So she leaned backward a bit, to feel the touch of the amulet against the skin of her upper chest –

She saw herself surrounded by a pale blue glow. She felt the man/ not man fumble with something, and she knew the time was right …

She put all of her energy into her spell, as the man/not man jabbed the little knife toward her … and into the invisible protective covering provided by her protective spell. The man/not man didn't see her little grin of victory as she pretended to slump forward in an unconscious heap.

As luck would have it, though, he shoved her hard into the cage, and she tripped backward over someone's unconscious form, striking her head against something –

And everything went black.

It was very quiet. Nothing could be heard save the drip, drip, drip of trickling water, which was uncomfortably familiar …

It was cool and damp, and the ground beneath was hard, like rock. Creda's head pounded. She dared not simply lie here, but her head cautioned her to move slowly, carefully. She opened her eyes just slightly, wondering if she should continue to feign unconsciousness. Moving her head slightly, she gazed to her right, then to her left –

And all around her, she saw people – or at least what once might have been active people. Now they looked like little more than empty shells of living beings.

She saw too, that she was in a cave – not the She-Serpent's, but a much larger one. Carefully she managed to raise her head a bit, fighting the dizziness and nausea as her body complained. Again she gazed to each side, trying to get a more complete picture of her surroundings and what they contained. More and more and more unconscious people! She had to lie back and close her eyes again, to take a deep breath and try to gain some sort of control. Shock and revulsion could do nothing to help this situation.

Taking another long breath, she opened her eyes once more. Beyond the bodies in one direction, there was an opening of some sort in the cavern wall –

And, across the opening was faint greyish haze …

A spell! This was a prison, and the spell would be as effective as iron bars. But she was a sorceress, and would prefer to be faced with a barrier of magic. She took another breath to steady herself and concentrated on the sound of voices coming from beyond the magic barrier. There was noise which resembled people moving about – the sounds of boots on the hard ground, wooden chairs being moved. She supposed that these were likely to be guards, or other men/not men from the warlock's army.

So then, it would appear that this was where the warlock housed the bodies of his prisoners. If she had wanted to find him, it seemed that she had managed it, albeit not as she had planned nor wished. Creda sighed, wondering what to do. Still she felt achy and weak, and knew that she must preserve her energies, yet she had no wish to remain here.

And where were the others? She lifted her head just a bit to scan the area for familiar faces, and then she could see slight movements here and there. Thankfully, these prisoners did not appear to be dead. Hopefully, her companions' spirits were with them still, and not being kept in the Icetombs!

But none of the prisoners around her were familiar. Sighing, she lay with eyes closed, gathering her strength. She *must* find the others ...

The rapport with Veras's spirit had increased and deepened considerably through their shared contact in the far north, and since the incident in the cave of the She-Serpent. It might not be difficult for Creda to sense Veras's location, should she be near –

She concentrated intensely, putting forth a light search of magic, not wanting to use a stronger spell for fear of risking detection.

And sighed. *Nothing.* She wasn't certain if she should be disappointed. True, it was good to know that Veras was not among the prisoners here ... but that didn't mean Veras was *safe*, either.

A bit of memory suddenly flashed through her mind. *She'd seen another wagon in addition to the one she'd been pushed into –*

She had to find them – she *would* find them! Still lying on her back, she reached a hand to the forehead of the man who lay next to her and focused on sensing his spirit. It was there. He did not lie dead. Yet his consciousness seemed to lie dormant, almost as though covered by a heavy blanket. Hmm. She might be able to revive this man's consciousness, and maybe some of the others –

But what would that accomplish?

Another sensation distracted her – and alarmed her – for this was something scurrying across her legs. Creda shuddered, imagining all kinds of vile little creatures just waiting for the prisoners' deaths, ready to sample their flesh –

But suddenly she *knew* that that wasn't true! Despite her weariness and aches, the thought came through quite clearly –

She turned her head in the rat's direction and touched its – *his*, she realized – mind. The rat stopped in his tracks, feeling the contact, and looked toward Creda, whiskers twitching vigorously above big yellowish teeth. Creda was in luck. The rat returned her eye contact quickly, speeding the task along.

Creda sent much of her spirit inside of the rat, careful to maintain a touch with her own body as well. (She had no desire to spend the rest of her days as a rat!) Through the rat's little eyes, the prison seemed filled with mountains of reclining humans, and through his nostrils the air was rich with the stench of sweat.

And his ears could hear the movements of the men/not men of the warlock's raiders beyond the magic barrier. As one, Creda inside the rat moved in that direction, instinctively seeking the security offered by the shadows and nearby walls. They scurried along, avoiding the humans who seemed most inclined to movement. Now, in the shadows they crouched, eyes, nose, ears drinking in the information they sought.

Two men/not men sat beyond the magic barrier. Both were eating. Yet neither appeared to be enjoying his – or its – meal. Their faces were almost identical, both in their features and their lack of expressions. It appeared that they, too, must have been drugged, or perhaps be under the effects of a spell, for they seemed to go about their business without conscious thought or feeling.

Creda/rat turned their gaze back from the guards and focused on the magic barrier. It had been intended to keep the humans inside, and Creda suspected that its weakest sections would be small spots where it met the walls. And suddenly Creda realized that this was not *her* area of experience – it was the *rat's*. So she simply conveyed to him a need to go past the barrier. Quickly they moved closer, and now Creda could see a small gap at the very bottom, just large enough for a rat to pass through. Through it they went, and scurried quickly around a corner. They hurried down the corridor to see another magic barrier, with more prisoners beyond. They stopped.

Creda could feel the rat's preference for going in the other direction – back to where the men/not men were eating their meal. She caught glimpses of the rat's hope that some crumbs or morsels might be available on the ground beneath the table. So they moved that way, scurrying along the corridor, seeking the shadows. They slowed their pace as they approached the guards, not wishing to attract their attention – although Creda wondered if these men/not men would react at all to the rat. Carefully, carefully, they made their way around the guards' boots until they were under the table nearest the wall. Sure enough, there were some tasty morsels which had fallen. The rat happily nibbled for a moment or two.

But Creda couldn't keep the rapport with the rat for a great length of time, and so they set out in the opposite direction to the one they'd explored first. Down the corridor, and around a corner –

And it was wonderful! A beautiful whiff of the scent of trees from somewhere in the distance. That was what Creda had needed to know!

They turned around and headed back up the corridor, and once again, back around the corner. They were approaching the guards once more. Their eyes were studying the men/not men who continued to sit silently as they nibbled on their meal. Now their eyes were studying the walls around them …

These were not smooth walls, but were the inside of a large cave, with crags and crannies. High up on some walls were torches which lit the surrounding areas. And, just above the men/not men, and slightly behind them, was a bit of rock which protruded from the rest of the wall. Creda/rat eyed this, but knew that this was too steep a section for climbing. So they went back down the corridor until they found a more gradual incline and slowly made their way, holding tightly with their sharp claws, until they were lying quietly atop the little rock, grateful to catch their breath.

From here, they had a clear view of the men/not men below and just in front. They appeared to have completed their meals. And now they just sat. Creda/rat watched them, taking in as much information about them as they could. Around each one's neck was a cord of hide. Creda/rat moved around a bit on the rock for a better vantage point. The light from the torch nearby was reflected by something near the neck of the shirt of the guard closest to them – something metal.

Creda/rat took a deep breath. The next move was clear …

Creda drew back into herself. Now she knew what she needed to know. But she didn't know if the rat would be able to do what was required. She pondered the situation. The men/not men were wearing amulets. A spell would be needed to remove the magic barrier. And that spell would be the reason for the amulets. She needed to gain possession of one of them. She might be able to use her own amulet to affect the magic barrier in some way. But the warlock would be aware of the interference if it was enacted by someone else's amulet. She had to have one of the guards' amulets. But *how?*

Despair was threatening to close in on her. She *knew* what she needed in order to escape. She *knew* how to find her way out. Yet here she was, unable to take any action. She let go a sigh and lay back with an arm across her eyes.

Veras was despondent. She lay in some sort of large cart – unable to move. With effort, she found that she was able to move her eyes to a degree, so could at least see something of what was around her. She knew that Nico lay beside her, for she knew the sound of his breathing and his odors. The cart had been moving, and she could see from the changing look of the treetops high above that they had travelled somewhere.

She had tried to move, especially at first, but her body simply would not obey her. It was as though she had a very heavy blanket thrown over her, so heavy that it kept her pinned down. She could breathe, she could hear, she could smell and she could see.

Although her sense of touch was somewhat numbed, she was grateful that she could still feel, for the warmth of Nico's hand against hers brought her some comfort. She knew that others from her group were here, too, from the familiarity of their breathing sounds and their smells ... but not Creda.

Veras moved her eyes around as much as she could, and saw Giever and Vander and Ferren, and Nico on her other side. But that was all. The captain and Tavis might be here as well, as she could not move her eyes enough to see all the cart's interior. But she was sure that Creda had been taken in the other wagon. Whether she had been taken elsewhere or was travelling in the same direction as this cart, she had no knowledge. Veras had tried sending her spirit to those around her. If Creda had been close, Veras was sure that she would have sensed her presence.

She sighed. She had been resting as much as she could despite the bumps and the jostling of the cart. Now she could feel a bit of energy inside, and she would use it try to send something of her spirit to Creda ... wherever she was. She could not move her hand to touch her amulet, but she was lying on her back, and could feel its metal against the skin of her upper chest. She would focus all her energy on it ... and on Creda.

Veras took a few seconds to enjoy the feel of Nico's hand against hers. Then she turned her focus to the task. She was grateful that her amulet lay where it did, for it was situated slightly to the left of her chest, and therefore closer to her heart. She inhaled very deeply, for what she was about to do would require a great deal of focus and energy combined –

She stopped, gasping. *She couldn't do this!* Well, perhaps she was capable of it, but she *dared* not do it!

If this cart was taking them to where the warlock was, she had no way of knowing if they might be close enough that *he* might be the one to sense her magic, rather than Creda! Or perhaps they *both* would sense her presence. How might the warlock respond to this?

She simply couldn't take this risk. Tears made their way down her cheeks.

Nico pressed his hand harder against hers. It was all that he could do. Veras was not the only one to feel despair.

Creda had not lain there for very long before she felt the presence of her friend. There had been only the slightest noise, and then she felt the tickling of his whiskers against her cheek, her arm. She pulled her arm away from her eyes and chuckled at the sight of what looked like an oversized mouse looking at her –

Oversized mouse …

She said those words over and over in her mind as she gazed at the rat. The rat was too large to do what she was thinking about … but a *mouse* …

She sat up, casting a glance toward the magic barrier to ensure that there was no man/not man guard peering in to see her. She searched the area with her eyes, certain that, if there were rats here, there would be mice as well …

Her rat friend watched her curiously. Creda sighed. She was fortunate, indeed, to possess this strange skill with beasts, but right now that didn't help her – for how could she get across to the rat that it was a *mouse* that she needed?

"We'll just have to search for one, won't we?" she whispered to her friend.

Once again, she was one with the rat. Together they scurried around the perimeter of the cave/prison. But the rat's vision was not good, and so they relied on the rat's sense of smell. Although Creda as a person might not have perceived the scent of mice, the rat certainly could. And it did not need long to find a tiny mouse which had a hole at the bottom of the rocky wall. Creda/rat hurried back to Creda's body. Once she had become herself again, Creda thanked the rat. Sending her spirit into the creature's body and then back into her own again drained her energy, but she had little choice at this point.

Again, she checked that the magic barrier was still in place with no guard looking in at her. Then she carefully picked her way among the unconscious humans, as quietly as – she hoped – a mouse. She crouched down at the bottom of the rocky wall where the hole was. Of course, at the sight of her approaching, the mouse had fled inside.

Now what to do? Could she entice it to come out to her? She searched the ground for food but saw nothing which resembled anything a mouse might eat. She flattened herself on the ground as best she could and tried to peer inside of the hole. All she could see was darkness. She looked up at the torch in its holder on the rocky wall, but it was too high for her to reach.

Hmm. She needed to send her spirit inside of the mouse. In the past, she had had physical contact with a beast, or at least could see it, and it had been in close proximity. All that she had now was the fact that she was close to the thing. Physical contact would certainly make the process easier –

Creda took a deep breath to prepare herself –

And thrust her hand – or at least all of it that would fit – into the hole. Nothing happened. She stretched her fingers in as far as she could –

Pain surged through her hand and instantly she sent her spirit into the mouse –

Together, they wriggled around Creda's bleeding hand where it still partially blocked the hole. Together, they hastened to the magic barrier and scurried through the space beneath it. Together, they clambered up the wall and looked at the cord fastened at the backs of both men/not men's necks.

Very quietly they made their way down the wall to the ground and to the base of one of the wooden chairs. As slowly and gently as they could, they climbed up the chair leg and to the top of the chair's back. There, just above them, was the cord of hide through which they must chew. They would need to be very, very careful and gentle in order to do so without alerting the man/not man.

One paw, then the next gripped the coarse material of the guard's shirt. Very slowly, Creda/mouse climbed up the back of the man/not man. Finally, the cord was in front of them. Very, *very* carefully, they nibbled at the cord, chewing through it a tiny bit at a time. But the man/not man moved slightly, and they almost lost their footing. They had to hold on and not fall, but at the same time, be very careful not to sink their claws through the shirt's material and into the man/not man's skin. They had come to a thicker section of the cord, and it was difficult to chew through it. They had to grip it more tightly with their teeth, and pull it closer –

But the guard felt the amulet move and spontaneously put his hand across it –

Creda/mouse leaped down to the ground and ran back past and around the unconscious bodies to the hole as fast as their little legs could carry them – *there wasn't much time* –

Quickly, quickly, back to Creda where she lay at the mouse's hole –

Creda, herself once again, gained her feet and raced to the prison entrance where the magic barrier had been stopped when the guard touched his amulet. Through it she crawled, hoping that they might not see her immediately if she was at the level of the floor. She looked in their direction to see both men/not men preoccupied with inspecting the cord which had been chewed. And so she moved as quietly as she could, but was still surprised that she was able to make her way past them unnoticed.

When she came to the corner, she stood and gazed back at them. These men/not men were certainly not functioning at the same level as the ones who had attacked her camp. Yet it made sense. Why would the warlock bother to have the guards at a higher skill level? After all, they were tasked with keeping watch over unconscious prisoners.

Creda tucked what she had learned about these men/not men into her memory, and turned in the direction of the trees which she and the rat had smelled earlier …

CHAPTER NINETEEN

Reunion, Yet Separation

The refreshing breeze, the sweet scent of trees and the wonder of the gleaming moon and stars above!

For a moment, Creda simply stood in the wooded area and enjoyed being free from her prison. But she shook her head. She had no time to dwell on such joys. She had to find the others! She moved to the base of a large tree, sinking down against the trunk. Her breath still came in pants. She took deeper breaths – she must concentrate in order to focus her thoughts.

Sitting quietly, she became aware of the stillness of the night. There came no sound, it seemed, at all. She would need the help of a spell. *The Seeking Spell …*

She rose, and quietly moved back in the direction of the prison. Just around the corner, there seemed to be sufficient light. Yes. But first she took a moment to look around and listen to her surroundings. It would not do for her to meet up with more of the men/not men now. She held her amulet so that its shadow would be in the moon's glow, and whispered the words of the spell …

And through the spell she saw them. They were in a cage. This had been removed from the wagon, apparently, when the wagon had lost a wheel –

They lay as though lifeless. It was difficult to look upon her friends in such a state. But Creda had been among unconscious humans herself, and she knew well that they still lived. She had to pull away from this view, so that she could gain more information about the surrounding area. Sadly, she did not have the energy to maintain the spell long enough to obtain a good picture of the surroundings. The only food she had had in what seemed a long time had been the crumbs which the rat and mouse had found, and those crumbs had gone into their bodies, not hers.

Back into herself, she quickly moved away from the prison area and back into the shelter of the woods. Returning to the base of the thick tree trunk, she took a few moments to breathe deeply and regain some strength. Now she knew what had happened to her friends, and she knew – if not exactly where they were – at least what the area looked like. Finding them might also be made easier by the fact that there been two lanterns.

But which way was it from here? She rose, walking slowly, and removed the fastener that held her long hair together at the back of her neck, tried to gather her tresses together again, and rebound them. As she had been so occupied, her eyes had been scanning the area around the outside of the prison for any information which might prove helpful –

And then, from around the far side of the prison, she saw the roadway. If the others had been in a wagon, then it must have been coming from somewhere along this road. She gazed upward to ask the constellations for their help.

If this prison was south of where they'd been captured, and the others had not yet arrived here, it would seem that they must be on the roadway which lay north –

But the stars above advised her that here, at least, the roadway travelled in more of an east-west direction …

She sighed and stepped among the trees in a northerly direction. Still she could see the roadway as it stretched forward away from her, but after walking for a time she became aware that it had turned and did indeed follow in a more northerly direction. She stepped toward it, but paused when she sensed animal life to the west. But suddenly there was something else –

Back at the roadway, there was a lantern, and it was bobbing along as though moving–

Not wanting to be seen, Creda stepped back into the shelter of the trees to the west, and quickly –

She and a buck were one. Suddenly the quivering of their nostrils told Creda far more than her eyes had been able to perceive. The men/not men. And there was something else familiar – some odour she'd smelled before –

The potion! And now they could hear the creaking of the cart as it moved along. Creda/buck moved closer to the roadway but remained hidden behind the trees. Here they could safely watch as the cart lumbered past, two men/not men on the front, holding the horses' reins. How odd it seemed to see these men/not men, for they were all almost completely identical in appearance. And all had that strange, detached, blank look on their similar faces. Now Creda/buck could see the cage in the back of the cart –

And suddenly she pulled back into her own body. The cage had been empty. She had hoped that this might be the cart bearing her friends, but even as the thought passed through her mind, she knew that it couldn't have been. Not enough time had gone by for the wagon's wheel to have been repaired and affixed to the cart.

She was not surprised to see that the buck was still near, watching her. She smiled at him, and then was with him once more. Through the trees they moved again, in the direction from which the empty cart had come. Yet again, Creda marveled at the tremendous sense of smell so many beasts shared. The buck's nostrils were sensitive, indeed, and soon she could make out the peculiar odour of the potion.

From here they could see the two lanterns ...

Sending the buck her gratitude, Creda returned to her own body. If only she could find some way of moving her *own body* with her when she became one with the creatures. For, now that she was in her own body once more, she would have to cover the same ground again that she'd travelled with the buck. As a human, this would seem to take an eternity. So she hurried as best she could, pushing aside low-hanging branches, and easing her way past brambles. She had to jump across a stream, and sank in almost to her knees. And all of this she must do as quietly as possible.

In her haste, she had almost stumbled right into the little camp. She gasped, put a hand over her mouth, and stepped gingerly back amid the bushes.

The men/not men sat silently as they worked at repairing the wheel. Again, it seemed so strange to see them, for they were almost completely identical to the others she had seen. They all wore amulets. She supposed that these must bring them communication from the warlock. She wondered what she would find if she sent her spirit inside one of them as she had the beasts –

But no. She must not ponder this. Becoming one with creatures was becoming easier. She must *not* allow herself to become one with a man/not man, for this might well alert the warlock.

Creda turned her attention to the prisoners inside of the cage. They were lying silently, unmoving. Although Creda's heart ached to see her friends like this, she knew that they were alive. She was close enough to try to sense Veras now. Creda closed her eyes and prepared herself to reach outward and feel the Superior's spirit. Poor Veras! She must be so very fatigued now. She would no doubt have been trying to somehow counter the effects of the potion which left her so helpless …

But she stopped. Yes, of course. To try to send something to one another over *any* distance might be too risky, for they had no idea how near or far the warlock himself might be. They must take no risks which could result in alerting him to their presence.

In order to assist Veras – or any of the others – Creda would require direct physical contact. But how could she accomplish this when the men/not men were there, with their potion-knives doubtlessly quite ready?

Suddenly her consciousness was distracted by an animal presence not far away –

She recognized him instantly. *Baru!* Quickly she sent a flash to him to tell him simply *no*, not to attack the men/not men. She sensed his plan and sent him her thanks. She was reasonably certain that the warlock would not sense this communication – after all, Creda seemed to be the only person of magic who used it. But still, she kept

Now she could focus her attention on her imprisoned friends.
And, as she moved quietly forward, she could sense Baru's movements
through bushes not far from here. Soon she could *hear* them, too,
for he intended that they be audible. Creda could almost smell the
unease and fear as it began to make its way among the horses – and
then the men/not men. Creda had wondered if these men/not men
were simply puppets, told by the warlock exactly what to do through
the amulets, but now she could see that they *did* have some ability to
think, or at least react, on their own.

Baru did not attack them. But he certainly knew how to *worry*
them. And the increasing fearful reactions of the horses were adding
to their unease, for they now had left the wheel to step toward the
horses and gaze into the trees and bushes, knives drawn.

Creda took the opportunity to slip over to the side of the cage
furthest from them, and, straining to reach it, touch her fingers to
Veras's forehead –

Joy filled Veras's every fibre! Although still powerless to move,
she could feel Creda's strength and energy as it intertwined with her
own. It felt wonderful, but she was still not able to make any use of
it. Veras could hear whinnies and the pounding of the horses' hoofs
as they moved as much as they could in their places. She could hear
the sound now of a wolf's yips, and knew that it must be Baru.

Creda, too, was aware of Baru's activities to distract the men/
not men, and sent him a quick message of caution, along with her
gratitude. Creda was as close to the Superior as she could be but
knew that she needed to be closer. She could reach in and touch
Veras's forehead, but to do so required her to stretch as far as was
possible. So she moved her hand from the Superior's forehead and
instead seized her robe to pull her closer to the bars. Now Creda held
her amulet gingerly in her right hand while her left sought to gain
hold of Veras's. It still felt *wrong* to touch the Superior's amulet. The
Tower had always taught that it was wrong. Yet this very action had
brought Veras back to them when it had seemed that they'd lost her,
back at the Icetombs. And so, once again, Creda held her own amulet

The communication very brief, to keep the chances of detection to a
minimum.

in one hand, and that of her dear friend and Superior in her other. Her eyes closed …

Nico waited, his own spirit straining once more against the awful invisible force which held him. He, too, had heard the restlessness of the horses, and the fuss created by Baru, and had surmised what was happening. Although pleased with this progress, he wished he could curse aloud, for so desperately he wanted to get out there and take his own revenge against their captors – and this warlock who had caused all the problems. But the Sister was here now, and soon would set things right …

A flash like lightning –

Veras could move! Quickly she turned and reached a hand to Nico.

He was lying still, and suddenly he turned his head to look at her. Yet what to do! Nico wanted to shout, to curse, to bang his fist against the side of the cage, but he lay still. The plan would come from the Sisters. The look on Creda's face had him turning his attention in the direction of the wolf –

Ferren too, now moved, having been touched by Creda and her amulet –

Both men/not men were still brandishing their blades in front of a growling Baru, the horses stamping their feet and tossing their heads behind him. Creda moved away from the cage, looking along the ground. Finally, she found what she had been seeking. Now she approached the men/not men from behind. As she came closer, she raised a strong branch with both hands. As the first man/not man collapsed, unconscious, the second turned, withdrawing his potion-filled knife and staring at Creda –

But, as he lunged toward her, Baru ran between his legs and the man/not man fell to the ground on his back with a loud thud. Creda used her branch to knock him unconscious. Careful not to touch his amulet, she checked his pockets. Nothing. She crawled over to the other man/not man, yet found nothing helpful there either. She gave a deep sigh. Now they were no further ahead! What good was it all if they had no keys to open the locked doors to the cage? Creda sat back on the ground, wondering if there was some sort of spell that

Veras and she might use to unlock a lock. She'd never had need of such before –

Startled, she jumped to her feet, reaching once more for the branch –

"Whoa! Easy there!" It was Nico! He smiled broadly, putting a hand on each of her shoulders. "Next time I'm trying to deal with a man who has too much ale in 'im, I'll just let *you* handle things! You and your branch." He embraced her warmly.

"But – but –" Creda didn't have a chance to ask any questions before she was surrounded by the whole grateful group.

After much hugging and a happy reunion, she finally asked: "But – but how did you get out? I was searching for the keys –"

Giever smiled. "It was a rusty lock. Likely they didn't see a need to keep it working properly, seeing as it was used to keep *spellbound* prisoners inside." He held up his knife. "A little maneuvering was all it needed."

Veras looked at the group, her heart happy now that they were together once more. "It is truly wonderful that we are finally ourselves again! Thank you, dear Sister Creda for rescuing us. We will all be anxious to hear your tales, but for now, we had best move away from this area. We do not want to be here when the guards regain their senses. We will take the horses. We have most of ours, which they were leading behind the wagon, and the two of theirs which pulled it. There might also be some food in the wagon which we can use."

She turned to Nico. "I'm so very, *very* sorry, but Thunder is not among the horses which they led from our camp."

She put her hand on his cheek, not minding the growth of stubble which had been unaffected by the potion that had bound them. "I know," he said. He took her hand from his cheek, put her fingers against his lips and kissed them. "Thunder would have hated this with all of his being. I know that he would have fled. Perhaps some small spell could be sent to find him."

But Veras shook her head. "We can't risk such, Nico. The warlock might sense it. I'm so sorry."

He smiled, and kissed her fingers once more before letting them go. "Thunder will be all right, Veras. We'll find each other eventually.

I'll check the horses that were hitched to the wagon and get them ready. *I'll* likely ride one of them, as they might not be used to riders."

"Thank you, Nico," she said softly.

Veras did not know that the Sister had overheard their exchange. Creda hoped with all of her might that the spell she'd used to find her friends had not been sensed by the warlock. She knelt beside Baru, placing a hand on his head. She was grateful that she could easily send *him* a message which would avoid detection, because of their physical contact.

CHAPTER TWENTY

Closer

They found some bread which the men/not men had been keeping with the wagon, and brought it with them while they rode away from the unconscious men/not men and the wagon with the broken wheel. They went in the direction leading away from the prison and the wagon and found a sheltered area in the forest.

Finally, a fire had been lit, and they sat near it, nibbling on what was left of their own supplies. Creda and Veras examined the men/not men's bread closely for any signs of the potion and found none.

"I know that we don't have a lot of our own supplies left, but we should eat whatever we have remaining in our own packs carried by the horses," Creda stated with firmness. "We don't know much about these men/not men, but there is most certainly enchantment involved. We can't be certain that what they have to eat doesn't contribute to their situation."

"But they have amulets, Sister," said Tavis. "I thought *that* was how the warlock made them follow his commands."

"Yes, Tavis. But we don't know if the food they eat might contribute to this. And so we don't know how or if their food might affect *us*."

Tavis looked deep in thought as he pulled some of his dried meat into two pieces, handing Nico one. Nico nodded his thanks.

Veras had been quiet – and she did not look very happy. Creda had shared much of what she had learned with the others, and now turned to her Superior. "Veras?"

The Superior sighed. "We are no doubt getting closer to finding the warlock, and we must be prepared as best we can. We do not have the talisman, although the Great Seer said nothing of one. So perhaps the talisman is not essential to our task. The Great Seer said that the *One* will defeat the warlock. Perhaps *together* we are the *One*, Creda."

Ferren turned her head at this, her interest sparked. But the Superior appeared to be speaking only to Creda. Ferren turned her eyes away but continued to listen.

"Both of us are weaker now," Veras continued, "yet it seems that our powers are now markedly stronger when we work together. We've known such to be the case among Tower Superiors and we've made deliberate use of it – but it is unusual for a Superior to be able to accomplish this with one of a lesser level."

"Ever since we used my amulet with yours to rescue you from the snow in the far north, we've had a deeper rapport," Creda added.

"Yes," Veras agreed. "This is certainly something to be investigated further … eventually."

"At any rate," offered Nico, "we're grateful to you, Sister Creda, for freeing us from that cursed potion!"

Creda shook her head, musing over the memory. "It was tremendous good fortune that I was quick enough to initiate a *Spell of Protection* for myself! Otherwise, I could not have avoided the potion!"

"Indeed," said Veras in a weary voice. "It was an especially frustrating situation. I felt as though all of my power was inside a container of some kind, and no matter what I tried, I could not make use of it."

"Yes," Ferren agreed. "And how awful for *us* – to be fighters, warriors, and be totally unable to move!"

"Are you rested?" It was Joul Zann's voice, and everyone gave him their full attention, for he had not spoken for a long time. "Are you ready to continue? We really should try to get a look around before daylight …" He had been anxiously glancing in the direction of the roadway, wondering what might await them. *Was he getting closer to his wife?*

But it was Ferren and Tavis who were anxious to scout ahead. They'd return quickly should they spot danger. The others finished their meals and began preparing to continue their mission. The two who scouted ahead found nothing threatening in the immediate area. Indeed, the night was waning, and it was quite beautiful to be riding while the first orangish tendrils of dawn stretched their limbs along the horizon. They came to some hills, and Ferren dismounted to climb higher, wondering what view this higher ground might offer.

Tavis following, she began to climb. After a steep beginning, the ground became more level, with soft green grasses. Above was a higher hill, but their view of it was obscured by bushy growth and more rocks. Ahead, though, was what looked like a small trail …

At the end of a short ledge, Ferren saw the most alarming sight she'd seen thus far…

Quickly they urged their mounts back to the others, for this was something which they *all* must see. Finally, they reached what remained of the encampment. They were pleased to see that the rest of the group was ready to go. The group urged their mounts to follow, Nico carefully riding one of the wagon's horses bareback, while holding the reins of the other so that it followed.

Ferren and Tavis led the others back toward the hills. It was difficult to keep from urging their mounts into a run, but they must attract as little attention as possible should there be any prying eyes. Ferren paused at the base of the hill and, somewhat impatiently, waited for the others to arrive and dismount. As they began to climb, Creda noticed Baru off to the right among some bushy growth, nibbling upon an unfortunate rabbit.

They made their ways to a higher level, where the flat grassy ground offered a comfortable view of what lay in the distance …

A huge, gleaming palace was catching the early rays of the sun. From where they watched, it looked almost to have been carved from marble. There was no wall surrounding it, not even one to protect the city on the near side. Beyond could be seen the glorious blue of the sea.

Veras felt her heart sink. Here was power, indeed! How could their little band defeat the like of this! No walls. No walls because he had no need for them. Or, if he had them, they were made of enchantment rather than rock.

Zann spoke softly to the entire group. "We must proceed with the utmost caution. Considering the strength which he evidently holds, he may be able to sense almost anything happening within a certain distance. We will be relying upon your judgement, Sisters." How could he rescue his wife from *this*?

"How are we – how are we to gain entrance?" Ferren asked with a frown.

"Let us watch," Veras said with a calmness which she did not feel. "We might gain entry as *they* do." She pointed in the direction of several small farms not far from the hill. Clearly visible to the watchers on the hill were activities beginning as the sun rose higher in the sky.

But what they saw was awful, for the farmers moved like mindless things. They did not resemble the men/not men, but were nonetheless obviously under the control of the warlock. Nico spat in disgust as he watched men and women walking woodenly, picking from their baskets of crops the best ones and depositing them into wagons –

Which were then driven straight to the warlock's city, for the warlock himself no doubt.

Nico was breathing more heavily. Prophecy or no prophecy, he wanted to storm in there and wring the tyrant's neck. He moved around the curve where there was a better view of the roadway …

"Over here." His voice was harsh and strained.

Zann and Veras moved quickly to follow him, Creda, Ferren and the others close behind them. Creda gave a low moan. Zann sighed.

Just below, where the roadway became wider to accommodate the increased traffic, was a huge likeness of what resembled a tall, richly robed man. It gleamed white in the sun – almost overpoweringly so – but the farmers who made their ways past it did not seem to notice it at all. They seemed incapable of noticing anything, their eyes blank and their faces empty as they trudged slowly along.

Further along the roadway were more of these likenesses of – they assumed – the warlock. Nico spat again, wishing it was the warlock upon whom he was spitting. He put his hand on the hilt of the sword, and let his mind enjoy an image of himself slicing the warlock's throat with the man/not man's sword which he had picked up.

"Perhaps that would be the best way," Joul said in a quiet voice, nodding toward the farmers and their wagons and baskets as they ambled to the city's edge.

"But still," Creda added, "I would certainly like to have a better view of the outskirts. Maybe we could see something more that might be helpful …"

No one replied. No one added anything further. There was so much to take in, so much to consider. Some sort of plan to be decided on –

Suddenly there was a tremendous howl from the other side of the hill, near the bottom –

"Baru!" Creda exclaimed, as they turned back in alarm.

Now, from around the curve, they could hear Tavis, Vander and Giever. When they rounded the curve to the grassy area, they found them –

Men/not men! They must have been on the hill above!

Nico cursed the blade which he now held, wishing it was his own, and not the one he'd taken from the wagon. But a sword it was, and he'd not hesitate to use it. Zann and Ferren were beside him in an instant –

Creda hung back in the area of the ledge – where was Veras? Creda touched her amulet, sent her spirit to seek that of her Superior –

No! Veras's was muted, as before! But, hoping that the potion had not yet blanketed Veras's spirit completely, Creda sent her a flash of strength –

That would likely be all that she could do for now. There were spells that she might bring into play, but none which would be effective against so many enemies at one time. And a stronger spell might alert the warlock. No, she had best bide her time, watch for the best opportunity to do more. She lay flat upon the ground, hoping to remain unseen, just where the ledge met the grassy, more open area.

Nico was deeply involved in the battle now. It felt *good* to have a chance to take action, to relieve his fury –

The sword flashed in the sun as he swung it with speed and strength. There was a *clang* as it collided with the blade of the nearest man/not man, the impact sending a jolt down his arm and into his shoulder. The man/not man's weapon was knocked from his grasp to land upon the ground. Nico grit his teeth and prepared to run the bastard through –

"No!"

Creda's cry startled him, but he didn't dare take his eyes from the enemy. Still he held his weapon ready, brandished it in the man/not man's direction.

Then came Creda's voice again. "Nico! It's a spell! You might be killing an innocent!"

Nico spat, considering the words. But they made sense, for, even in the heat of battle, the man/not man was expressionless ... and looked remarkably the same as the other men/not men. But how Nico wanted to finish him off – finish them *all* off. And then take the warlock's head! But quickly he reversed his hold on the weapon and brought the hilt against the thing's head not once, but twice, and the man/not man fell heavily. He turned then to help Tavis to do the same to his attacker.

Unfortunately for Creda, her shout to Nico had alerted some of the men/not men to her nearby presence, and she found herself face-to-face with one of them. She reached beneath her robe for her amulet –

But the man/not man seized her arm, pulling her from the shelter of the ledge and into the open. All around her seemed to be bodies engaged in battle. Her attacker seemed to have thought that Creda, too, was reaching for a weapon, for he gave her arm a shove as though wanting her to keep it visible –

Then he saw the gleam of her amulet ...

His face changed. Some of the mindless obedience left his eyes to reveal deep sorrow as his stare met that of the Sister ...

He knew what she was –

He hesitated, weapon drawn but his sword arm motionless. His lips moved, and very softly, he begged her –

"Help me," he whispered hoarsely.

But suddenly, two other things were fighting for Creda's attention. She heard another man/not man from behind move closer –

And she felt the touch of Baru upon her mind, but there was something *else* –

As she felt the potion-knife suddenly against her skin, she sent as much of her spirit as she could over to the wolf –

She heard and felt the howl which filled the air before the potion left her powerless.

CHAPTER TWENTY-ONE

Inside

It was agony – absolute agony – to fight the almost overpowering urge and *need* to get to the attackers and rip them, tear them to shreds, feel their warm, sticky blood –

Although together Creda/Baru knew that their spirits were united for now, they could also smell, hear and see their dearest friend and her companions as their bodies were dragged away and shoved into some sort of conveyance.

The desire to throw back their head and howl their misery was strong. But they knew what they must do …

The humans needed help. There was no doubt about this. All of these men/not men forming the army and guards, and the farmers tending the land – and, no doubt, all of the people inside the city – seemed to be firmly under the control of the warlock. Still, their Creda part was thinking, it had been encouraging to see that one man/not man begging for her help. It was clear, though, that if this warlock was to be defeated, they would need the help of everyone. Every*one*, not just the humans …

And so off Creda/Baru ran. Quickly, quickly they backtracked through the woods. Their paws moved as fast as they could, for this quarry was the most challenging they'd ever imagined. Over fallen logs, through the shadows of the trees, under thick brambles they went. Gradually their pace began to slow. They began to feel much warmer – warmer than this wolf-body was accustomed to. Finally, they needed to stop. The dryness of their throat could no longer be ignored. They trod slowly now, tongue hanging from their jaws. Their nostrils quivered constantly as they analyzed every scent which passed their way –

Finally – what they'd been seeking was close. They stopped to sniff the air a moment, to ensure that they were heading in the right direction. Yes. Down a little hill they moved, clambering over a fallen log. Ah, there it was.

Water.

They crept forward to the little stream, letting their muzzle caress the surface of the cool water before drinking deeply. They let their legs fold beneath them, to give them time to regain strength. And the Creda part thought.

The plan would not work, it seemed. They could not simply go back to the last place they'd been together with the pack. They had already gone past the spot where they'd last had contact with them, only to find that there was no new smell of them. And all the scents they'd found were too faint to be recent.

Too faint, too far. Whatever could they do? The Creda part tried to think of different ways that she and the wolf might work together to help her friends, but ...

Suddenly their nostrils began to quiver. Although they were lying still, allowing weary limbs to recover, a familiar scent was beginning to waft its way to their sensitive nose.

Baru's howl had been heard! Hastily they regained their tired feet, moving away from the stream as the scent became stronger. A whimper escaped their throat as familiar and welcome creatures hurried into the area. The pack leader stopped, eyed them, then looked over his shoulder. In response to his gesture, a greyish female came bounding happily to greet Creda/Baru, nuzzling them with great enthusiasm. Creda/Baru couldn't help but respond, although they turned their attention to the leader quickly.

The Creda part knew only vaguely what was occurring, and had no conscious understanding of how they communicated, especially with the dominant wolf. All she knew was that her human friends needed assistance – the details of how her beast friends might help were up to Baru.

Their yip-yipping seemed to have spurred the others of the pack to some sort of action. Evidently, they knew what must be done.

Creda/Baru and the pack stood together amid the trees by the brook, threw back their heads and shared their message with every creature who might understand it. They sang loud and long, sharing the tale (Creda assumed) of the terrible human who had the powerful magic, and the sorceress who was a friend.

Then the pack leader yipped softly, looking from one to another of the smaller wolves. These apparently knew exactly what was being asked of them, as they turned to run quickly from the area.

Creda/Baru lowered their head, ears flat, in a gesture of appreciation (Creda assumed). She could sense Baru's longing to return to where they could feel Creda's body to be. And Baru's concerns made good sense to Creda. Should she remain within a creature for too long, or be too far away from her own body, the link which remained with her own body might be weakened beyond repair. Perhaps even severed. She had no way to know what the limit might be …

If the link with her own body was severed, and Creda was the *One*, then she would not be able to defeat the warlock – unless, of course, *Baru* was the *One*. After all, the Seer had said that the *One* was not a *man* –

But Creda allowed her reasonings to take a rest, and allowed Baru's sensations to dominate as they hurried in the direction of the city.

They moved cautiously through the woods and long grasses – a wolf in daylight near a city is not a comfortable creature! The Creda part was appalled by the sight of the mindless-looking peasants. Sad things they seemed as they urged their horses forward, pulled their produce toward the city for the *Great Lord*, which Creda now realized the inscriptions on the bases of the statues said.

Great Lord, indeed!

They crouched beneath some prickly bushes just outside of the entrance to the city. Their nostrils picked up a sweet scent, which the Creda part recognized as magic.

The Baru part also sniffed a bird, which held appeal as a meal. They looked toward it, and the Creda part was grateful for the unexpected information which the experience provided ...

A hawk glided downward, something in the city apparently attracting its attention. But it was stopped abruptly by something. It tried again in another spot, only to fly once more against a barrier which couldn't be seen ...

Magic. She had been able to see the magic barrier inside of the cavern she'd been imprisoned in. From where they were now, though, she could not see this particular one. But she remembered the barrier in her prison, and how its weakest areas were at its perimeter. This one might be similar ...

As they crouched in their hiding place, Baru's sensitive nostrils told them that members of Creda's group were not too far away. Keeping low to the ground, they crept from beneath the bush and carefully made their way through the longer grasses, away from the city's entrance. Crouching behind rocks, ears flattened to help them avoid detection, they could sense more easily now the presence of the escort as well as Creda's body. Then, finally, they could *see* them. They were lying in the back of a wagon as it moved jerkily along. There was no cage in this one. Apparently, it hadn't been intended to hold prisoners.

Creda/Baru could feel more of Creda now – her spirit, her power. Now this was muted beneath the blanket of the potion. But it was only a part of her power, for a good deal of it was here with Baru.

Had Creda been one with her own body, her jaw would have dropped in astonishment, for even though so much of her was here with Baru, she could sense a small amount of Veras's deep blue spirit. This seemed strange, as when Veras had been drugged before, Creda had been able to sense only Veras's struggles to throw off the 'blanket'.

But now Creda felt her ... and she knew why.

The strength which she'd sent the Superior just as she'd been drugged must have been enough to allow part of her spirit to remain free of the potion. Creda could sense Veras's efforts to revive Creda, she could see the deep blue tendrils struggling to touch the pale blue that was Creda's power and spirit –

But there wasn't enough of Creda there!

She gathered her strength like a cat pulling its legs beneath it, in preparation for a great leap. She saw the almost lifeless Creda inside of her own mind and, leaving a flash of gratitude and love for Baru, she hurtled her energy in the direction of her own body –

Instantly she felt a feeble touch from Veras, as well as Veras's surprise and joy when she felt the sudden increase in Creda's strength. Although Creda's eyes were closed, she could now hear the faint crackle of the magic surrounding the *Great Lord's* city. They did not have much time, for the wagon would pass through the city's entrance soon –

Quickly Creda asserted herself easily over the faint deep blue of Veras. And, as carefully as anything she had ever attempted before, she tried to emulate the warlock's potion as it muted their spirits. She envisioned her own azure power as a dead thing –told her body that it was unconscious –

For a time, she felt nothing. But then suddenly there was the welcome touch of gentle Veras upon Creda's spirit. It was wonderful to know that the magic of the warlock could be outsmarted, and that she had found a limit to this power. The strength which she'd sent Veras, as well as her recollection of the potion had enabled her to maintain something of herself *beyond* the blanket-potion's influence. And Creda's emulation of the potion had enabled them to pass through the city's magic barrier undetected.

Of course, she reminded herself, one had to bear in mind that the samples of the warlock's power which they had seen had been intended for use with common folk, not people who had knowledge of and skills in the arts of enchantment …

Veras was delighted. She had been aware that Creda had sent her a flash of strength just as the warlock's potion had entered her system, which had enabled her to keep some control over her powers. But she had been so – so worried when she had sent her own contacts to Creda and received no reaction. Then, suddenly, Creda was back!

And she was strong! Veras had been trying to help *her*, yet now it was Creda who was sending more strength to her Superior. It was glorious to feel that strength combining with her own power, enabling her to pull more of her spirit through that blanket-potion. Perhaps they *were* the *One* together. For the strength of their powers when together seemed to be growing even greater …

Creda turned her attention to the sounds which surrounded them. Dead sounds they seemed. There was no joy here. Any conversation which occurred seemed strictly for the purpose of exchanging information. There was no laughter, no greeting of one friend to another –

No *life*, really. And they had the warlock with his lust for power to thank for it.

The anger this aroused inside of Creda had her feeling stronger. She *was* the *One*. She was certain of it now!

She risked a glance around, taking care to keep her eyelids open just a tiny bit. They were being wheeled along the city streets – and in the direction of something which might be a prison, or some sort of holding facility. She studied the sky and found that, if she moved her fingers to her amulet cautiously, she could gain enough power to see the magic above her which was obviously designed to keep the city safe from intrusion. It glittered like a fine film of gold, high above. The magic barrier in the prison had been a grayish haze. She wondered if the warlock might have preferred to use gold for this one to impress possible adversaries. But she noticed that the gold appeared to be thinner in some places than in others –

What might that mean? Could it be that the warlock was like any other powerful being – allowing his defences to grow weaker when he believes that there is no one who can compete with him? Or might he have used so much of his power that he now needed to use it with more restraint?

The wagon suddenly creaked to a halt. Creda found it difficult to resist the urge to open her eyes more widely and turn her head to see just where they were …

The men/not men were standing together, as though waiting. Creda frowned, wondering what this might be all about. But then she realized that they might be awaiting instructions or orders or something through their amulets. Then they appeared to be moving from one to another of the captives. From what Creda could see, they were giving each of them another bit of potion … and she could see from the responses that this potion enabled each of them to regain enough consciousness to move about, at least a little.

But what might this do to Creda, when so little of her spirit had been affected?

Then she remembered earlier contact with one of the men/not men …

As he reached toward her, she forced herself to breathe evenly, and to prepare herself for quick movement. Her heart feeling like it was caught in her throat, she suddenly seized his wrist. He stopped in surprise. Her other hand grasped her amulet, while her eyes stared into his. His mouth had dropped open, but he stood, seemingly dumbfounded. Creda gazed into his eyes until she could see the helpless spirit trapped inside. Still she held his gaze

He put the potion into his pocket, and blinking in disorientation, pulled away from the contact.

Creda turned her attention to her comrades. She felt a twinge inside – grateful to see them able to rise from the wagon, yet hating their inability to move according to their own wishes. Determined, she focused on keeping her facial expressions neutral. She glanced at Veras and was happy to see a flash of life and determination. As inconspicuously as possible, Creda eased herself to stand close to the Superior.

In front of them, she could now see the reason for reviving the captors, at least to some degree. Before them was a narrow, twisting stairwell, leading downward. There were no windows in it that she could see. Only shadows and darkness …

One of the men/not men gestured toward the stairwell, with Nico instantly stepping in that direction. Creda could imagine how frustrated Nico must be to find himself doing the man/not man's bidding so apparently willingly. Veras followed him, and Creda stepped quickly behind her so that they'd not be separated –

Veras had been grateful when the new potion had given them the ability to move their limbs, but still she could only move them when and how the men/not men commanded. As she made her way to the stairwell, though, she felt Creda's hand grip her own from behind, and the joy of anticipation filled her. She could see movement from the corner of her eye, and knew that Creda would be reaching her other hand to hold her amulet –

And she knew instantly when that had happened, for the all effects of the potion were gone, and she was free. She breathed deeply, and quickly reminded herself to maintain a passive look upon her face.

By now they had almost reached the bottom of the staircase. The door there opened from the inside, and a man/not man stood staring. Veras stood very still, hoping that she had been convincing enough with her attempt at passivity. But then she realized that he appeared to be looking, not at them, but at something above, at the top of the staircase. Nico had been bowing his head to fit his large frame under the top of the doorway, but a sound from the man/not man had him pausing. He stood perfectly still, waiting, his back to Veras. The man/not man gestured, and Nico and the others who were under the effects of the potion were turning, apparently to go back up the staircase. Veras and Creda had to be quick to follow their example, but at the same time, appear as though they were not hurrying …

As they turned to ascend the stairs, Veras managed to time her step so that Nico stepped upward before she did. In this way, she was able to keep one hand hanging back so that, as he raised his leg to the next stair, she could grip him, just above the knee. This she squeezed, sending all her attention into sharing as much of her spirit with him as she could –

Nico gave a little gasp, then recovered himself quickly. It was a strange and wonderful sensation, yet it also required much self-control. The potion had been like a heavy blanket which had been weighing him down – and now it was gone. He felt free again. But he must maintain control, and not give away the sorceresses' plan – whatever it was.

The man/not man prodded them forward, to the top of the stairwell where the others stood. Nico stopped, trying to eye the others, wondering if they, too, were free. But he had to force himself to gaze straight ahead ...

They were being led to another door, this one leading to the main floor of the building. Creda stumbled suddenly and bumped against Joul Zann for just a moment. As they continued, Nico could see that Zann's gait had changed slightly. Nico began to grin, then forced the corner of his mouth back down to a neutral position.

They stepped inside, into a narrow corridor. It was relatively dark here, the way lit only by torches whose flames cast long shadows, making the prisoners seem much taller than they really were. They walked for what seemed like a long time. Finally, the long corridor came to an end. They were about to enter a grand hall, it seemed. They were prodded to enter and to stand to one side before a raised area with steps on three sides.

At the top of the raised area, was a rich, golden throne. When Nico thought of the warlock sitting on it, hatred swirled in his stomach. He bit the inside of his lower lip in an effort to remain expressionless. They stood silently and almost still, yet from the corner of his eye Nico could now see tiny movements among their group. Quickly the Sisters had been touching hands to the others, to free them, too, from the potion.

Then *he* came in. And a grand procession it must be –

They could not see it, for as soon as *he* began to enter, the men/not men were ensuring that the group knelt, bending over so far that their foreheads touched the floor. Nico couldn't help himself. After the first contact between his forehead and the floor, he deliberately eased his head up just a tiny bit. He would *not* bend forward to that extent for this tyrant! He would *not*!

Creda was hoping that the men/not men were not becoming suspicious, for they did not know that all the members of this group were free from the potion. It was requiring more communication from the men/not men to make their commands understood.

Now there was silence. No music, no chanting, no cheers, no talking. Silence. All they could hear was the sound of footsteps as the warlock was carried past on his cushioned platform. Evidently, it was time to rise, for the members of the group were poked until they stood. And finally, they had the opportunity to gaze upon the warlock who'd caused so much fear and misery and pain to the lives of so many.

Creda stared at him in amazement. After the dream she had had of him, with his flaming beard –

He was just a man, or so he seemed. He had no beard but was shaven clean. He was not a large man – he was much smaller than Nico. He seemed thin, and his hair was graying. He wore thick red and gold robes, though, which spoke of great richness.

His face was breath-taking. Not in physical beauty, but in its expression. Here, it said, is a man of power. This is a man of complete confidence, a man who had managed to bend county after county to his will. A man so powerful that he seems almost ... almost *bored*.

And he yawned then, almost as though to confirm this impression. He made a brief gesture with one small hand, and suddenly an attractive woman was pulled from where she'd stood with a group of empty-looking prisoners across the room. She wore the diaphanous costume of a dancer, an entertainer of men.

The 'Great Lord' looked at her as she stood thus, expressionless, as though not caring whether she lived or died. Then he snapped his fingers, and she began to dance.

It seemed very strange to the Sisters and their group to watch this woman, whose face continued to be completely empty of any expression, going through the movements of a very sensuous dance. Without music.

He watched her, at first with interest, but then even her most alluring undulations failed to offer him what he wished. He motioned quickly with a hand, and a man/not man moved to grasp the woman's arm. Emotionlessly she allowed him to pull her to the 'Great Lord'. He reached forward to her. He stood, and grasped her by her shoulders. Then he pulled her to him in what looked to be some sort of embrace.

Nico was close to trembling now. He yearned to see the blood spurt from this man's throat! A touch from Veras's hand against his own helped him to be still –

Creda had to turn her eyes away, locking her gaze on the floor ahead of her.

Were the stories true? What were they about to see?

Veras whispered something, and Creda looked up –

CHAPTER TWENTY-TWO

The 'Great Lord'

Ferren's fingers twitched. How she longed for the feel of her sword in her hand! How she longed to leap upon that dais and run the man through! She wanted to spit, to give vent to her disgust at this vile creature. Now unrestrained by any potion, it was more difficult for her to control her outrage. She cast a glance at Veras, and the Superior's eyes bade Ferren to be still ...

How can I defeat him? How can any of us? Ferren could not – *would* not stop herself from planning how she might do it. She scanned the area, looking for weapons, and memorizing which of the men/not men were bearing them –

She looked back at the raised platform. With a mixture of fascination and revulsion, she stared as he put his lips upon the woman, almost as would a man with a woman whom he loved. But, as his lips sought hers, he began to breathe inward, deeply. Then even more deeply. It was almost as though he was sucking from her every breath she had –

And, as he did, he began to change, rather remarkably. At first he trembled with pleasure like a young man on his wedding night. Then he seemed to – to *grow*, somehow...

He began to gleam, to glitter like gold. It began with his eyes, then spread downward until his entire body shone like the sun. *Now* he resembled the warlock from Creda's dreams – the one with streams of fire running through his hair. He released the woman's limp form now and stood, arms wide, standing so tall that he almost reached the ceiling of the grand room.

And he laughed.

It was both horrible and beautiful to hear, for there was a musical quality about it that – despite the awful reason for it – was actually quite pleasing to the ear.

Nico was finding it harder and harder to stand impassively and bear witness to this. He had been nibbling on the inside of his lower lip, and now he tasted his own blood. The realization only added fuel to the fire inside of him, knowing he wanted to spill the blood of this beast in front of him. Veras intertwined her fingers with his, and a cooling sensation of calm filled him. He closed his eyes for a moment to collect himself.

The 'Great Lord' was slowly shrinking back into himself, the joy apparently having left him. Now he began to store what was left of the woman's energies in places around the large room.

With a flash from his fingertip, he sent a blast of gold upward, toward a corner of the room where the top of the wall met the magic golden protection which formed the 'roof'. There it came to rest in some sort of confined space, apparently with the energies of others. And, as the group took this in, they saw that there seemed to be more of these in other corners of the room.

Then he picked up the woman's body and, with a word, rendered her tiny. With a quick gesture, he called out "*Icetombs*" – and she was gone.

Creda pondered the details of what they had witnessed. The woman's body was to be stored at the Icetombs with the others that she and Veras had seen. Perhaps those bodies in the Icetombs were like trophies to him. Perhaps he could send himself there, too, to admire his collection –

But then she sensed something from Veras, and reached her fingers over to grasp those of the Superior –

And sensed her spell. Veras had found the minuscule opening in the that roof of magic – the opening through which the woman's tiny form had been sent. And now, with a hair-thin deep blue tendril, Veras prevented that access from closing once more. There wouldn't be much time. Quickly Creda sent her paler blue energy to support the Superior's, and they felt the opening being forced open more widely –

But to a person of the magic arts, those tendrils were as visible as the threads of clothing –

Quickly an order was barked by the warlock, and as one of the men/not men came to Creda, she withdrew from the spell. She turned to face the man/not man and gazed directly into his eyes. He returned her stare, apparently unaware of the spell that Veras was continuing – and of the orders which the 'Great Lord' was directing to him.

If I can keep him distracted, we will have more time! Creda could feel that the man/not man was unable to pull away from her –

Nico swallowed. How long should they stand here? How much time could the Sisters continue doing ... whatever they were doing? Curse it! He was here to protect them! He took a deep breath and let it out slowly.

But a second man/not man grasped Creda's arm from behind and he began to escort her up the stairs to the 'Great Lord'.

When Nico saw the warlock gazing upon Creda, it almost more than he could bear. He turned to Veras, but her face was focused. Nico knew her well enough now to know that she was involved with some sort of spell. *Creda would be all right, then! Veras would save her!* Yet he watched in horror as the warlock inhaled deeply of the energies stored around the hall. As he did so, he grew taller once more, and obviously enjoyed the opportunity to look down upon the small sorceress who, held by the man/not man, now stood upon the dais.

Nico's fingers were clenching and unclenching. Why wasn't Veras stopping the warlock? Creda was trembling now – Nico could see it from down here! He couldn't stand it if the tyrant took Creda's spirit too – he simply couldn't –

"So," boomed the voice of the warlock from up high near the glittering gold ceiling, "you think *your* little spells can compare with *mine?*" He laughed heartily, staring into the pale face of the Sister.

But, as he did, he extended an arm to point in Veras's direction –

He was aware of her spell too. Veras moaned, and Zann supported her with an arm as Nico turned to look at her. The captain and Nico exchanged looks. They must be careful not to give themselves away. They must try to look impassive. They would be of no help whatsoever if they were captured.

Nico forced himself to take his gaze from the Superior and look back toward the dais. He was grateful to see that Creda was caressing her amulet and mouthing words –

Creda sent a *Spell of Protection* to the Superior. Instantly it surrounded her – everywhere *except* for that pinpoint of contact from the warlock's fingertip to Veras's mind –

Creda gasped. She couldn't penetrate his spell! He was simply too strong. The look upon Veras's face showed her determination, yet also the wavering of her ability to resist him.

And then the warlock did something, although Creda couldn't see exactly what. Whatever it was, it was powerful, for the entire floor began shaking, trembling, as though it was about to open and devour any who stood in his way.

His magic was just too powerful! And then a bit of stone fell from above –

Parts of the top of the wall had fallen in. Was this more of the warlock's demonstration of power?

But no, for he, too, was looking about in some confusion, and began to shrink back to his original size. He tried to pull more of the stored energy into himself, but some of their locations were now blocked as more sections of the wall tops began to sag around and above them. Creda dodged a thick slab and backed away to a corner of the dais where the walls joined.

From here she watched as the warlock enacted his own *Spell of Protection*, and a translucent coating of gold had the blocks from the tops of the walls easily bouncing off him as they fell.

Suddenly, something blocked the sunlight which had been peering through. Darkness began to pour inside, and a rush of wind blew the torches out, leaving the area eerily encased in shadow.

And there, upon the platform, the warlock glowed like the sun itself, the only source of light in the area. Men/not men were blinking in apparent confusion, messages from the warlock apparently no longer clear for them. Some were instinctively backing away toward the doors, while others sought refuge in corners of the large room.

And now something familiar – a touch upon Creda's spirit –

Veras's steadfast continuance of her spell had brought what they'd needed – help! Through the gap she had helped open in the magic protection through and beyond the roof came assistance ...

Creda watched in awe as huge claws were extended through what was now a *large* hole in the magical roof. The beautiful bluish green of dragon scales was followed by a blast of fire from the mouth of the Large Dragon.

Golden flames met the glimmering protection which surrounded the warlock and bounced off only to light something else afire. The warlock looked upward at this opponent, no fear or concern visible on his face. He directed what looked like a tiny arrow from each fingertip. With a roar, the Large Dragon blew smoke into the room –

Creda managed to send a *Spell of Protection* to her friend. She was almost too late, but was relieved to see the arrow stopped by her azure force just in front of the dragon.

The Large Dragon roared again, reaching that clawed foot for the warlock. But, with a gesture, he surrounded himself with a fire of his own. The dragon could not get hold of him.

And she was beginning to tire from attempting to hold her position in the sky while carrying out the attacks.

There had to be a way –

Creda fired her own energy into the shield surrounding the warlock. She watched as a pinpoint of azure flew from her fingertip to bore into that golden armour – at least, she hoped that it was doing so –

But it was weakening. Unable to maintain the energy for the spell, she stopped. She just wasn't strong enough. She stole a glance in Veras's direction, and suddenly realized that the Superior had taken advantage of the confusion to come to Creda's side upon the dais. She had been attempting a similar approach at penetrating the warlock's protection. But, even with the two of them, it seemed that their powers were insufficient.

They were dimly aware of the escort, who continued to do as they had been asked to do. They were preoccupied with keeping the men/not men from interfering – without killing them in the process.

Veras's hand was suddenly on Creda's arm. She spoke into Creda's ear so that she could be heard above the din, without alerting the warlock to their plans. "While he is preoccupied with the dragon, support my energies while I enact a *Spell of Undoing*, to set these men/not men free from his spell."

Veras was grateful to feel Creda's energy added to her own, for the Spell of Undoing was certainly not an easy one. She focused, holding her amulet and directing the energies to the minds of the men/not men, trying to find what was real and not part of the warlock's hold on them. But there were so many of them! She managed to free two – but so many remained!

She faltered, but Creda supported her to keep her from falling. "We just haven't the strength," Creda gasped. *How could the Seer have been wrong?*

The dragon was obviously becoming exhausted. Although she'd drained him of some of his energies, weakened him, she'd been unable to break through the warlock's defences and bring him to an end. And this would seem to mean that the Sisters, too, would be unable …

"Where did we go wrong, Veras?" Creda watched in horror as the Large Dragon began to pull away from the castle's roof.

Veras's insides were filled with despair. "Perhaps – perhaps we misunderstood. Perhaps we were hasty. Perhaps we are simply *not* the One –"

And it seemed that this must certainly be true. The dragon was gone. The men/not men and the escort ceased their battles as an eerie silence filled the large hall and beyond. Eyes turned in the direction of the warlock –

He turned to the Sisters, a trace of amusement upon his face. Still he glowed with his magic protection, although it was a slightly paler colour now. Obviously, it was thinner in response to the attacks upon it. Yet still it seemed impenetrable.

Creda's insides had become nothing more than a dull ache. The pain of being wrong after being certain of success. The pain of looking an enemy in the face and now knowing that nothing she could do – nothing at all – would be enough.

The agony of knowing that this being had sucked her own dear sister dry of her life-energy for his own pleasure.

She hated him, despised him …

And was powerless to do anything at all to stop his senseless plunder –

Creda hated *herself* now, too.

She felt almost nothing at all as he pulled her toward him with an unseen force. She no longer felt fear as she stood before him, knowing what he would do –

She wondered dully what it would be like as he sucked her spirit from within her …

CHAPTER TWENTY-THREE

The End

Creda stared blankly into the face of the being who had changed her life, whose defeat had become the entire purpose of her life –

The being who had taken her sister.

And now he would have her, too, simply save her life-energies somewhere should he wish to feast upon them again. What would it feel like? Would she feel anything at all?

Now there seemed only numbness, a dull ache somewhere inside as he pulled her face closer, closer to his. He opened his lips, licking them with a moist tongue. He moved closer, closer. She could feel his hot, sour breath –

Ferren could watch no more of this! *She* was the *One*! *She*'d defeat him, seize him while he was distracted, break his neck! That must be the way! Ferren leaped from the grasp of a man/not man, pulling herself onto the dais. She felt as light as the wind, saw herself as a bolt of lightning here to strike him down –

But suddenly she was falling as the warlock sent a blast of energy to burn into her. With a gasp, she fell heavily to the floor, holding her wounded hand –

It was over. No one could help Creda. No one.

Feebly Veras reached for her amulet, shaking her head all the while, knowing that no spell she had was strong enough, that he would simply strike her down if she dared to make a move. "Creda," she moaned softly, "I'm so sorry."

Ferren wasn't about to surrender. Grimacing, she crawled forward. She would destroy this beast in the name of the Royal Family, of Prince Yurmar. But suddenly a wave of dizziness was shaking her – no! The dais was trembling, the very floor was trembling. She wondered if the others felt it too –

And now, above and beyond the face of the warlock, she saw it –

Through the huge hole in the roof, and beyond the golden haze of the protection which the warlock had repaired when the Large Dragon departed, came again something familiar – and yet not.

The warlock turned his gaze upward –

Something was coming. It was huge, enormous, colossal – and sparkling with greenish-gray energy.

Creda pulled away from the warlock and looked toward Veras. Did she see it too? Did she recognize this thing? Hastily she made her way to the Superior's side, down the stairs. Veras had a look of astonishment on her face. Two strong arms now held them from behind –

A lightning bolt of greenish-gray magic penetrated the warlock's gold protection above the city. They could hear the warlock gasp, as though he'd thought this to be quite impossible, even though the protective layer had been weakened by the Large Dragon.

When Creda turned to look at him once more, he resembled only a mere mortal.

But he pointed a finger in the direction of one of his energy containers that was no longer obscured now that more of the tops of the walls had fallen in. A thin line of gold flashed into his fingertip, and he directed this upward to once more repair his protection.

But the greenish-gray energy stopped him – yes, stopped him! And, as it did, it seemed to fall inward in little clouds. Suddenly, they could see little beyond the mist which now blocked their vision. They knew that the others around them were in the midst of it, too, for it filled the great hall –

It did not seem to affect the warlock. Through the haze, dimly, they could make out his form as he stood upon the dais, gazing upward.

And then the thing spoke:

> *Yesss! And that isss very good!*
> *You've looked into my eyesss ssso fine!*
> *Little man, come to the She-SSSerpent –*
> *From now on, you are mine!*

The greenish mist seemed to clear, just a bit, and a long, greenish-grey tentacle reached downward to take him. And her magic was strong – stronger than his –

And now it was clear why.

Around that tentacle was a chain, and from the chain hung a familiar, yet unfamiliar decoration.

"The talisman," gasped Veras. "It's complete!"

The She-Serpent pulled the warlock effortlessly through the destroyed roof and upward. She held him firmly, and the sorceresses knew that still she would be holding his eyes with her own ...

> *Sssuch crimes have you done!*
> *I empty you of the energy*
> *You have taken without caussse.*
> *And now all prisssonersss free!*

> *My own abundant magic now*
> *I give to replaccce all*
> *That you took from innocccentsss –*
> *What onccce wasss, again isss now!*

There was a great murmur throughout the entire palace now. As the greenish mist dissipated, the people gazed about themselves in wonder ...

A young man stood before Creda. He was fair-haired like the people from the area around Espri. He shifted about somewhat uncomfortably in the man/not man clothing which was now too large for him. Then realization suddenly struck him, and he stared about himself in sudden joy. He was *free!*

All around there seemed to be more and more of these people … and even more, for the She-Serpent's spell had returned all the prisoners' bodies to be reunited with their spirits. Nico touched Creda's arm and, happily, she followed him. They walked together into a large corridor. It, too, was filled with confused and joyful people.

Past another large room and then a smaller one they went – and each one was filled to capacity with freed people. As they headed outside though the great door, they heard the voice of Joul Zann –

He was embracing a woman, tears cascading down both of their faces –

Suddenly Creda felt something furry beneath her fingertips, and quickly began caressing the wonderful head. "Oh Baru," she murmured, kneeling beside him. "We *did* it! We *did* get help! The message was heard and understood – and carried far! What would I ever have done without you?" She threw her arms around his thick neck and set her own tears free. Through the embrace, though, she could feel Baru's discomfort at being so close to so many humans. And so, after one more hug, and a spell to protect and keep him well, they parted for now.

"We've checked the dungeons, Nico," came Tavis's jubilant voice. "We didn't need to them free! When that – that *thing* cast its spell, all of the magic barriers disappeared."

And then Creda felt a hand upon her shoulder. She assumed it to be Nico's and joined it with her own. But this was no warrior's hand –

"Carlida!" That was all she could say. Something blocked her throat. She couldn't produce anything other than sobs. As she embraced her sister, through the curtain of tears she saw Carlida's husband and extended a hand to him.

Finally, the initial excitement and astonishment lessened a bit. Now it was simply time for joy. The entire city and beyond would be filled with celebration this night.

Creda was happy to sink down into a comfortable, upholstered chair which had been brought out of one of the warlock's buildings. Gratefully she lifted the cup of hot tea to her lips and gazed into the fire, enjoying the peacefulness of watching the dancing flames. She gazed across the top of the fire and watched Carlida and her husband as they danced joyfully. Past them were many other happy folk, talking, singing, dancing or just walking together, enjoying their freedom, including Creda's nephews.

She felt the presence of someone nearby and gazed up to see Nico's grinning face. He glistened with perspiration, having been very active in the celebrations.

"Well, Sister Creda! Now, will you honour me with a dance?" He gave an exaggerated bow, as though she were a queen.

She couldn't help but laugh. Their situation had been such a serious one for what seemed a long time. It was so good to see this side of Nico once more! She smiled but shook her head. "I – I don't dance, Nico. And, anyway, I am much too exhausted."

He could see the truth of that upon her pale face. He knelt beside her chair and watched the celebration for a few moments. "And so, it has come to pass just as you and the Superior said it would." He turned his eyes to meet hers, noting how tired she appeared. But it was good to see a smile upon this good Sister's lips.

"So it seems," she murmured, gazing downward into her cup.

Nico cleared his throat. There seemed so much that he should say … but suddenly he grinned.

He rose and took her hand in his. Gazing into her eyes, he held her hand with both of his big ones. With great bravado, glancing about to ensure that others were watching, he kissed her hand and bowed. "All right then, Sister! Refuse my attentions! I'll not be miffed! While, I'll just dance with –"

He paused, stepped around the fire, and waited until the right moment. "I'll just dance with *this* kind lady!" And he moved in to take Carlida's hand from her husband's, bowed grandly, and, pulling the joyful woman into his arms, revealed himself to be astonishingly light on his feet for a larger man. Carlida laughed gaily, for Creda had introduced her to Nico, and she was quite prepared to enjoy some fun. Nico looked past Carlida at Creda and winked.

She shook her head at Nico's antics, but smiled back at him.

Veras managed to pull herself from the embrace of a grateful couple and headed in Creda's direction. She was stopped, though, by Ferren.

"Sister," she said, putting a hand on Veras's arm. "I – I mean Superior. I want to tell you how much I've learned from this journey." She bit her lower lip, uncertain of her words.

Veras nodded, and put her hand atop Ferren's, giving hers a squeeze. She waited, wanting to allow Ferren the time she needed to form her thoughts. Suddenly, Ferren looked into Veras's eyes. "So then, Ferren." Veras spoke gently. "You are *not* the *One*. Does this disturb you?"

Ferren continued to frown. "Well, to have had any part in this at all has been quite wonderful." She looked around at the continuing festivities. "Look at these people, Superior! Look at the joy, the love!" Now she looked back at Veras. "It doesn't matter who the *One* was, does it? *This* is the important thing!" She gestured, to include as much as she could of the gaiety which surrounded them.

"It was *all* of us, Ferren," Veras said softly. "It was the townspeople, and the people of the Royal Family and their army, and the people of the Tower, the Witch, The Large Dragon, the She-Serpent. It was all of us, all working together, who brought this to pass."

Suddenly Giever was there, too, and he swept Ferren up in his arms and danced away with her. There was a look of confusion and surprise on Ferren's face which, after a few moments, turned to enjoyment.

Veras watched them another moment, smiling slightly, and turned back toward Creda. She pulled an empty chair beside Creda's. With a contented sigh, she sank down beside her. She chuckled. "For now, they're contented simply to rejoice. But, despite all the explaining we've done, there will no doubt be more questions!"

"What – what exactly *did* happen, Veras?" Creda had her suspicions, but still things seemed jumbled and unclear.

"Well, it would appear that the She-Serpent took the talisman segments, and that enabled her to add the power of the warlock's talisman to her own power –"

"I realize that," Creda interjected. "But – but –"

"Why was it the She-Serpent who was the *One*, do you mean? The witches must have known that she possessed the power needed – with the warlock's talisman, and the energy which she took from us – to defeat him after his protection was weakened by the Large Dragon –"

"The She-Serpent was the *One*," Creda repeated quietly.

"Well, she isn't a *man*, not even human –"

"Yes, Veras. But ..."

"But what?"

"I was – I was certain that you or I was the *One!*"

Veras laughed. "What we *were* is just as important."

Creda gave her a puzzled stare.

"Creda. You and I were the *Way*."

CHAPTER TWENTY-FOUR

The End and The Beginning

The sun was bright and comfortably warm as the sorceress made her way along the path, astride her mare. The weather made the day pleasant enough, and the woman considered herself fortunate indeed. She was in the process of making the short journey from the Tower of Giefan to the Hidden Caves of the Abufan, for there were to be final Tests and Completions taking place on the morrow.

She had ridden quite comfortably, and the woman had been humming a song as the sunlight warmed her. Rather suddenly, though, her mount had faltered, and following this she could hear a clicking sound.

She dismounted, leading the horse off the pathway, so that she could check the mare's hoofs. She sighed. She sat back and considered what options were available. There were some problems which even her magic spells could not solve.

The sorceress heard hoofbeats from over the hill which she had crossed not too long before. She rose to her feet, her hands seeking the feel of her saddlebag. She opened the top of it so that her knife was within reach. She had no desire to deal with highwaymen, but between her knives and her spells, she intended to be prepared.

Then she saw him as he made his way down the hill. He was clad as a warrior, with his broad chest covered by thick hide. He wore a brown cape which would quite adequately ward off the evening chill – yet it was not adequate to keep the rather large, very muscular arms from view. He pulled his black horse to a stop. He peered down at the sorceress and her mare, his dark brown eyes crinkling with laugh lines at their corners.

"Good thing I happened to come along," he was saying in what appeared to be a serious tone but was obviously not really intended to be. "I'd hate to think of the two of you spending the entire night at an impasse." He dismounted and walked over to her. He extended a hand toward her. "Veras," he said.

She took his hand, smiling wryly as he kissed it. She paused as their eyes met. "Have you been following me?"

He gave a look of mock insult. "Madam, please! It just so happens that a friend of mine will be participating in her final Tests and Completions at the Hidden Caves of the Abufan tomorrow!"

Veras laughed. "Oh, Nico! You are always full of surprises. I will be there as an honoured guest. What will *you* do while Creda is being tested?"

"As I am *not* an honoured guest, then I will simply wait." He frowned then. "I thought that, because of her involvement in the defeat of the warlock, she would not be required to complete the tests."

"She is not *required* to do so, Nico. She chose to."

"Well, if I am not welcome to attend the formalities, I am certain that I can pass the time in the local tavern until I am permitted to visit with my friend. Now," he nodded in the direction of Veras's mare, "what is the problem here?"

Veras sighed. "I believe she has a loose shoe, and I am hesitant to have her travel if there is any danger to her."

"Well, good madam, you are fortunate indeed." Dismounting, he patted Thunder with affection, happy that he'd found him again, and continued his bravado, "for I have a thorough knowledge of horses and such beasts."

Indeed, he does. Veras watched, gratefully, as Nico approached the mare and spoke gently to her, stroking her neck and her nose, reassuring her. The sorceress smiled, remembering the many times he'd tended to the mounts during their past journey. She watched as he inspected what seemed to be every aspect of the mare.

He turned to her. "I think that fortune is with you, good madam. A nail has come a bit loose, but if she walks in the grass, she should be all right until we find a blacksmith." He paused. "It would be best if she did not bear a rider until repairs have been made."

"Oh," Veras replied, wondering how long the rest of the journey would take if she walked with the mare. Her eyes were on the horse.

There was silence a moment.

"Veras," Nico said. His bravado was gone. "You will ride with me, and we will lead the mare."

She looked at him. There was something about the idea of riding with him which left her disquieted. But what else to do?

He had taken the mare's reins and pulled her close to Thunder. He mounted the black stallion and reached his arms down to the sorceress. She put her foot into the mare's stirrup, and Nico easily lifted her the rest of the way to sit in front of him. He clicked his tongue, and Thunder began to walk.

They had not ridden together before, and each was very conscious of the other's presence. For some reason, suddenly neither could think of anything to say.

Finally, Nico spoke. "Is it true that Sister Creda will return to the Tower when she has completed the formality of her tests?"

"Yes. Yes, Nico. It is quite wonderful to think of! My student will be a Superior! She has much to teach others. I don't know how many others of the world of the magic arts can work with animals as Creda can. I don't know if there are *any*. But she can certainly be a teacher for those who might have the skill."

"And you, Superior. How soon will you be returning to the Tower?"

Veras was silent. There were many possibilities about her future which had been occupying her mind. Finally, she spoke. "I really don't know, Nico. Our journey has had such an effect on me. I – I don't know. I feel drawn to working with the people in the community … as a healer, perhaps. There are many ways in which sorcery can aid in healing. I don't know …"

Silence returned. For a time, the only sounds were the muffled hoofbeats of the horses as they walked through the grasses at the edge of the pathway. And there was birdsong, with the pleasant sunshine to help to make the afternoon enjoyable. Veras was finding the nearness of the man who rode with her quite agreeable, as well.

"What is your name, Nico?" Veras's voice broke the stillness. "We have all heard what you *say* you've been called."

"Ah, yes. The Quickest and The Bravest – Might and Right –"

"Fornico?" Veras laughed as she said it.

Nico smiled wryly, although Veras couldn't see it. "Another time," he murmured. "Another place."

"So ... what is your *name*?"

He was silent a moment. "You want to know what my mother called me?"

Aware of how this man could choose his words for a certain purpose, she clarified, "what did your mother *name* you when you were born?"

He sighed. "My mother was older when she brought me into the world. And I had many brothers and sisters ..."

Veras was becoming quite curious. "And? What did your mother *name* you?"

He sighed again. "Bairn."

"Bairn? Your mother named you *Child?"* She was chuckling at the absurdity of such a large and powerful man having such a name. It was no wonder that he had made up his own!

Veras noticed that he did not join in her laughter. "Nico," she said after a moment, "what would you like for me to call you? Is Nico your preference? I will call you whatever you wish."

"You are asking me what I would like for you to call me?"

"Yes. Whatever you wish."

He tightened his arm around her waist, pulling her closer. He caressed her ear with his lips, and then whispered into it.

"Husband."

Veras smiled.

Made in the USA
Monee, IL
05 November 2019

16368088R00139